ALL THE WRONG PLAYS

C.W. FARNSWORTH

CONTENTS

PROLOGUE

WILL

Age Ten

"Will! Will, come on!"

I glance over one shoulder at my little brother, Tripp. He's annoyed with me. Or as annoyed as Tripp can get.

"Five more minutes," I tell him.

"We've been here for *hours*. All my friends left a long time ago. I'm bored. How are you not bored? You've just been kicking that ball the whole time."

What Tripp doesn't get—what *no one* seems to get—is that playing soccer is the only time I'm *not* bored.

I'm bored in school.

I'm bored at home.

Out here on the field, I feel *alive*. I feel like I'm doing what I'm supposed to be doing.

No one else understands that. Not my mom. Not my dad. Not Tripp. Not Wyatt, my best friend, who lives a couple of blocks away and headed home a while ago because he got sick of playing soccer.

1

I've never gotten sick of playing soccer. Can't imagine it ever happening.

"Three minutes," I say.

Tripp sighs, then wanders back toward the playground. He's ten times more patient than I am. I could stay out here for another hour, and he probably wouldn't come over again.

It'll be pitch-black in another hour, though. It's already late; the August sky a colorful blaze of pink and orange as the sun dips. The other kids who were here when we arrived already headed home for dinner.

The lines covering the stretch of grass I'm standing on are faded. It's rained a lot lately, and the park in our neighborhood gets forgotten most of the time. The trash bin by the picnic table is almost always overflowing. The netting of the soccer goal is torn and tattered. But the barest tint of white lightening the blades of grass is all I need to pace to the perfect spot. The metal frame is all that's necessary to adjust my aim.

I take a deep breath, pretending I'm standing on a famous field in front of thousands of people instead of in a run-down park at dusk. Tap my thigh three times, exhale, and then kick. Not only does the ball sail through the goal's opening, but it also goes right through the foot-long tear in the top left corner of the netting—exactly where I was aiming. I smile before jogging forward to retrieve the soccer ball, then start all over again. Coach Wilson told me my aim is the best he's ever seen. He thinks I'll definitely make the all-state team if I try out in September.

Six shots later, I tuck the ball under one arm and head for the playground.

Tripp is sitting on one of the swings, his expression glum as he drags his shabby sandals through the wood chips.

"Come on," I tell him, heading for the gate that leads to the sidewalk.

We walk in silence along the cracked pavement, which is unlike my little brother. Usually, he's chattering away at a million miles a minute.

"What's wrong?" I finally ask.

"Nothing."

"Tripp, tell me."

My little brother exhales. "Cooper was saying some stuff about Dad earlier."

My grip on the soccer ball tightens. I already knew Cooper Mason had been running his mouth. I thought I'd taken care of it before Tripp heard.

"You should have told me."

He shrugs. "I didn't want you to get in trouble."

At that, I scoff. Any trouble I get into, I talk myself out of. "Tell me next time. Promise?"

"Fine. I promise." Tripp smiles, his small shoulders no longer hunched.

My brother is three years younger than me, but he's half my size. Both his height and his easygoing personality favor our calm, short mom. I'm more like our unpredictable, towering dad.

"Can we get Popsicles?"

We're about to pass the small convenience store two buildings down from our house. The owner, Mr. Henry, used to babysit us the evenings our mom had to work and our dad wasn't around. Now that I'm ten, I watch Tripp on my own.

"Sure." There's a five-dollar bill in my pocket leftover from weeding our neighbors' flower beds last week.

Mr. Henry only charges us a dollar each. I choose grape, Tripp gets orange, and then we continue toward our house. The front yard is small enough to cut with scissors, just a couple square feet of grass. And the back of our house looks out at an alley, where lots of stray cats live. I can hear them meowing at night sometimes.

Our dad is in the garage with the door wide open, working on the old muscle car that's been sitting in there for as long as I can remember. My parents argue about it a lot. They argue about a lot of things a lot.

When I was younger, I'd sit in the front seat, pretending to drive it. I haven't done that in a long time. Now, I prefer to play with my friends. Or play soccer. Not spend time around my father, who's usually in a bad mood.

He emerges from beneath the raised hood when he hears our approaching footsteps, some sort of wrench in one hand. I don't know what he spends so much time doing out here. He's never gotten the engine running, not once. Seems like a lost cause to me.

"Where you been, boys?"

Tripp stays silent, so I answer, "We were at the park."

"It's nearly dark. Get inside."

Tripp scrambles toward the front door, and I follow at a slower pace.

"Will."

I stop. Glance back at my father. "What?"

His eyebrows rise at my sharp tone, but he doesn't tell me off. "Your mother is at work. I have to head out for a bit. Look after Tripp."

"You're leaving?"

"You want new soccer cleats, don't you?"

Hesitantly, I nod. Mine were secondhand when I got them.

4

Now, they're so small that they pinch my toes, in addition to being so worn that the rubber sole is falling apart.

My dad nods too. "Then I gotta go do some stuff." He closes the hood of the useless Pontiac and wipes his oily hands on a dirty rag. "Don't cause any trouble."

"I won't," I say.

I might.

I often do when I'm bored.

"Get inside, son."

I listen without saying anything else.

Without glancing back.

Had I known that was the last time I'd ever see my dad, I would have at least looked back.

CHAPTER ONE

SOPHIA

There's something inspiring about sunshine.

Even when you want to ignore it, you can't. It beams and brightens and continues shining. It forces you to acknowledge its presence.

It never hides, which is exactly what I'm currently doing.

Some irritation seeps away as I slouch against the back of the plastic chair and prop my Adidas up on the empty seat in front of me.

The sneakers don't go with the rest of my outfit. They were a last-minute change before leaving my apartment, after Noah told me the fun afternoon he had planned for us was taking place *here*.

It's bad enough that I'm stuck in the last place I'd voluntarily choose to spend a Saturday afternoon. I wasn't going to chance the heeled sandals I was planning to wear with this dress getting ruined. Or waste cute shoes on a visit to a football stadium.

At least the sunshine is out.

And all the way up here, away from the commotion and the

fans, it's easy to pretend that I'm soaking up vitamin D somewhere else.

For the first time since we arrived at Sieg Stadium, I relax.

The hard, hot plastic isn't the most comfortable of resting spots, but at least there's no one blabbing in my ear and rattling off stats anyone with access to a computer could learn. If they *wanted* to.

Noah Hahn heard my last name and thought *football*, same as everyone else. Assumed I love the sport, same as everyone else, proving he didn't listen to much of what I said when we flirted in a bar last weekend. And then decided the perfect surprise outing this weekend would be to take me to a FC Kluvberg scrimmage.

I've never actually said the words *I hate football* to him, but I obviously should have. I thought quickly changing the subject each and every time he brought the sport up would convey that clearly.

I was wrong.

Or Noah is just that oblivious.

Same result—me, here.

There's no need to pretend I'm watching the pitch from the fourth-to-last row of the balcony, so I tilt my head back to let the afternoon sunlight warm my face. Basking in the bright rays helps wash away more of my lingering annoyance. The barest of breezes blows a few blonde strands across my cheek.

I told Noah I was getting a soda five minutes ago. The stadium is nowhere near its full capacity of seventy thousand, as evidenced by all the empty seats around me. Any self-respecting fan committed enough to come to a friendly game—a preseason scrimmage before the season officially begins in mid-August—

purchased seats in one of the lower levels, closer to the action, like Noah.

I'm up here for the solitude, not the view. I figure I can enjoy this respite for another ten minutes before heading back down to the edge of the field. I should be planning out what I'll say to Noah after the game ends—*It's not you; it's your obsession with football,* maybe?—but instead I tilt my head back, close my eyes, and soak in the sun. It's too nice out today to stew. Maybe I'll go for a walk after Noah drops me back off at my apartment.

"You're in my seat."

The sentence startles me. Last I looked, I was completely alone up here. The voice comes from my left, delivered in a deep baritone that raises goose bumps on my skin despite the heat. I've never given much thought to someone's speaking voice —more what they're saying. But the syllables seem to linger in the summer air, a tangible presence besides the humidity.

My head turns toward the sound automatically, and my eyes fly open.

I squint up at the shadow partially blocking the bright sun. He's tall, and he has dark hair, and that's about all my burning retinas are able to absorb before I have to look away at a more muted sight.

I make a show of looking around at the sea of empty chairs surrounding us.

"Um, *seriously?*" I answer in English since that's what he spoke to me in.

His accent is American. His tone is rude, which translates in any language.

A rectangle of glossy paper is thrust directly in front of my face. I scan the ticket until I find the row—E—and the seat number—four—printed toward the bottom, then glance at the chair to the right of the one I'm currently slouched in. Five. Turns out I actually *am* in his seat.

But who marches up to a stranger and demands they move when there are other seats—*lots* of other seats—available? When it's not even a *good* seat? The football field looks like a green-and-white postage stamp from all the way up here.

I raise a hand to shield my eyes from the sun. I'm not willing to risk permanent vision loss to face off with this guy.

But, *fuck*, is looking at him a mistake. I should have taken my chances with blindness.

He's wearing a ball cap and sunglasses and an annoyed expression. None of that disguises the fact that he's undoubtedly the hottest guy I've ever seen.

My older brother, Adler, plays football professionally. He's an international celebrity. Girls I went to secondary school with had his poster up on their wall, which will never not be weird. My parents are both considered football legends as well, long retired, but still relevant. I've been around lots of famous actors and models and athletes because of my family members' successes. Most of them were good-looking in addition to being talented in their respective industries. Meeting them never felt like *this*, though.

This guy has a presence that burns. His golden skin and dark hair remind me of the sun and soot.

Oxygen feeds flames.

I'm suddenly having trouble pulling enough out of the warm air, which should contain plenty.

I clear my throat and look away. Prolonged eye contact with him is more damaging than it would be with the sun.

This is a shorter break from Noah than I was hoping for.

I could *actually* get a soda, I guess. Returning empty-handed wasn't a piece of the deception puzzle I thought through. Although I'm confident Noah will be too focused on the scrimmage to even notice my prolonged absence.

"Fine. I'll move," I say.

"Forget it." The stranger folds his tall frame into the seat right beside me. His bare arm brushes mine as he settles into the plastic.

My every nerve ending feels it.

"Can't believe people sit through a full game in these." He shifts in the chair until he adopts the same pose I'm in—feet up and slouched down.

All he's done so far is scowl at me. I should give him the silent treatment.

Instead, curiosity has me asking, "You haven't been to many Kluvberg games?"

"This is my first one."

His face is focused on the pitch. All I can see is his perfect profile, shaded by the brim of his hat.

I trace the straight lines and sharp angles with my eyes. His jaw is covered with a light layer of dark stubble, but it doesn't do much—anything—to camouflage the fact that his bone structure would make a modeling scout weep. He's wearing a black T-shirt and black athletic shorts. And he's ridiculously in shape. I can see the definition of his broad shoulders and his strong thighs through the clothes he's wearing. Watch the ripple of tendons as he reaches up for the brim of his ball cap and tugs it even lower. His left arm is covered with a sleeve of tattoos, the black ink a swirl of shapes I can't make out in the short time I allow myself to ogle him before looking away, worried he'll catch me checking him out. He seems intent on watching the game, but I can't tell exactly where his eyes are looking behind the barrier of his aviator sunglasses.

His deep voice isn't the only appealing thing about him.

Aside from his prickly personality and weird obsession with assigned seats, I haven't found anything I don't like about this stranger, which is disturbing.

Yeah, he's ridiculously good-looking, but I'm not usually *this* superficial. Obvious beauty can hide other ugliness.

"You're American?" I question.

"Yep."

"What are you doing here, then?"

He looks over at me. *Smirks.*

And my brain sort of short-circuits because, *wow*, is he attractive. Attractive always, but especially when he's amused.

I forget what I asked him. I just stare.

Suddenly, I'm grateful for the extra time I spent on my appearance this morning before I knew it'd be wasted on attending a football match. It's gone mostly unappreciated by Noah, who has barely looked away from the pitch since we got here, completely enamored by the players while I hid yawns behind my hand.

"My dick got me in trouble," the stranger tells me. Still looking this way. Still smirking.

Again, it feels like my lungs forgot how to breathe.

I shake off the bizarre reaction. I haven't been the wide-eyed girl with a crush in a long time. I forgot what this giddiness felt like; it's been so long since I wasn't the one in control. Since I wasn't begging my brain to stop overthinking and let go.

"Can't relate," I respond.

His smile grows, making me feel dizzy. My inhales and exhales still aren't following a regular schedule.

"You?" he asks, as if discussing his penis with a stranger is a normal occurrence for him. Maybe it is. I'm definitely getting strong *I don't give a fuck* vibes from this guy. He doesn't seem the type to embarrass easily or to care what anyone thinks of him.

"I'm on a date."

He makes a show of looking around at the empty seats surrounding us. "And...what happened to your date?"

"He's busy drooling over the team."

His attention is back on me. I can feel the intensity searing through the sunglasses he's wearing, making me want to squirm.

"You don't like soccer."

Two minutes, and he's surmised what Noah couldn't comprehend after hours of my company.

"*Football*. And, no, I don't."

"Why?" It comes out more as a demand than a question.

I shrug. "Overexposure, I guess."

For some reason, my answer amuses him.

"Interesting."

"Are you a big fan?"

"Depends on the day."

I feel my brow wrinkle, not sure what to make of that response. "Are you in Kluvberg for long?"

"Not sure yet."

"Not very committal, are you?"

He makes a sound of amusement in the back of his throat, but doesn't gift me with another full smile. "You got a pen?"

"Uh, yeah."

He holds out a hand. I dig through my bag until I find a ballpoint and pass it to him. He scribbles something on his ticket and then hands it to me, along with my pen.

I squint at what he wrote, the digits only making sense when I remember he's American. Scoff. "Your phone number? I'm here on a *date*."

"Seems like you're up here, *avoiding* your *date*. Besides, I'm not hitting on you."

His smirk is infuriating. Like he knows exactly how bored I was until he showed up and totally captured my attention. I'm tempted to rip his ticket to shreds, just to wipe that smug expression off his face.

But I don't. I keep staring at it.

"You're not?" My voice is thick with skepticism. Self-centered as it sounds, that's what usually happens.

"Nope." He pops the *P* obnoxiously.

"So, you're giving me your number because..."

He shrugs. "We'll see what happens."

"You think I'm going to use it?"

"I don't know. I've never done this before."

"You've *never* given someone your number before?"

He's lying, right? How is that even possible?

"Not to a chick."

"Why not?"

"It sort of gives the impression you want them to contact you, I hear."

I snort. "Wow. You're...that's...wow."

I'm almost...not *impressed*, but close.

Disbelieving. Disgusted. A *little* flattered.

It takes an epic amount of swagger to make confessing you're a shameless player sound charming.

Warning lights flash in my head. This guy has all the right moves.

He stands.

"Is this your dick getting you into trouble?" I can't help but ask, holding up the ticket he bought to only watch a few minutes of the match.

"Dunno. We'll find out." A nod and a smirk, and then he's gone.

Instead of crumpling up and tossing the piece of paper, I fold it in half.

I won't use his number, but I keep it.

CHAPTER TWO

WILL

So far, I hate Germany. Absolutely everything about it. The food and the lack of air-conditioning and the no window screens and the fact that I can't read a damn sign anywhere I go. I took Spanish in high school, and what little I remember besides *gracias* doesn't appear to have any overlap with the German language.

When I'm in the gym, at least I can pretend I'm somewhere else.

Kluvberg's facilities are outrageous. I knew Europeans took their soccer—or football, as I should probably get used to referring to it as—seriously.

I underestimated just how much based on the amount of money this facility must have cost. Forget sports. It's the nicest space I've ever been inside, period.

Every surface gleams. There are no smudges on the glass windows, no balls of dust collected in corners. It doesn't smell like stale sweat and chemical cleaner, the way the facility in Seattle always did. Constant dampness never helped, mildew mixing in more often than not. The air in here is fresh, the purest I've ever breathed indoors. It must have just been cleaned.

The workout room I'm currently inside is right by the indoor field, large glass windows revealing green turf and stark white lines. I focus on the familiar sight as I run through my usual routine of squats, deadlifts, and pull-ups.

I have the facility to myself, as far as I can tell.

My formal introduction to the team hasn't happened yet. I was cleared by the team doctor yesterday after the obligatory medical check. All the paperwork has been processed by the national governing agency, and my player's permit was approved. But the club has yet to make any official announcement about my arrival, as far as I know. Avoiding social media and news sites became necessary unless I wanted to lose my damn mind.

The transfer window doesn't close until the end of August. Roster changes among clubs this close to the start of the season aren't rare. But they're usually a reshuffling of the lower ranks. They rarely involve players who will make much of an impact on the team. Who will influence game outcomes.

I plan to make my presence known.

There's also the fact that I'm American. Most of the team is German, unsurprisingly. There are a few players from England or France or Cameroon. One Portuguese goaltender. An Austrian fullback.

And now, me...the American striker. My main job is to score goals, and I'm fucking good at it.

But it's been a long time since I played with a group of total strangers. Since I felt like my value to a team needed to be proved. I'd be lying if I said that didn't breed some apprehension about what playing on a different continent will be like.

I finish my reps and head for the treadmill, rotating my shoulders as I walk.

Physically, I'm in the best shape of my life—and I wasn't a straggler to begin with. Being the fastest, most aggressive player on the field is a reputation you have to back up with an exhausting regimen. And that's exactly what I've done for *years*.

Destroyed in minutes.

I push the dark thought away. The past month has been filled with plenty of punishing self-pity and regret.

This is a clean start. In theory, at least.

I didn't leave all my problems behind in Washington. Every single article announcing my signing with FC Kluvberg will dredge up some narrative of the events that made it a necessary move in the first place, which is probably why no announcement has been made yet.

Drake blasts my eardrums as I step on the treadmill and start sprinting. I wonder if Germans listen to Drake. I know nothing about the country I'm now living in. Certainly nothing complimentary. I was always more of a slacker than a star student, but I remember some of what we covered in world history.

Maybe I would hate it here less if coming to Germany had been a choice—not a last resort.

Kluvberg was the only organization willing to touch me with a ten-foot pole. I signed a contract worth pennies compared to the value I'll bring to this team. FC Kluvberg is a decent club, but it's been a while since they accomplished anything spectacular.

For over a decade, their best player has been Adler Beck. He became a national icon as a teenager on the world stage. Partly because of his famous family, according to the basic research I did about my new team. Both of his parents played and accomplished impressive levels of success.

Beck hasn't been as successful in his home city as in international tournaments that kicked off his early career. FC Kluvberg has averaged more draws or losses than wins during their past few seasons. They're one of the oldest and most respected football clubs in Europe. But they're boring. Mediocre. Classic. Their hallowed reputation is the most interesting thing about them. They play like all that storied history is weighing them down.

Adler Beck is a solid player and a respected captain. But he's been around for a while. And he's never taken the risks in big games that I take on a regular basis. He's precise and skilled. Controlled talent.

I play to prove a point, and it's obvious each and every time I step out onto the field. It's the one thing that doesn't change, no matter what color jersey I'm wearing. What country I'm playing in.

I run until sweat is pouring off of me, dripping down my face and coating my back with a sticky layer.

As soon as I step off the treadmill, I rub my face with a towel that smells like laundry detergent and chug some water. Maybe I should steal a few of these. My apartment came fully *un*furnished. I bought the absolute essentials—a mattress and sheets and some toiletries once the travel sizes I brought ran out —but I haven't bothered to purchase anything else. Doing so feels like accepting this is a permanent change, not just an unfortunate blip, and I guess some part of me is still in denial about that.

My phone buzzes with an incoming call, cutting off "One Dance."

It's my agent, Shawn, calling.

I strongly consider not answering.

Our conversations are rarely pleasant. I'm a total headache to deal with, admittedly.

I take a seat on one of the weight benches, scrubbing the terry-cloth towel through my short hair. I had several inches shorn off before leaving Seattle, both because of the summer heat and because it seemed like a fitting move before a fresh start.

"Shawn," I greet, looping the towel around my neck.

"How's it going?" He doesn't bother so much as a hello.

"Fine."

"Actually?" His tone is thick with disbelief. As if I'm incapable of not causing trouble just by breathing.

"*Actually*," I reply, scuffing the toe of my running shoe against the edge of one of the black rubber mats. "I'm not going to fuck things up. I know what's at stake here."

His snort echoes across the Pacific loud and clear. Shawn works for Garner Sports Agency, a big company headquartered in LA. He's probably staring out at sunshine and palm trees right now. "Excuse me for not thinking you take your career seriously after the shitstorm I've spent the last couple of months dealing with."

I pinch the bridge of my nose and exhale. "Did you call me for any reason *besides* bringing that up?"

All the tension eased from running until my muscles were shaking starts seeping back in.

Forget the last few years of hard work. My *entire career* has been reduced to that one night. At this point, I could win every award or trophy available, and if you searched my name, the first article to come up would still be related to a drunken mistake.

"Have you met with anyone on the team yet?" Shawn asks.

"No. I'm supposed to meet with Wagner tomorrow afternoon. Maybe he'll want to go out for some bratwurst and a beer afterward."

"Will, I swear, if you—"

"Relax, Shawn. I watched their scrimmage yesterday." Well, a few minutes of it. "They need me. And I'm already under contract for the year."

"You were under contract in Washington too, remember?"

I clench my jaw until a muscle pops. "Yeah, I fucking remember."

I refrain from adding, *Thanks for bringing it up—again.*

Shawn is the only reason I have any career left. The one person who's remained in my corner.

He sighs. "Okay. Call me if anything comes up. No booze and no *women*. I'm a fucking miracle worker, Aster. Kluvberg could save your career. But if you muck this up, the closest you'll get to a job involving a soccer ball is as a middle school gym teacher in a teeny little town that no one has ever heard of. Got it?"

God, he's dramatic. But I don't think he's wrong.

I'm the punch line. The guy who can't keep his cock in his soccer shorts. Before banning myself from reading more of them, I saw most of the articles. Scrolled through the social media posts.

There *is* such a thing as bad publicity, and I'm a walking, talking prime example of it. Clubs want to point to me as an example of what *not* to do, and they don't want to sign me to their roster and deal with a deluge of embarrassing press coverage speculating if they'll be able to straighten me out.

"Got it." I hang up.

Music immediately starts blasting through my headphones again. But all the endorphins from exercising are long gone.

My body feels heavy and lethargic. My evening plans consist of heading back to the empty apartment the team is putting me up in. Go to bed early and wake up early, like I've been doing every damn day since I got here.

I've spent most of my life on a soccer field or inside a gym. And when I'm not exercising or sleeping, I'm partying.

Work hard, play hard has always been my motto.

But all of the things I used to do for fun aren't options right now, as Shawn loves to remind me every time we talk. Excessive drinking and one-night stands are how I ended up here, thousands of miles from anything familiar.

I stand, stretch, then head for the weight rack.

Years of routines are ingrained in my head. All I have to do is count the number of reps as I rotate through working different muscles, music blaring in my ears and blocking out the rest of the world.

By the time I've finished my workout and showered in the nicest bathroom I've ever been inside, the sun is setting. I shove my hands into my pockets as I walk past the separate administrative building and outdoor soccer fields in the direction of what I *think* is the nearest S-Bahn station.

Kluvberg's practice facility is on the fringes of the city in a more industrial, less developed area. The twenty-minute train ride takes me right into the city center, which looks completely different from the sleek, modern facility I just left. Now, I'm looking at stone facades and half-timbered exteriors. Cobblestone streets littered with greenery and abandoned cigarette butts.

If I wasn't here as a twisted form of penance, I guess I could see why someone might want to visit. It's very different from Dorchester, the Boston suburb where I grew up. And from rainy Seattle, where I lived for the past four years.

It's impossible to forget I'm in another country. The architecture and the chatter of foreign words around me are an incessant reminder.

There's a small sushi restaurant tucked in a storefront just before the end of the block. I duck in. The tiny fridge in my apartment is empty, and I've never been anything close to a chef. The house I shared with three teammates overlooking the Sound was stocked by the team's nutritionist. If Kluvberg has one, they haven't contacted me.

The sushi menu is in Japanese, German, and English. I order three spicy tuna rolls, then add on an order of beef udon and seaweed salad for good measure. I just burned about a thousand calories.

Takeout bag in hand, I continue down the street. The last of today's sunshine has almost entirely faded, city lights turning on as I pass by buildings.

Before this trip, I'd never left North America. I took a college spring break trip to Mexico. I traveled with the US team to the Summer Olympics in Montreal two years ago. But I'd never been to Europe before—until I had no choice *but* to come here.

One year.

Time away from the scandal and a kick-ass season overseas are all I need to get back to where I want—need—to be.

I just can't fuck it up.

This is my final chance.

CHAPTER THREE

SOPHIA

Harry's office smells like stale coffee and old paper. I lean back in the overstuffed armchair he keeps opposite to his desk, toeing a stack of old issues as I wait anxiously for him to hang up the phone. My fingers tap out a rapid tempo against my thigh.

My assignments at *Neues Kluvberg*, the regional paper where I'm interning this semester, were determined weeks ago.

This meeting means something changed. Or that I messed up and might be getting let go.

Neither is ideal.

Finally, Harry's call ends.

"Sorry about that." He pushes his wire-rimmed glasses up his nose and takes a sip from the mug next to his keyboard. "Look, you've done excellent work here, Sophia."

"Am I getting let go?" I blurt. That feels like a sentence that's followed by a *but*.

Harry shakes his head. "No, no."

I relax.

"But..."

The tension that just dissipated reappears. My spine straightens, and my shoulders tense.

"You heard about Alex's accident?"

"Yes."

Alex Bauer, a jovial forty-something who spearheads the paper's small Sports section, got into a cycling accident over the weekend.

"Marie said he'll be fine."

Marie works as—I'm actually not sure what her official role here is defined as. But she's beloved, and she knows everyone else's business at all times. Since I started here at the beginning of the semester, she's the one who's helped me navigate photographing for different departments the most.

"He will be. But he broke his wrist and has a nasty sprain in his leg. He'll have a hard time getting around for a little while."

"Okay..." I'm not seeing where this is headed. Signing a *Get Well Soon* card?

Harry sighs. Presses his fingers together so they form a small bridge. "Look...I need you to help Alex cover FC Kluvberg. He'll still be able to write the articles. All you'll need to do is take photos from the sidelines. For a few weeks, until his cast is off."

I blink.

Once.

Twice.

I'm still staring at Harry with his balding hair and his wrinkled button-down. No joking expression in sight.

He's serious, I decide.

Harry shifts in his chair with a *creak*. "I know this might be uncomfortable for you, what with your brother and all. But you're the only photographer we have available. Everyone else is swamped. And you said you were looking for a challenge when you started here."

That "challenge" wasn't supposed to include *football*.

"Harry, I'm not a sports photographer. I've never photographed athletes. I'm not...qualified."

"We're a small paper, Sophia. Frankly, I don't have another option. Alex is a veteran. He'll tell you exactly where to stand on the sidelines, and he can give you guidance on taking the actual photos as well. You've been a real asset here. I have full confidence you can handle this assignment. You're an excellent option for many reasons."

I know exactly what the *many reasons* he's alluding to are, and if he won't state the most obvious one, I will.

"You mean my last name," I say.

Being a Beck is the equivalent of a crown and a throne in monarchist countries. Automatic interest and attention. A spotlight you can't shake. Even if you're the black sheep of the family who's shunned the sport that made the rest of your family famous.

"I believe you covering the team will receive some extra attention, yes. That's good for the paper. It will also be good for your career."

I exhale. "I try to keep my professional life separate from my personal one."

"I understand that, Sophia. I respect that. We Brits prop footballers up on pedestals too. I'm sure the amount of attention your family receives is not always welcome. But it will be there regardless, as I'm sure you've realized by now. Why not use it?"

I contemplate that and sigh. I've told myself the same thing before—many times. The problem is, acknowledging that people fixate on my last name as soon as they find it out and accepting it aren't really the same thing.

"Is this optional or..."

"Of course." Harry pauses. "I can't make any promises this internship will lead to a permanent position here. But our Kluvberg coverage is our most popular section by far. This will get your name out more than anything else you work on here."

It's a shiny incentive, considering many photographers work freelance. My parents think photography is a passing phase for me, a hobby, which I've admittedly cycled through many of. I talked about studying fashion or interior design or music at university before settling on photography. I know neither of them believes I'll actually be able to make a living at taking photos. They're waiting for me to announce what I'm moving on to next. Getting a staff position at *Neues Kluvberg* would go a long way toward proving to my family that I take it seriously. Toward proving to myself that I have what it takes.

Everyone will think I was handed this opportunity because I'm a *Beck*. And they'll be right. But they'll also think I angled for this chance. Used my connections to get it.

I've worked hard to separate myself from the rest of my family, and yet all roads seem to lead back to football, no matter what I do. At some point, I'll have to accept it, just like Harry suggested.

I exhale again, then agree. "Okay. I'll do it."

Harry beams. "Excellent. I'll let Alex know. He's supposed to be back in the office early next week. You two can meet then to discuss more details before the first game of the season."

I nod. "Sounds good. Have a good weekend."

I stand.

Harry clears his throat before I can leave. "One other thing

27

you should know." He grimaces a little. "Kluvberg is rumored to have just signed a new striker. According to my sources, the official announcement is coming out tomorrow. It'll...well, if it's true, it will stir up some controversy. Draw some more attention to the club."

I raise an eyebrow. "Why? Is he coming from Ludlin?" I ask, referring to Kluvberg's main rival.

Harry laughs. He's enough of a football fan to get the joke. "No. He's never played in Europe, actually. He's American."

Rare, but not unheard of.

"Plenty of teams have foreign players."

"His nationality isn't what's most controversial. More the way he left his last team. He was, uh, he was photographed with the team owner's wife. In an intimate situation."

I widen my eyes, understanding Harry's awkwardness.

"Even before *that* particular incident, he had a reputation. Partying. Fights. Clashing with coaches. Issues with other players. He's rumored to have a hair-trigger temper."

"I'm surprised Kluvberg signed him."

More like shocked. The club's head coach, Leon Wagner, is known for not tolerating that kind of behavior. Before Adler settled down with Saylor, his wife, photos of him leaving clubs with different women were regularly splashed across tabloids. I know my brother received several slaps on the wrist for that behavior. And that was tame in comparison to what Harry is describing.

Harry grins. "You wouldn't be if you'd seen him play. He's a beast on the pitch. Never seen a more dominant player. Here." He reaches across his desk to grab a folder and tosses it my way. "Take a look."

I skim the sheet of stats. The numbers are impressive, but that's about all I take note of.

His name is Will Aster. The name prompts no recognition, which is unsurprising. Following the American league isn't on my list of priorities. I steer as clear of football as I possibly can. Or I *did*, rather. That's temporarily changing. Going to the scrimmage last week was a bad omen, I guess.

"He'll be a focus of articles about the team, so I wanted to make sure you were up-to-date."

"Okay."

"I won't forget this, Sophia. I really appreciate you stepping up."

That's the problem with having a boss you actually like. Harry is the dorkiest, sweetest man you'll ever meet with his constantly slipping glasses and his British accent.

"No problem."

It's a *massive* problem, which I acknowledge now that I've committed.

I can't imagine what Adler will say. What my *parents* will say. Football and I are like oil and water—we don't mix. I'd fake a stomachache when we played it at school. As soon as the black-and-white ball came out, I knew everyone was looking at me. The *Beck*.

With admiration.

Respect.

Expectations.

I leave those to my brother. And he's lived up to them, letting me off the hook to do my own nonathletic thing.

The hallway is empty when I leave Harry's office. It's the end of the day. Everyone is in their office, wrapping up, or has already left.

Marie is perched on the edge of my desk when I reach my cubicle. She's a few years older than me, and she's been working here for about eight months, transferring from a larger paper in Frankfurt.

She's quirky and eccentric, but she's never once asked to meet my brother. That's more than I can say for most of the "friends" I have.

"So?" Marie asks eagerly, swinging her legs back and forth. She suggested at lunch we go out for drinks tonight, but I wasn't sure I'd have time.

I'm supposed to have dinner at Adler and Saylor's place tonight. Knowing the news I'll have to break makes showing up late and a little buzzed sound a lot more enticing. It's not like Adler won't notice me standing on the sidelines, snapping photos. I'll have to tell them.

"Yeah. Sure. Let's go."

Marie slides off my desk and claps her hands in excitement. "Yay! I'll go grab my stuff."

I smile at her exuberance, then sit down at my desk to close out of everything I was working on earlier. The meeting in Harry's office took longer than I realized.

I finish quitting all the applications, then open up a new browser window and type *Will Aster*.

Harry isn't the type to exaggerate. I have a hard time believing he'd make up any of what he just told me. And am equally dubious Kluvberg really would have signed a player with that questionable of a reputation.

Last it came up, Adler was excited about the team's roster for this year. I wonder if he knows about the new addition yet. He must, if it's leaked to the press.

The first news result is an article titled "Will's Wrong

Plays." I click on it, registering it was published by an American magazine I'm not familiar with. Black text covers the screen. I skim the article, enough to glean that, if anything, Harry was glossing over details.

But then I reach a photograph of a man standing in profile next to a goalpost, and other details fade away. I might not recognize his name, but I recognize the guy wearing a purple jersey and scowling. His arms are crossed, the left one covered with black ink.

Dark hair. Straight jaw. Full lips.

I've met Will Aster.

Ogled him.

And if I wanted to, I could call him right now.

CHAPTER FOUR

WILL

The first FC Kluvberg player I encounter is Friedrich Schneider.

My meeting yesterday with Leon Wagner, Kluvberg's head coach, was just between the two of us in the office building on the opposite side of the parking lot. There was no warm welcome and definitely no bratwurst or beer. Just a curt overview of the team with a heavy emphasis on its behavior guidelines. Then I was handed off to a bubbly brunette named Ella, who made it clear she was available to assist me with more than navigating the practice facility as she showed me around. Showed me around space I'd already made myself at home in as soon as the paperwork was signed and I received my badge.

Friedrich is seated on one of the benches that lines the pool deck with a leg stretched in front of him. A young woman with short blonde hair is flexing and rotating his ankle. She's dressed in a tracksuit embroidered with Kluvberg's logo, making me think she's a trainer or physical therapist for the club. I suppose I'll meet more of the staff at my first official practice tomorrow.

As soon as Friedrich looks up and spots me, he says something to her in German—at least, I think it's German—and stands. There's no limp in his stride, so his injury can't be that severe.

He looks a few years younger than me. I've only skimmed Kluvberg's roster a few times to try to match names with faces since I'm at a significant disadvantage among guys who have mostly played together for years. I can't remember Friedrich's age, and I'm impressed I recall his name. I do recall that he's a center back.

He emanates the swagger of a kid finally called up to the big leagues, shoving a hand into his hair as he looks me up and down with a growing smirk. "So...you're Will Aster."

His English is good. Heavily accented, but good. Hell of a lot better than my nonexistent German.

"Yep."

He holds a hand out. "Friedrich Schneider."

"Nice to meet you, Friedrich," I tell him as we shake.

His grip is tight, but not exaggerated. "You can call me Fritz." His head tilts to the left, scanning me again. "I've heard a lot about you."

"I'm sure you have." And I'd rather he admit it than pretend not to know how I ended up here.

Fritz shifts back and forth between his feet, still appraising me with an intensity that doesn't match his laid-back expression. "Watched some tape of you playing last night."

I don't react, waiting for what else he might say.

"You're good."

An unconscious smile tugs at one corner of my mouth. I missed the easy camaraderie of being around a teammate, someone who's invested in your performance on the pitch.

Once shit hit the fan in Seattle, none of the guys knew how

to act around me. No one wanted to show support toward a pariah they were no longer playing with. Any loyalty ended at the same time my contract did.

"I know."

Fritz grins back. "You want to grab a drink later?"

I can hear Shawn cussing me out in my head, talking about small towns and big consequences. But sitting alone in my empty apartment for another night might end with me banging my head against a blank wall. I still haven't bought any furniture. Or groceries. I've been picking up takeout every night. It's a pathetic ritual that I need a break from. One drink with a teammate won't wreck everything. I'm capable of self-control and restraint; I've just rarely chosen to show it.

"Yeah. Sure." I glance toward the empty pool. "Give me an hour?"

Fritz nods. "I'll meet you in the locker room."

"Sounds good," I tell him, then head for the stairs that lead into the water.

Fritz returns to the bench, where the woman is waiting to finish his treatment.

I shuck off my shirt and then step into the pool. The water is cool, but I've taken too many ice baths to let the colder temperature dissuade me. I dive in as soon as it's deep enough, chlorine burning my nose as I accidentally inhale some water when I surface. I start to swim laps, the steady rhythm of strokes soothing me the same way exercise always does. My pace is punishing, even though I already worked out for an hour. The ache in my muscles is more pleasant to focus on than any of the shit in my head.

By the time I climb out of the pool, Fritz is gone.

I towel off, deciding to skip the sauna before I shower. Grab my shirt and then head for the locker room, wondering what drinks with Fritz will be like. He seemed friendly enough, but I can't help but feel like I should have my guard up. That it won't be as easy as a compliment and a shared beer to settle in with Kluvberg's team. This is an uncommon situation for everyone involved, but I'm the one at the biggest disadvantage.

Meeting my new teammates will have to happen eventually. We'll be training together. Winning together. Losing together. Traveling together. There's no fucking *I* in team, which has been drilled into my head since I started playing.

I'm not all that worried about the *why* I'm here. The judgment has all been about the foolishness of getting caught, not what I was caught doing. The idiocy and arrogance of not bothering to hide an affair with a married woman.

I'm less concerned with what Kluvberg players will think about the narrative Cassandra Owens spun for the media and more with the fact that I'm an American—an outsider. I've watched enough footage of previous games to know my usual on-field antics won't be a natural integration into the team. I'll stand out in more ways than the color of my passport's cover.

I play most aggressively—most impressively—when I have something to prove.

And I've never had more to prove than I do now.

All thanks to Mark Owens and the fit he threw because his wife had propositioned a man closer to her age than his. He called in a lot of favors to decimate my career, and I intend to make him regret every single one. For people to call him a fool for prioritizing his ego over good business sense. Arrogantly, I thought the team's administration would value my performance on the field over my antics off of it. They didn't, and I'm determined to make them wish that they had.

Fritz is waiting in the locker room when I enter. So is another player I immediately recognize.

Adler Beck is sitting on the ledge in front of his locker, scrolling on his phone. His shorts are Kluvberg's colors, his shirt covered with sponsor logos. He looks like he belongs here every bit I feel like I don't.

Beck stands as soon as he sees me, walking over and holding out a hand. "Adler Beck."

Even if I wasn't aware of his legendary reputation, that move would earn him some respect. He's won every individual or international accolade you can in this sport. We both know I know who he is, just like most of the world. Him introducing himself, humble enough to act like I might not know who he is, doesn't really fit with the arrogant, cocky guy I was expecting to meet. The one who ripped his shirt open after scoring the game-winning goal in the World Cup final.

I shake it, tightening my grip when he does. "Will Aster."

Neither of us drops a hand, silently sizing the other up.

I only have an inch on him, maybe two. He's obviously fit, but he has the sleeker build of a runner. His shoulders aren't as broad as mine, and I could probably beat him in an arm-wrestling contest.

He's still intimidating. Guy has had one hell of a career. There's no air of oversized ego, like the unchecked swagger that Fritz radiated. Just the steady thrum of confidence that comes with being football royalty, I guess. I wouldn't know what that's like.

Even Wagner didn't study me this closely, and I wonder if that was because he knew I had this inspection waiting for me. Leon Wagner might be the head coach, but this is Adler Beck's team in every way that counts. He holds more power over my career right now than a single other person on the planet.

If he accepts me, the rest of the club will fall in line. If he doesn't...I'm probably screwed. More screwed.

A quick glance at Friedrich reveals the younger player is studying us closely, watching and waiting to see how this interaction will go.

I bite the inside of my cheek, trying to hide any apprehension as Beck scrutinizes me.

"You're settling in well?" Beck drops my hand and crosses his arms. He's not exactly *glowering*, but definitely not looking pleased to see me.

I'm guessing his stoicism has something to do with how I was here, training before him. How it's obvious I've been here a while. How I tightened my grip when he squeezed tighter.

I respect him, but I won't be another person who worships the ground he walks on.

"Yeah. It's a nice facility."

Beck doesn't react at first, still staring at me. I'm not sure what he's looking for. Maybe it's just an intimidation tactic. "Yes, it is," he finally says.

"Your English is very good."

Better than Fritz's. He barely has any accent at all.

"My wife is American."

"I know."

One of Beck's eyebrows rises, displaying more interest in those two words than anything else I've said.

"I grew up about an hour from Lancaster University. Saylor Scott attracted a lot of attention."

Honestly, finding out he's married to Saylor Scott was the only part of my research on Adler Beck that provided any reassurance I'd like the guy. I went to college in Philly, but I could have been on the opposite coast in California and heard about the woman dominating the soccer world. I'd heard she'd opted to play overseas, not shocking considering the struggle of the women's league in the US, but still disappointing.

His stern expression shifts into what *almost* looks like amusement. "Yeah, she has a tendency to do that."

Maybe me being American won't be the black mark I figured it would be—at least where Beck is concerned. I doubt he's bothered to watch any footage of me playing the way Fritz has. If he knows anything about me, it's probably just the mistake that landed me here.

He takes a step closer, and I don't move.

Beck is used to being the top player on the team.

So am I.

"This is a clean club, Aster," he tells me. "I don't know what your last team let you get away with, but—"

"I wouldn't be here if they let me get away with shit, would I?"

It's not totally true. Up until Mark Owens got personally involved, Seattle was happy to look the other way whenever I got into trouble. But I'm well aware even the smallest infraction would be treated a lot differently here.

"I'm here to play," I tell him. "To *win*. That's it."

Beck's expression makes it obvious people don't interrupt him often. Maybe ever.

I hold my breath, waiting for his response.

I need his support. His respect, at a minimum. *Yes, sir,* wouldn't accomplish that. But pissing him off won't serve my purposes either. I'm walking a fine fucking line, holding my ground, but not impeding on his territory.

Fritz is the one who breaks the heavy tension thickening the air. "I'll meet you in the lobby, Will."

I'm surprised he's getting involved. Shocked he's letting Beck know we have plans to hang out. I figured any friendliness from the club would be kept on the down-low until the team captain decided how he felt toward me. I guess Fritz is young and reckless enough not to care.

"Okay," I reply.

Beck doesn't comment on my evening plans after Fritz leaves. He just says, "See you at practice," before turning and walking away.

"I'll be there, Captain," I call after him.

As long as he judges me for my performance on the pitch, it'll be fine. Off the field is where I have the tendency to fuck up.

CHAPTER FIVE

WILL

The club I walk into with Fritz doesn't *look* German. Aside from my time in the gym, it's the first time I've felt like I might be back in the States.

Some techno song blares through invisible speakers—in English.

Girls are clustered in giggling groups, wearing short, low-cut dresses. There's the same distinctive smell to the air, like possibilities and promiscuity.

Our appearance causes a bit of a stir. Attention immediately swings our way as I follow Fritz toward the back. He heads for a corner booth two guys are already seated in, tucked away in some sort of VIP section raised two steps above the rest of the club. There's a velvet rope that gets removed for our entrance.

Soccer comes in a distant fourth—if that—to football and baseball and hockey in the US when it comes to sports. I could count on getting recognized anytime I went out in Seattle, but that wasn't the case for most of the players on the team. And it probably had more to do with how frequently I went out than me being a professional soccer player.

I knew football was the most popular sport in Europe. It's different to know that than to *experience* it. Strange to realize my choice of career is why strangers are looking this way and whispering. At least no one seems to be taking photos that might make their way to Shawn.

Both guys in the booth look up as we approach. I recognize one of them as Otto Berger, Kluvberg's goaltender. I assume the other guy must be on the team as well, but I can't immediately place him.

Fritz says something in German that makes both guys grin, then glances at me. "This is Will," he tells them.

Otto holds out a hand first. "Otto Berger."

"Will Aster. Nice to meet you."

"Olivier Pires." The other guy shakes my hand as well. He has a thick French accent.

More scrutiny, only slightly less intense than Adler Beck's. They study me like I'm a science experiment or a foreign species—the American teammate. With more curiosity than animosity, but it's still unpleasant.

My ass has barely hit the booth when a waitress appears to take our drink order. Both Otto and Olivier flirt with her, and she laps up the attention with a few flirty smiles and a hair flip.

I pay more attention to surveying the club than the way her full tits are practically spilling out of her low-cut top. The walls are paneled with some dark wood. I'd guess it's walnut or mahogany, based on my limited knowledge of lumber after working for a construction company a couple of summers back in high school. The lighting in here is dim, the fixtures on the walls all brass. The booth we're sitting on is upholstered with what looks like dark green velvet. Basically, it's a hell of a lot classier than the sports bars I frequented in Seattle. Those were all scarred wood and sticky floors.

After taking Fritz's order, the waitress turns her attention to me. I reluctantly order a club soda instead of the beer I'm craving. Just like I look toward the dance floor when she leans closer, so her cleavage is right in my face.

Avoiding temptation.

Shawn would likely never know if I broke his two rules tonight. If I blew off a little steam and enjoyed myself for the first time since landing in Berlin. But I never thought he'd know about Cassandra either.

I could do a couple of shots. Fuck this waitress.

And someone could see us, record us, photograph us, and I could be on a flight before morning.

To where, I don't even know. I swore I'd never go back to Boston on any permanent basis, and any positive memories of Seattle were washed away. If I return to the States without the bargaining chip of an incredible season with Kluvberg, there's no way my career will be resuscitated.

I hate that I'm in this situation. And I especially hate how it's my own damn fault. I can look back and see so fucking clearly the exact moment when I should have made a different decision. I'd be in Nashville right now, on the road with a group of guys who looked up to me. Instead of in a club in Germany, forcing a fake smile at the hot waitress as she sets my club soda down. I take a sip, the bland, bubbly water as disappointing as I expected.

Olivier is talking about...honestly, I'm not really sure what— it's hard to hear in here, and his French accent is thick, and I have a short attention span when it comes to anything unrelated to soccer—when I see her.

It's like one of those ridiculous movie moments where the crowd parts and everything goes quiet. Four guys move closer to the dance floor, allowing me a clear view of that section of the bar top. I fully tune out Olivier's chatter and the loud music. My eyes stop scanning the shifting crowd or any of the other booths.

It's a singular focus I've only ever experienced on a soccer field.

But it's *here*, now, in a club I've never been to before and in a country I don't want to be living in, staring at the gorgeous blonde leaning against the bar top, talking to the bartender.

Realizing *I know her* in a place where I expected to know absolutely no one.

The list of people I've talked to in Germany out of anything except necessity is a very short one.

I gave her my number, which is even rarer than my sudden focus. She hasn't used it, and I'm torn on how I feel about that, especially now that I'm looking at her again. She's a much more challenging test of my self-control than the beer or the waitress was.

She was beautiful at the scrimmage—endless legs and blonde hair and sass. Freckles on her nose and slouched with her feet up, like a little kid pouting about not getting ice cream.

There's nothing childish about her appearance tonight. She's wearing a short black dress with a pair of high heels that draw even more attention to her legs. The bartender says something that makes her laugh before she takes the drink he hands her.

I look away, focusing on two brunettes at the opposite end of the bar. One catches my eye, giggling into her palm. But my eyes keep skimming, the features of every woman I look at appearing blurred. Boring. And then my gaze swerves back to the blonde, whose name I don't even know.

Why didn't I ask for her name?

I want to know it. Just like I want to know why she hasn't used my number. Why she hates soccer. How the rest of her date went.

I'm bored, I tell myself. I'm bored, and I'm horny, and she's a gorgeous distraction. A challenge since she didn't reach out. The *one* time I gave my number to a woman, and she didn't use it. I snort, shaking my head.

Under the table, my knee bounces wildly as I battle the urge to get up and walk over to her. She's standing alone, staring down into her glass. As indifferent to everything going on around her as I suddenly am to everything, except her.

"All the rumors seem right."

I startle, glancing at Otto. He's studying me. Fritz and Olivier are still talking about something.

"What?"

"Everyone says you stir up trouble, and you're staring at Sophia Beck like that."

My eyes wheel toward the blonde, then back to Otto. "The blonde woman? That's Sophia Beck?"

He nods, smirking as he sips some of his drink.

Sophia *Beck*. I'm on a legendary losing streak, it appears.

"Beck. As in..."

Otto's grin widens as he registers my obvious surprise. "She's his little sister."

I replay what I recall of our short conversation at the stadium. It started with me telling her she was in my seat. Followed by at least one mention of my dick. *Jesus.* It definitely didn't involve her mentioning that her brother was the fucking captain of the team we were watching. *That* I'd remember.

Although I guess I never mentioned *I* was on the team. Didn't seem like the smartest idea, after she just made her dislike of the sport obvious.

I move to stand.

Otto grabs my arm with the rapid reflexes of a goalie. "What are you doing?"

"Fresh drink."

Otto glances at my full glass, then mutters something in German before I walk away, which, I'm guessing, means he knows where I'm really headed.

And I agree; this is stupid. But maybe he's messing with me.

Maybe I'm just using this as an excuse to indulge my selfishness.

I haven't gotten laid since I arrived here. I'm stuck in a foreign country, surrounded by strangers. Soccer, my one constant, is a different game here. More attention, a name change, nicer facilities, new teammates. I need to do something I know I shouldn't, something stupid, just to feel like myself again.

And Kluvberg has a bigger population than Seattle. What are the chances I run into her a third time?

I approach the bar a few feet away from where she's standing, now animatedly talking to a curvy brunette. Sophia towers over her friend. She was sitting for the entirety of our first interaction. But I'd guess she's five-nine, maybe even five-ten with heels on. At six-four, I'm used to cricking my neck to talk to a woman.

The moment Sophia spots me, I *feel* it.

I focus on flagging down the bartender and ordering another

club soda, trying to act oblivious to the eyes burning holes in the side of my head.

It only takes a few minutes for her to abandon her friend and walk over.

She says nothing. Just shoves into the space between me and the redhead who was inching nearer, close enough that I can feel her body heat through her short dress and smell the floral scent of her perfume. It's subtle, not fruity or sweet or cloying in that way that's suffocating. My dick hardens as I battle the urge to lean closer, and it has nothing to do with my recent celibacy. Everything to do with how she's easily the most stunning woman I've ever seen.

Her last name is Beck, I remind myself. At least, I think it is. I haven't come up with any reason why Otto would be lying.

If I'm going to break Shawn's rules, there are a million other women who would be much better options. Frankly, *any* other woman would be a better option. Touching Adler Beck's little sister would be career suicide.

When I glance over, Sophia's head is already turned toward me. Her eyes widen slightly when they meet mine, the blue swirling with secret thoughts. The same intense shade that glared at me in the locker room earlier. Her hair is the same blonde color as her brother's too.

I can't study her as well in here as I could in the sunshine at Kluvberg's stadium. Heavier makeup hides the sprinkling of freckles on her nose. The dimmed lights shade the subtler shifts in her expression.

"Hi."

I pivot so I'm half turned toward her instead of fully facing the bar. "Have we met before?"

Her eyes narrow. Most guys probably fall over themselves

just to get a scrap of her attention. She's the sort of stunning that stands out. That attracts attention.

I grin. Her lips press together in an unimpressed line that looks remarkably similar to the non-smile Adler Beck gave me earlier.

"Nice to see you again…" I let an elongated pause fill where I'd use her name if I wasn't pretending I didn't know it.

"Sophia," she supplies.

Dammit. Otto wasn't fucking with me.

"Sophia." I roll the syllables of her name around in my mouth like they're a taste of the expensive liquor lining the back of the bar.

Intrigue replaces the indifference in her expression when I hold eye contact, which I'm extremely satisfied by.

I doubt she knows who I am. If she's as affronted by soccer as she acted last Saturday, she doesn't pay much attention to Kluvberg's roster changes.

Overexposure. That was her answer for why she hated soccer. I found it amusing then, and I'm even more entertained by it now. Having Adler Beck as your brother would mean lots of exposure to the sport, I guess. I didn't extend my research to any details about his family. I didn't even know he had a sister. But most of what I read included some reference to his—their— parents playing. To a Beck family legacy. To them being football royalty.

I wonder if Sophia ever played.

Add it to the growing list of questions I want to ask her.

Questions I *won't* ask her.

I should tell her to have a nice night and walk away. I've always been good at doing the opposite of what I should. But that's the attention-seeker and the shit-stirrer in me. It's rarely because I *want* to do the thing I shouldn't.

I want to keep talking to Sophia Beck very badly. Almost as badly as I want those long legs wrapped around my waist as I thrust inside of her.

But only one of those actions will end my soccer career.

Words are harmless, so I reach out to pick up her glass. Give it a hearty sniff. "Tequila?"

Sophia shrugs a delicate shoulder at me. The straps of her dress are thin, barely hanging on to her smooth skin. They'd be so easy to tear.

"This was supposed to be a fun night. I had a crappy day."

I hum. "Another bad date?"

She rolls her eyes. "School stuff."

"You're still in school?"

"My last year of university."

I would have guessed she was older. She looks it, composed and worldly.

"And how fun has your night been?" I ask.

"I haven't decided yet."

I try to pin down her tone, and it's like a shifting kaleidoscope. She's younger than me, but I'm not sure by how much. Her features are delicate but proud. Her expression cautious but compelling. I can't tell if she's oblivious to her allure or a practiced seductress. If she frequents spots like this or if it's a crappy day exception.

And I shouldn't care about any of it.

I hum again in response, buying time before I walk away. Studying her the way I assess opponents on the field, trying to satisfy a burning interest with a final glimpse. I'll forget about her. I always do. The only woman I could name from the *fun nights* of *my* past is Cassandra Owens—and not for any flattering reason.

The bartender sets down my drink. I slide him my card, opting not to keep the tab open.

I justified coming here as a social outing to get to know my new teammates better. But a quick glance back at where I left Otto reveals he's got a woman in his lap. Olivier has moved to the dance floor. Fritz is nowhere to be seen. We won't be bonding tonight. I'm better off heading out and getting a decent night's sleep before practice tomorrow.

When I look back at the bar, Sophia is copying my earlier move, lifting the drink and smelling it. "You're not drinking?"

"Not tonight."

"Does it get you in *trouble*?"

I smile at the taunt in her tone. And the revelation that she recalls our conversation. Appreciate knowing my crude summary of how I'd ended up here didn't scare her away and also kind of wish that I'd never known that. I'm interested in her enough already. I don't need to wonder why she looks like a fairy-tale princess but is bold enough to remind me that I mentioned my cock in our first conversation.

"Sometimes."

"Have you decided how long you'll stay?" she asks.

The season is on the tip of my tongue. I'm accustomed to women who want to screw a professional athlete, not someone who views my career choice with the same detachment my family does. It should be more of a turnoff than it is. So, I lie because it's easier. Because I know the dynamic will shift as soon as she knows I'm on the team. That I play the sport she loathes.

"Nope." I pop the *P*, then swallow some soda. "You didn't use my number."

Fucking hell. I wasn't going to mention it.

One corner of her mouth curves upward. It's a tease of a smile, a shift I wouldn't have even noticed if I wasn't studying her expression so closely. "I lost the ticket."

"I don't believe you."

Sophia looks down at her glass. Swishes the clear contents round a couple of times before she looks up and smirks. "I'm not that kind of girl."

"What kind of girl is that?" Without realizing, I fully turned toward her, drawn into her orbit like a planet circling the sun. So close that I can see she has a few freckles sprinkled on her shoulders as well.

"The *casual sex* kind of girl. And you seem like the *casual sex* sort of guy." She raises a challenging eyebrow, daring me to deny it, and it's hot as hell. "Was I wrong?"

"Is there a guy who *doesn't* enjoy casual sex?"

No drama. No expectations. No complications.

Sophia nods. "That's what I thought."

We stand and stare at each other, energy buzzing beneath my skin and in the air around us.

Do I want to kiss her? Touch her? Fuck her?

Absolutely.

But none of that can happen, and I've accepted that. She just ensured that, and I'm grateful. But this...interest hasn't faded. Neither has the pull to continue talking to her, even though I know it won't end with sex. I enjoy being around her, which I rarely experience with women unless we're fucking. Which I rarely experience with *anyone,* actually. I've always been popular, but a lone wolf. Part of why I got the tattoo on my forearm rather than an ode to Seattle's mascot, the way most people assume.

I shove the lust far, far away and refocus on her.

Words are harmless.

"I don't know German," I say.

"I mean, I assumed since we're talking in English."

I scoff. "Coming here wasn't...planned. And it's looking like I'll be here awhile. Few months at least. My apartment is empty, and so is my fridge. I don't have a car or know where to go shopping."

"Buy a guidebook," she suggests, then sips her drink.

"I'm more of an auditory learner. If you were willing to show me around—once—I'd appreciate it."

Even for me, this is impulsive. I know nothing about this girl, except she hates soccer and her last name is Beck. But her last name means she grew up here. Means she knows this city a lot better than I ever will. I'm not going to ask a teammate for help. Shawn's an ocean away, and he would laugh at the idea of assisting me with something like this. I'm not just unaccustomed to asking for help, I avoid it at all costs. But it's easy, asking her.

And...I want to ensure I see her again. Just once more. Then, I'll forget about her.

Twin lines wrinkle Sophia's forehead as she studies me. "You want me to be your tour guide? We don't even know each other."

That's the point.

If she did know me, know why I was here, she'd probably be disgusted.

"Does it get you in trouble?" Her sly tone echoes in my head, and I reconsider. I can't get a clear read on her, figure out if she scares easily, and it's part of the fascination.

But the furrow in her brow is deepening, and that's my answer. She doesn't even know me, probably thinks I ended up here after chasing a work promotion or something, and she's hesitating.

"Never mind. I'll figure it out. Hope you have some fun tonight."

Finally, I walk away.

Resisting the urge to look back with each step.

CHAPTER SIX

SOPHIA

I knock twice before the door swings open.

"Hey!" I throw up my arms.

"You're late." My sister-in-law, Saylor, shakes her head in mock annoyance, but she's smiling.

"I know; I know. But I actually *rushed* to see the cutest niece in the *whole wide world*." I scoop Greta—Gigi, as she's called right now—out of Saylor's arms, lifting her up in the air.

She giggles the cutest baby gurgle that makes me smile.

"My parents here?"

"They were early."

"Of course they were."

My mom considers on time to be late, and my dad follows her schedule. Even for Germans, they're ridiculously punctual.

I press a kiss to Gigi's chubby cheek and then hand her back to Saylor so I can kick off my heels and sling my bag on a wall hook.

"Everyone's in the living room," my sister-in-law says, then continues down the hallway.

She and Adler moved into this ten-million-euro penthouse

right after they got married. It's close to both of their practice facilities and an incredible location right in downtown Kluvberg, but I'm guessing they'll move out of the city once Greta is a little older.

Adler and I grew up running through the gardens of our parents' estate—me chasing butterflies and him after a football—and I'm guessing that's the kind of upbringing he'll want for his own child.

My parents are seated on one of the couches in the living room, grazing on the appetizers that have been laid out.

I kiss both their cheeks, ignoring the headshakes my dress garners. I changed in a haste after leaving the paper so I wouldn't keep Marie waiting for too long. And this is a laundry weekend, which means options were limited. It left me in a short black dress that worked well for 32nd Lounge, the bar we went to, but not so great for a family dinner. Neither of them comments on my outfit, though. My parents gave up on policing my decisions a while ago. Adler is the one who gets their criticism and the bulk of their attention.

No part of me wanted the pressure of carrying on their football legacy. But I also gave up their investment in my choices in exchange, it feels like. They love and support and indulge me, but it's never felt like they expect much. Like now, their matching expressions say, *Of course Sophia wore this to dinner.*

"Are you eating enough, Sophia?" my mom asks as I grab a handful of crackers and shove a couple into my mouth.

It's common knowledge in my family that I'm a terrible cook and essentially live off reheating and takeout.

"Yes," I reply after swallowing, settling onto the couch across from her and then leaning forward to grab a piece of cheese. "How's the patio project going?"

My parents are redoing several parts of their sprawling yard over the summer.

"They're ahead of schedule," my mom says.

"Really?"

"Your papa has been spending a lot of time outside," she explains, glancing at my father.

"Ah." I shove another cracker in my mouth.

My father's default setting is intimidating. Even now, relaxing on the couch, he's wearing what could easily be categorized as a frown. I can only imagine what the workmen are thinking as he appraises their every move.

"Dinner is almost ready," Saylor announces, entering the living room with Gigi on her hip.

My mom immediately opens her arms. Saylor sets Gigi on her lap, then takes the seat next to me, reaching out for the open wine bottle and filling a glass with a generous splash. She downs half of it in one gulp, then glances at me.

I smirk. "Rough day?"

"Rough week. Doctor thinks she's close to teething or it's colic. Either way, it's not much sleep."

"I can recommend a few names for a night nurse," my mom says.

"No." Saylor's response is swift. "Thank you, but I'll get through it."

"*We'll* get through it." Adler walks into the dining room, kissing the top of Saylor's head before taking the seat next to her. Like her, he immediately helps himself to some wine.

I cover my smile with my glass.

My brother has dark circles under his eyes too. But aside from his obvious exhaustion, he looks happier than I've ever seen him, watching our mom cradle his daughter.

"Where was that *go team* mentality at three a.m.?" Saylor teases.

"I didn't hear her!"

Saylor rolls her eyes, then sips more wine.

"Last scrimmage went poorly," my father comments.

Five minutes. We went five minutes with no one bringing up football. And my dad mentions it in his typical no-nonsense fashion. Most of the time, he's measured and serious. Just like Adler. And my mom. None of them knew quite what to do with my exuberance or flair for drama. And it's probably why I felt an immediate kinship with Saylor the first time I met her. She lives life loudly too.

"Adler played well, though," I comment, trying to be a supportive sister. It always feels like the least I can do since Adler shouldered the burden of being a Beck when I shunned it.

"You saw the match?" Adler asks, glancing at me in surprise.

"No," I lie. "Just assuming you did."

If I admit I went to the friendly match last weekend, I'll have to share why I went. Which will lead to an unnecessary conversation about Noah and our short-lived relationship.

I lose interest in guys fast. There's an initial flash of appeal and attraction that always dwindles away. So, I've stopped mentioning guys to my family to avoid the knowing looks when I tell them we're no longer seeing each other.

Adler looks fond and a little exasperated as he nods. "Wagner signed a new striker," he tells our father. "He starts practicing with the team tomorrow."

My stomach does a strange clench when my brother mentions Will. His vulnerable, defeated expression when he asked for a tour guide flashes in front of my face.

"Really?" Unsurprisingly, that captures my father's total attention. "You've met him?"

Adler nods, which captures mine.

"And?" my father prompts.

"He's...it'll be interesting." Adler rubs his jaw, shrugging.

Having met Will, I know exactly what my brother means. Everyone else looks confused.

Adler glances at Saylor. "He's American."

"He is?"

"Yeah. Knew who you were. He said he grew up near Lancaster."

"In Connecticut?"

"I guess?"

"You didn't ask?" Saylor rolls her eyes.

"It was a brief conversation," Adler says defensively.

"What's his name?" She pulls out her phone.

"Will Aster."

Saylor types something, then smirks. "You didn't mention he's *hot*."

"*Saylor*."

My sister-in-law laughs, then turns the screen toward me. She found a shirtless photo, not the photo of him leaning against the goalpost, and I almost swallow my tongue. I knew he was good-looking, but...*fuck*. His muscles look like they were carved from marble; they're so sharply defined.

"His stats aren't bad," Saylor comments, continuing to scroll.

"His stats aren't what I'm worried about," Adler says.

"Then what are you worried about?"

"He's arrogant."

"So are you," Saylor shoots back.

"I've proven myself, though."

"He scored *thirty-three* goals last season."

I have no idea how many goals Adler scored last season. Based on his scowl, less than thirty-three.

"So?"

"*So*, he's not an idiot to be arrogant."

Adler scoffs.

"He played in Seattle and—*oh*."

I'm guessing Saylor just saw something about why Will Aster is here. Something that, shockingly, I didn't think about once while I was talking to him. It wasn't until I was watching him walk away that I remembered he doesn't just like casual sex. He likes casual sex with married women. Or with *a* married woman, at least.

Gigi suddenly starts screaming.

She's the cutest baby I've ever seen. But, *wow*, does she have a pair of lungs on her. Both Saylor and Adler stand to help my mom soothe her.

The ear-splitting sound stops the socializing in the living room and prompts a move to the dining room. Dinner gets served, most of the meal monopolized by Gigi getting handed around as everyone else tries to pacify her. One of the perks of being the only person at the table with no kids is that I get skipped over. Instead of patting a miniature back or cooing, I just shovel the roast chicken Saylor made into my mouth between sips of wine.

Once Gigi has finally fallen asleep in Adler's arms and conversation is possible again, my mom asks about my classes. I complain about my most boring one—media law—and explain my advertising photography project for a fake fashion line.

"How's your internship going, Sophia?" Saylor wonders.

The perfect opening. I fiddle with the slender stem of my wineglass. "Uh, okay."

My tentative tone gains Adler's attention. "Just okay? I thought you were really enjoying it."

"I was. I mean, I am. I..." I take a deep breath. "I got a new assignment today. A guy who works on the Sports section got into a cycling accident over the weekend."

"That's awful. Is he all right?" my mom asks.

"He'll be fine. Just got a little banged up. He needs an assistant to cover the club, though. A photographer, so..." I glance at Adler. Muster a smile. "I'll wave at you from the sidelines."

Adler starts laughing. Then realizes, "You're serious?"

"Yeah. My boss made a big deal about it, so..." I shrug, like I'm truly unbothered and try my best not to be. "It'll be a new challenge, doing sports photography."

"Good for you, *schatz*," my father tells me.

He says some similar version of that every time the topic of photography comes up. Supportive, but not understanding. Paired with the childhood endearment, it feels like his usual indulgence.

My father thinks taking photos is a hobby, not a career, and I've never been bold enough to ask him why kicking a ball around a field qualifies as a higher pursuit in his eyes. My dad is an older, sterner version of Adler, but I've never seen him display any of the warmer affection my brother does. He shows his love in subtler ways, like the apartment he bought me in the city center before I started university. Like the wine we're drinking, the same bottle he brings every time we do one of these family dinners because Saylor once commented how much she liked it. He never makes a scene about showing his affection. He handed me the apartment's keys in the same matter-of-fact way he sets the bottle on the table.

I'm terrified to disappoint him, desperate to impress him. And that's a large part of why Harry's request was too hard to pass up. Plenty of successful photographers work freelance. But I'm hoping I'll be able to tell my family—my dad, in particular— that I have a steady staff position. That they won't need to support me post-university as I continue to waffle around on what to do with my life. Hopefully my short stint as a sports photographer will be my ticket to accomplishing that.

One obvious difference from my intended career and my brother's: Adler has made millions through football. Not only is he the highest-paid player in the German league, he has sponsorships and endorsements and has been gifted so many free sports cars that he gave me one. I'm proud of my family's accomplishments. But I don't want to be supported by them any more than I want to be defined by them.

"Does that mean we'll see you on Saturday?" my mom asks.

Kluvberg's first game of the season.

"If you look at the sidelines, yeah. I don't know exactly where I'll be standing."

"I'm sure you'll do an amazing job," Saylor says. "Your photos are incredible."

"Thanks." I smile at her.

Gigi starts wailing again, and everyone's attention shifts off of me.

———

I glance over when I hear the door slide open. My parents left about twenty minutes ago since they have a longer drive home.

After helping with the dishes, I opted to carry my wineglass out onto the enclosed patio that boasts an expensive view of Kluvberg. I'm sprawled out on the couch, staring up at the few stars whose light isn't drowned out by the brightness of the city.

Saylor walks out with her own wineglass and takes a seat on the matching couch, tucking her feet underneath her.

"So...where did you go tonight?"

I raise one eyebrow.

Saylor smirks, glancing at my dress. "Come on. That's what you picked out for dinner *here*? What a waste of a cute dress."

No matter how much Adler pisses me off sometimes, I owe him majorly for getting me Saylor as a sister-in-law. For a while there, I thought he'd end up with one of the aloof models he'd "dated" for years.

"32nd Lounge."

"Ooh. Is that the place with the velvet booths?"

"Yep. Exactly." I take a sip of wine.

"And? Any cute guys?"

"*Saylor*."

The screen door slides open again, and Adler appears on the balcony.

My sister-in-law laughs, lifts her legs, and then drops them on his lap once he's sat down. She wiggles her toes, and he starts rubbing her feet.

"I was just *asking*."

"Sophia still has a semester left of university. She should be focused on finishing school."

Saylor rolls her eyes. "Right. Because we all know you were hitting the books *hard* at twenty-two."

"Sophia's smarter than I am."

"She's also *young*. She should be going out and enjoying herself, which is *exactly* what you did at her age. *Hypocrite*."

I smile before taking another sip from my wineglass. Saylor is the one person my brother tolerates pushback from, and it's always entertaining to see him fold.

Sure enough, he sighs, but says nothing else.

Cries start to come through the baby monitor. No wonder Saylor and Beck look so exhausted.

As adorable as my niece is, being over here makes me very glad there's no possible chance I could be pregnant.

"I'll get her," Beck says, standing.

Saylor straightens and stretches. "I'm grabbing more wine. Want some?"

"Sure. Thanks."

I lie back and stare at the lights of Kluvberg.

Rather than relax and enjoy the pricey wine and expensive view, I tighten my fingers around the glass, my teeth worrying my lower lip.

I wasn't expecting to see Will Aster again, except from a distance with the barrier of a camera lens between us. Wasn't expecting to be close enough to discover that his eyes are the same shadowy shade of pines. Or that one of the tattoos on his forearm is a wolf. Details I didn't get to absorb during our memorable first meeting.

I grab my phone and scroll through the contacts until I find his number. I lied to him about losing his ticket. Even if I had, what he wrote down is saved here. I'm irritated with myself that I even put his number in my phone, especially now that I know who he is. I pegged him as a player, and I was right.

Except what was just supposed to be part of a funny, strange story has become infinitely more complicated. Not only because he's one of Adler's teammates—and a controversial one at that. Or that he's American. Or that I'm now assigned to taking photos of the team.

The main problem is that my memory didn't twist my recollection of him. Part of me thought—hoped—the bright sun and Noah's underwhelming company were what made Will stand out like a shooting star.

But he was equally compelling earlier. Just as gorgeous and magnetic. Charm that's so easy to get lost in.

So, now, his number is a tease that I wasn't counting on.

Usually, mysteriousness fades the more you learn about a stranger. But everything I've learned about Will—both from others and our two brief conversations—has only piqued my interest in him more.

I'll have to see him again, starting at the first game of the season on Saturday.

I'm apprehensive. Unsure.

Excited.

CHAPTER SEVEN

WILL

"A ster!" Leon Wagner follows up his shout of my surname with a series of harsh syllables.

"Is that how you say *good job* in German?" I ask Olivier, who's standing nearest to me.

His lips press together into one thin, flat line.

Guess not.

I sigh and jog back toward the center line, where Kluvberg's head coach is waiting.

"Why did you not pass?" Wagner barks, his arms crossed.

He's standing in a warrior stance, legs spread and chin lifted. Looking just as intimidating beneath the bright sun as he appeared beneath the fluorescents in his office. He told me not to make him regret taking a chance on me during that meeting.

He looks like he's regretting it right now.

"I had the shot." Made the goal, too, but that seems unnecessary to point out. The whole squad saw, and I even caught a few impressed expressions before Wagner called me over.

"Because the point was to pass," Wagner tells me. "No one expected you to shoot."

It was an awkward angle, and Otto Berger was in the goal, even if he wasn't expecting me to be the one taking the shot. As a goaltender, his entire role on the team is to be prepared for anything when the ball is in play.

I'm positive reminding Wagner of that won't go over well.

"I'm trained to shoot."

Wagner's expression doesn't change, remaining the same hard, unflinching one I've only ever seen him wear. "Americans have benches, no?"

"I wouldn't know. I wasn't the one riding 'em."

I only catch the barest glimmer of amusement on Wagner's face, but it's there. And it inflates my chest with hope that maybe Kluvberg isn't the jail sentence I imagined. I'm used to coaches showing me total deference. If I'd pulled that move in Seattle, Garcia would have nodded and told me to save some for the game. My former coach couldn't have cared less about me disobeying his instructions as long as the soccer ball ended up in the back of the net.

I thought I loved that autonomy. I'm realizing now it's also a little...boring. Wagner holding me accountable isn't terrible, but I don't want to be closeted by close confines either. No game goes according to plan, so training like it will seems pointless. My first instinct is to shoot, not pass.

"Go practice." Wagner jerks his chin toward the bench, his expression reverting to stoicism so quickly that I might have imagined any warmth.

I nod before taking a seat on the bench and accepting a water bottle from one of the trainers. I swallow several sips, then lean forward to watch the activity on the field.

Beck is dribbling toward the goal. He sends a clean pass over to Stefan Herrmann, another veteran on the team.

Herrmann shoots...and it lands directly in the waiting arms of Otto Berger.

I scoff, then lean back against the hot metal bench.

Rather than continue to watch my teammates follow instructions, I let my gaze drift.

I'm trying a new thing—focusing on the positives of playing here, and one of them is the stadium we're inside. Since tomorrow is a match day, today's practice is taking place in Sieg Stadium to prepare.

I've been inside before, during the friendly match I witnessed. But this is my first time on the field itself, and I'm appreciating the opposite view. Looking around instead of down.

For all the upsides of playing in the States—the main one being it's where I chose to play—I never would have experienced *this* there.

The stadium in Seattle had a maximum capacity of twenty thousand and was rarely half full. This place seats *seventy* thousand, and tomorrow's game is sold out.

There have been a lot of humbling moments recently.

This is another big one, looking at the thousands and thousands of empty seats. Imagining what this place *sounds* like when full.

In Seattle, I was the main attraction. People came to see me. There was an importance and a responsibility intrinsic in that, one I lived up to the only way I knew how. By being entertainment. By putting on a show that included risks and hamming it up when I was on the field. I'm excellent at getting the ball in the back of the net, and I'm just as good at putting on a show as I score.

Here, I'm part of an institution. Of history, it feels like.

Everyone who shows up tomorrow will be here to see FC Kluvberg play, to pledge allegiance to a club that's one of the oldest and most respected in Europe. Most of them probably won't even know my name.

Two defensive midfielders, Böhm and Winter, take seats at the opposite end of the bench.

I glance toward them.

Neither meets my gaze. The heat isn't keeping them from giving me the same cool shoulder.

I pick up the water bottle and take another sip, feeling beads of sweat dribble down my back.

Aside from Fritz's drinks invitation, indifference is the warmest reception I've received.

It's a jarring contrast from every other team I've played on. Starting in elementary school, I've always been the player who gets noticed. Who draws attention. Who other guys gather around.

Being banished to the outskirts is fucking uncomfortable. It's like I'm on the other side of a window, watching the rest of the team through a glass wall.

I get the uncertainty. I came in right before the start of the season as a foreigner with a colorful past, to put it mildly. I haven't looked up any of the press coverage surrounding me signing with Kluvberg because I know it'll just piss me the fuck off. But it's not hard to imagine what's being said about me.

I keep my gaze on the trampled blades of grass right in front of the bench, watching them slowly straighten.

Tomorrow, I'll have the chance to prove myself.

Unless, of course, Wagner decides I need more "practice," sitting on a bench.

CHAPTER EIGHT

SOPHIA

Nerves swirl in my stomach as I approach a waiting Alex, the laminated plastic of my press badge banging against my chest with each step. He advised wearing neutral colors since we'll be standing on the sideline. So, I'm dressed in all black, and my skin is already prickling with sweat. From the heat and because...

I'm *so* nervous.

And it has nothing to do with this being a position I'm not properly qualified for. Or my brother. Or my distaste for football.

It has everything to do with knowing I'm about to see Will Aster.

I barely know him. Owe him nothing. But there's a persistent fluttering when I think about seeing him. When I consider *he* might see *me.*

Alex greets me with a cheerful, *"Wie geht's?"*

"Es geht," I reply.

His forehead creases with concern, so I quickly amend my answer to a more enthusiastic one than *fine.*

Honesty isn't always the best policy.

My pace matches Alex's slow steps. I'm not wearing a cast or walking with a crutch. Just carrying a bag of heavy equipment and apprehensive about seeing a hot guy.

Alex heads for the press entrance, and I follow him.

As we walk, he coaches me on everything we already covered during our meeting this past week. The main one is to avoid drawing attention from the field or from the stands. Spectators should be focused on the pitch. Players should be focused on the game. He also reminds me to keep an eye on my surroundings, to make certain I'm not blocking another photographer's shot and to play attention if a player's close to getting shoved out of bounds. He then teases me about not asking for autographs or cheering when Kluvberg scores. My lack of appreciation for football also came up during our meeting, which Alex found entertaining.

Despite my anxiety, it feels very professional to flash my badge at the security guard monitoring the side entrance and walk beneath the stadium.

There are nearly two hours before the match is set to start, so the stands are still empty. It's so quiet that I can hear the rubber soles of my sneakers hitting the concrete floor as we pass by the colorful posters hanging on the walls. Adler is in a lot of them, mid-kick or celebrating a goal with teammates. My stomach twists as I realize those are the type of shots I'm meant to take today. The only living, moving subjects I've photographed before are wildlife and my niece. I took a three-week trip to Kenya for a photography workshop that was offered through the university. Those photographs were only for myself. And Saylor asked me to do Gigi's newborn photo shoot, but my niece slept through most of it, so she was a much easier subject than a sprinting athlete.

The tunnel leads right out onto the field.

Alex is a steady presence beside me as we enter the stadium, despite his limp. He didn't need to show up since he's technically on medical leave from the paper and I'm the one with the responsibility of taking photos today. But I'm very relieved he offered to accompany me.

Ahead, Kluvberg's pitch is a familiar sight. I've been to this stadium before. Many, many times.

But those visits were all in the stands with spectators, usually making up a sold-out crowd. Never when the pitch and the seats were empty, the sprinklers sending arcs of water over the green grass. Standing by the field, rather than looking down at it, means the stretch of green ahead appears almost endless.

And...I see a *little* of the appeal of the view, I suppose.

A tiny shot of excitement mixes with apprehension and uncertainty as I stare at the damp stripes in contrasting shades of green, alternating between darker and lighter. The thousands of empty seats are patterned with Kluvberg's colors and letters, spelling out the club's name. There's a presence to a place like this. A majesty. Like standing in the center of a giant cathedral. Plenty of people pray here, so it seems like a fitting comparison.

"Sophia!"

I pause a few feet from the field, glancing back at an approaching Adler. He's already dressed for the upcoming match, his expression bright and animated as he jogs over to give me a quick hug, careful not to jostle my camera bag.

He hands me the bottle of water he's holding, the plastic side so cold that condensation is dripping down. "Stay hydrated. It'll be a warm one."

Adler has always been overprotective, but it's gone into overdrive since he became a father.

"I'm not the one who will be running around in the sun."

"You're not the one with sidelines staff either." He holds the bottle closer. "Just take it."

I do. "Thanks." Then glance at Alex. Adler does the same. "This is Alex."

My brother holds out a hand. "Adler Beck."

"Alex Bauer." Alex smiles. "Wouldn't consider myself much of a sports reporter if I didn't already know who you were, *Kaiser*."

Adler offers his polite smile, the one that doesn't reach all the way to his eyes. His business one that says he's ready to play and in business mode. The one that earned him the nickname Alex just referred to. Emperors are supposed to be untouchable and domineering.

If I hadn't seen it happen so many times before, the starstruck expression on Alex's face would be funnier. I guess the other times he's been around FC Kluvberg players have been far less intimate than the three of us standing together.

His awed reaction is basically what I expect now. Whenever I mention my last name or my family to anyone—professors, friends, guys—they either try to play it cool to the extreme or pepper me with questions. Both are irritating.

"Enjoy the game," Adler says, then jogs back the way he came.

"Good way to start the day," Alex comments as we walk along the sideline.

I can feel the excitement radiating off of him the same way the sun is beating down.

I nod and return his smile. I can see the group we're headed toward, other photographers with press credentials, mostly gathered next to the corner flag near the edge of the penalty box.

The sprinklers are on, and a few errant droplets of spray reach me. The cool water feels good. I try to focus on the feel of it dripping down my bare forearm rather than the apprehension about where we're headed. I'm not normally intimidated in new situations, and I hate that I am now. Not only is this my big chance to prove my worth as a photographer, according to Harry, but the stakes are also higher. My grip tightens on the water bottle, a physical reminder of what I'm taking photos of today.

I've always strived to keep my identity totally separate from my brother's. To not let my last name overtake my decisions or my interests or my life.

And it's been a fine line to walk. To balance pride and to also set some boundaries. To support but to try to ignore the circus that's the national interest in my family's ability to kick a ball into a goal. As much as I adore Saylor, she's only amplified it. Women's soccer has never been more popular than since Adler Beck started showing up at matches. They're this athletic power couple. And Saylor is always happy to discuss football with my dad or to go for runs with my mom. She fits in with my family better than I do. Better than the guys I've introduced to my family, specifically chosen because they didn't seem to care who my family members were.

I pull my camera out of my bag and snap a few photos of the glistening turf and the empty stands. Having the familiar weight in my hands, my fingers curled around the smooth plastic, helps soothe some anxiety.

"Impressive, isn't it?" Alex asks. He's looking around with

the same awe on his face as when Adler stopped us despite the fact that he's undoubtedly been here many times before.

"Yeah, it is." I admire one of the shots I just took—arcing water, backlit by sunshine, the green glint of grass obvious beneath. Maybe I won't be terrible at this.

"And very different from how it'll look during the game. You'll have to tune out all the activity. It gets overwhelming. And remember to never turn your back to the pitch. I've seen pros get taken out by wayward kicks."

Wonderful.

Alex runs through the names of the other photographers assembled once we reach the group. He doesn't mention my last name during the introductions, which I appreciate. After some polite conversation, I busy myself with checking over my equipment when Alex continues chatting. The other photographers are mostly middle-aged men and all seem to be people he knows well.

He fits in here. I don't.

My palms and the back of my neck prickle with sweat as I fiddle with settings.

Last week, I was assigned to photograph a symphony performance for the Arts section. It was boring, honestly, because there was hardly any movement on stage, except the conductor. All the photos were identical, aside from the position of the conductor's hand.

This? This is the total opposite.

Soon, I'll be surrounded by rowdiness and distractions. Spectators cheering, coaches yelling, players running. And as if the commotion wasn't an overwhelming enough work environment, goals get scored in seconds. The shots that will be valuable aren't the ones you can sit around and wait for. You have to be ready to react instantly. Reading plays and spotting openings, just like the players on the pitch.

This isn't an assignment for a class that I can retake photos of until I'm satisfied with the final result. This is the first true test of my skills, and I'm scared I'll fall short. Especially since I know any photo of football taken by a Beck will be scrutinized extra closely.

Once I've made sure all the equipment is ready—even if I'm not—I pull my phone out and distract myself by looking through my messages.

Not that professional, but this isn't technically a job. I'm an unpaid intern, spending my Saturday afternoon watching the national pastime I've spent years avoiding.

Alex is still busy socializing, and the field is empty.

Most of my unread messages are from the group chat I'm in with my closest friends. I didn't tell a single one of them about this assignment, which summarizes our friendship well. They all care who my brother is, even if they pretend not to. It's exhausting, filtering everything I share, but it's what I've had to do for as long as I can remember. Never knowing what will get spread around.

I told *one* person I was busy because of my brother's engagement party, and it was in the papers the next day. Adler told me not to worry about it, that he'd shared the news with plenty of people, but I'm still certain it was my fault that him proposing to Saylor was leaked.

According to my many messages, my friends are all headed to Queen Victoria tonight. It's a new club that opened up downtown a few weeks ago. I'll probably end up going.

As predictable as those evenings have become, they're

expiring soon. Summer semester is going to end, my time at university right along with it.

"So, you hate football, huh?"

I freeze before looking up from my phone, knowing exactly what I'll see. Or having an idea, at least.

I'm not fully prepared for the sight of a smirking Will Aster wearing a Kluvberg jersey. It's a collision of two worlds. The guy I met in the stands and ogled at a bar. The sport I *hate*.

He's stopped on the other side of the white goal line, a football trapped under his left foot. But he's not looking this way. He's focused on the filling seats surrounding the field, so I can admire his perfect profile without him noticing.

Perfect is not an opinion. More fact. It's strong and striking.

I swallow as I take in the other players scattered across the field for warm-ups. None of them are talking to any of the other photographers.

"Waste of a perfectly good Saturday afternoon, if you ask me."

Will glances at me, smirks, and I learn he has a dimple. Just one on his right cheek. My heart takes off at a gallop.

"Say that a little louder, and you and I'll be the two most popular people in this stadium."

"The team is giving you trouble?" I ask. I know hardly anything about the club's dynamics because I've always tried to block out Adler and my dad's conversations about the topic. But I know enough to know there must be some politicking, especially with a new player.

Will tilts his head. "Who's wondering? The girl who's been overexposed to soccer? Adler Beck's sister? Or the woman who's here as...press?"

I don't know him. I don't owe him any explanation, and he's not asking for one.

But I feel the odd urge to give him one.

"Those are all the same person, Aster," I reply instead, not bothering to ask who told him who my brother is. Not bothering to pretend him playing for Kluvberg is some sort of shock to me.

He runs a hand through his hair, those piercing green eyes remaining on mine the whole time. Filled with questions I doubt he'll ask and I won't answer.

"Guess I know why you never asked for my name."

I had no idea who he was the first time we met, and I said nothing in the club because I knew it would shift the flirty dynamic I was enjoying. That's not an explanation I want to share with him. "I'm just here for a school assignment."

Will nods. "Good luck."

"That's what I'm supposed to tell you."

"Nah. I don't believe in luck." He winks at me, and my traitorous heart does a somersault. "Get that fancy camera ready. I'll score a goal for you, Sophia."

"Only one?"

"Only one because you never texted me. So, if we lose..." He shrugs, smirks, then kicks the ball up and catches it neatly before jogging away.

I'm pretty sure my mouth is slightly agape as I watch him head back toward where the rest of the team is warming up. For the first time—ever—I'm focused on a football field for a reason other than obligation.

I want to watch Will Aster score a goal for me.

CHAPTER NINE

WILL

My knee bounces incessantly as I watch Olivier kick to Beck. My elbows dig into my thighs as I focus on the action in front of me, my restless leg jostling my entire body.

God, I hate this view. It doesn't matter that I'm underneath a shaded overhang covered with sponsor logos. Or that the seats are leather and comfortable. I'm stuck *watching* the game I should be *playing* in.

I could count on one hand the number of times I've sat as a reserve player instead of a starter during a game. I need zero fingers to count how many of those times I wasn't injured or sick.

It's humiliating. It burns, like salt sprinkled on an open, untreated wound.

My back is to the crowded stands closest to the bench, and the seats on the opposite side of the field are too far away for me to make out any spectator expressions. I doubt many—any—of them are looking at me. They're focused on the action on the field. The action I'm not a part of for the first time in my career.

We're probably going to lose.

FC Ludlin, the club we're playing today, is good. Better than Kluvberg is. Better than *we* are, I guess I should start getting comfortable saying.

I'd probably feel a lot more invested in the team if I'd stepped on the field since warm-up ended. According to the mutterings around me, playing Ludlin in Sieg Stadium is the German equivalent of the Yankees coming to Fenway Park. No one *wants* to lose. None of them seem to care I could help them win either. Least of all Wagner, who hasn't glanced away from the field since the second half started.

I glance down the field, past the low barrier flashing advertisements, where the photographers are standing. Where Sophia Beck is standing.

Sophia didn't seem surprised to see me. Or that I knew her last name. Both of which threw me.

And a woman is the last thing I should be thinking about during a game.

Normally, I'm excellent at keeping my focus on the field. A tornado could be passing by, and I'd keep running unless it crossed the touchline.

But I'm usually playing in the game.

So, I let myself scan the sideline for a minute, my annoyance mounting when I can't spot her. Doubling when I can't figure out why I'm even looking.

I shouldn't be fixated on any woman. I definitely shouldn't be fixated on *her*.

Trent Banks, Otto's backup, is nearest to me on the bench. He glances at my wildly bouncing knee, the only part of me getting a workout, then at me. "Calm the fuck down, mate."

He means it to be reassuring, I think. But the only thing that'll *calm me the fuck down* is getting out on the field. That's the only way I'll be able to pretend I'm somewhere else. That I'm someone else—a guy who still gets to play soccer.

I wasn't thrilled about coming here, to put it mildly. Regardless of how big the stadium is or how nice the facilities are, Kluvberg isn't where I wanted to play. But I thought I *would* get to play, and I feel stupid for assuming so. There are a lot more than eleven guys on the roster. I assumed I would be one of the eleven because I always have been, and this is yet another humbling moment, as I realize I might not be. I can't forget where I am if I'm sitting on the bench. I can't prove to the team signing me wasn't a mistake if I don't even get to touch a ball.

There's a whistle on the field, followed by the waving of a yellow card toward a Ludlin midfielder.

Fuck it.

I stand, ignoring the questions being called behind me as I leave the shade and march right up to a suit-wearing Wagner. "Am I going to play?" I demand.

He doesn't look away from the field as he tells me, "Sit down, Aster."

"I've been sitting for the past hour."

Wagner doesn't respond, his gaze still on the field. Play will resume any second, and I'll look even stupider for pushing this than I already do. But he can't release me for being belligerent—at least, I don't think he can—and I'm already not playing. I don't have much to lose. And if this is what my career has already been reduced to—watching—I don't really care if this has consequences.

"Why did you sign me if you weren't even going to let me play?"

"*Sit down*, Aster." Wagner's tone says *or else.*

I listen, this time, deciding not to discover what that *or else* might be.

As soon as I sit back down beside him, Trent glances over. His expression is incredulous. "You crazy?"

"Probably," I respond.

You have to be a little bit nuts to dedicate your life to something the way I committed mine to soccer. Normal people have multiple passions. Different interests. Stable relationships. They don't consider chasing a ball around a rectangle of grass to be as good as life gets.

And if that's gone, if I lost that the minute the photos with Cassandra hit the internet, I'd rather have never come here. Never had the hope dangled that my career isn't over. I could have retired in disgrace, moved somewhere remote like Maine or Vermont or Colorado. I've always wanted to snowboard more. I wouldn't have to worry about breaking a leg or not being able to afford a lift ticket the way I did last time I hit the slopes.

I crack my knuckles, close my eyes, and exhale. I'm stuck in Kluvberg. I signed a contract. At the very least, I'm getting paid a decent amount just to sit here.

A sudden, loud chorus of boos captures my attention.

Ludlin just scored.

"Offside," Trent says.

On the field, a review is already being requested. Everyone, except me, looks relieved when the goal is ruled offside, and the score reverts to an even zero. Maybe us officially losing would have been enough to convince Wagner to give me a shot.

Minutes keep ticking by. We're up to seventy-five minutes of play—fifteen minutes of remaining time, plus whatever the officials decide to add—when Wagner barks, "Aster!"

I jump to my feet and stride over to him. "Coach."

Wagner just nods toward the field.

Herrmann is jogging this way. I glance at the sub board, my heart leaping when I see the glowing lines showing. When I read the number on the right. When it registers that Wagner is giving me a shot.

I don't ask him why. I don't thank him. I start to run, relieved breaths filling my lungs as I fly across the grass.

I'm *home* again, thousands of miles from where I last played a soccer game.

Play resumes.

I experience a heavy dose of nostalgia and gratefulness as I chase the ball up the field. There was a brief period where I thought I might never play professionally again. When I realized this was a privilege, not something to take for granted, no matter how hard I'd worked to get here.

Other players are tired. Most of the guys on the pitch have already run a few miles. Bouncing my knee didn't burn much energy. I'm raring to go, like a racehorse that's been locked in a starting stall, staring at the expanse of raked dirt ahead.

Beck has possession of the ball. I watch him scan the field, our eyes briefly meeting.

I'm the best and worst option. There's a Ludlin defender ten feet away, struggling to cover me. Beck knows I've been relaxing on the sideline for the entire game so far. But he's never played with me before. Knows I've never played here before.

He passes to me. I trap it neatly and then start dribbling upfield.

The tackle comes out of nowhere.

I go down hard, my shoulder slamming into the grass. I've hammed up hits before. This time, it's completely unnecessary.

My groan is genuine, and so is the way I don't immediately stand up.

There's a flurry of German around me. Blue jerseys matching my own, not just Ludlin players. I can't understand a fucking word that's being said as I slowly climb to my feet. A Kluvberg trainer reaches me, his tone urgent as he peppers me with questions.

I repeat, "I'm fine," over and over, more focused on the heated conversation between Beck and a couple of Ludlin players.

An official is standing between them, mediating.

Another yellow card gets pulled.

I shake my head and spit on the grass, trying to smother my irritation. That should've been a red card.

Everyone lines up for the direct kick. I catch a few concerned glances from my teammates, probably worried I'm going to miss.

I'm not.

My shoulder is throbbing. I'm pissed about the dirty tackle. He wasn't even trying to avoid contact.

But I push it all away.

Tune out the entire world, even the loud shouts from the stands. Everything fades to a dull roar as I glance between the net and the ball, like I've done a thousand times before. Tap the outside of my thigh three times, like I've done a thousand times before. Then kick, like I've done a thousand times before.

Ludlin's goalie lunges—too late.

The back of the net bulges from the impact of the ball's momentum.

I grin. Glance over at the cluster of cameras.

I don't make many promises. But the ones I make, I keep.

CHAPTER TEN

SOPHIA

"Sophia!"

I turn toward my name. Spot Clara and stride toward her, regretting my ridiculously high heels more with each step. They're new, and I've been looking for an excuse to wear them. Now that I'm wearing them, I wish I'd thought of an excuse *not* to.

Queen Victoria is different and a little edgier than our usual weekend spots. The floor is concrete, each unforgiving step making the balls of my feet ache. One wall is decorated with graffiti. It's in an older, industrial building, the space stretching long and low.

"What do you think?" Clara asks when I reach her.

I glance around, exhaling a quiet sigh of relief as my butt hits the bench seat. They're wooden with metal joints, similar to ones at an outdoor beer garden. Not that comfortable, but way better than standing.

"It's cool."

She frowns at my lackluster tone. "We can go somewhere else. Mia and Emilia aren't here yet."

"No, it's fine."

The restlessness I'm experiencing will follow wherever we end up. It's been simmering under my skin ever since the game earlier. Ever since I realized some part of me enjoyed the challenge of taking pictures of football players. Ever since Will Aster scored the goal he'd promised and then—in one of the most thrilling moments of my life—sent a smirk to exactly where I was standing. The harder I try not to think about this afternoon's unexpected events, the more persistent the thoughts become.

"Get that fancy camera ready. I'll score a goal for you, Sophia."

Worse than Will's cocky delivery is that he actually delivered. Ludlin scored in extra time. But the game still ended as a draw instead of a loss, which is how Kluvberg's matches against Ludlin have gone the past few years.

"First round!" Andrea appears, a tray of shots in one hand that she carefully sets on the table before sliding in next to Clara.

"Not wasting any time?"

"You're the one who was late," Andrea says, smirking before she slings one of the little glasses back.

"I know. I had a...busy afternoon."

"Taking photos?" Andrea rolls her eyes.

My "friends"—mostly wealthy girls who grew up in the same affluent area I did but always wanted to come over to my house—encouraged my passing interest in fashion and interior design far more than photography. I'm expecting that to change as soon as I say who I was taking photos of. The most interesting thing about me, according to most people I've met—especially women—is who my brother is.

"Yes," I reply airily. "At the FC Kluvberg game."

Sure enough, Clara's and Andrea's full attention is immediately on me.

"You were at the match earlier?" Clara asks.

"Why didn't you tell us you were going?" Andrea questions.

My friends are aware of my disdain for football. They definitely don't share it.

"I was there for *work*." I pick up a shot and toss it back, certain I'll need it. The vodka sears my throat, forming a warm puddle in my empty stomach.

"Did Kluvberg win?"

I shake my head. "No."

I'm not faking the disappointment in my voice for once. Because of my brother, I always want Kluvberg to win. But I've never been that invested in a game's outcome.

It's a *game*. No matter how it ends, who wins or who loses, there will always be another one. That doesn't seem like high stakes to me.

I swipe my tongue along the inside of my bottom lip, tasting the split that's smarting from the alcohol. The one from too much gnawing.

From the first second Will stepped on the field, I was transfixed. I was determined not to miss his goal, and it had little to do with how I'd been tasked with taking photos of it.

I did take some, though.

Before I had to get ready to come here, I edited all the photos from the game on my laptop. A few were blurry, but most came out well. My favorite is one of Will, mid-kick, and it bothers me that it is. Bothers me that I keep thinking about a *football player*.

Something is seriously wrong with me. Maybe it's end-of-university jitters.

I'm looking for a distraction from the uncertainty of not knowing exactly what I'll be doing, and Will Aster is *very* distracting. The whole group of photographers I was standing with was talking about his performance on the field. Excited about what his arrival might mean for Kluvberg's season.

Emilia and Mia arrive a couple of minutes later. It doesn't take long for Andrea to mention where I was this afternoon. I answer their questions about the match as simply as possible before standing and heading to the bar to get a proper cocktail. My pinched toes protest each step. I'm going to have blisters from these heels by the end of the night.

Three bartenders are working, and they're all currently busy. So, I lean against the metal bar top, letting my elbow support most of my weight so I can give my feet a little bit of a break.

"*Hallo.*"

I turn, taking in the guy who's standing next to me at the bar. He's wearing black jeans and a black T-shirt, giving off the musician, artsy vibe I've gone for in the past. They rarely play sports. Follow sports.

He swipes a hand through his blond hair, then holds it out. "Axel Klein."

"Sophia Beck," I say, shaking his hand.

His thumb brushes the back of my knuckles as he smiles at me.

Beck is a somewhat common last name, but it's always associated with the same thing in Kluvberg. Sure enough...

"Beck? Like the football player?" Axel asks.

I shrug, then glance at the nearest bartender. Still busy. Sigh, then admit, "He's my brother."

Sharing that is always a good test of a guy's interest in me. He came over here, having no clue who I was, presumably—although there are plenty of photos of me with my famous family taken at various public events floating around online, so I never know for sure. But there's a better chance a guy doesn't know who I am at a place like this than the bars closer to campus. Who my brother is happens to be common knowledge at the university.

"Oh. Wow." Axel's surprise seems genuine. "That's cool."

"Uh-huh."

I wait, but he doesn't ask any more questions about my brother. Just, "Can I buy you a drink?"

"Yeah, sure."

While we wait for the bartender, I learn that Axel's working in Kluvberg as an engineer and grew up in Bremen. He asks me a few questions about photography after I mention that's what I'm studying.

We order drinks, and they arrive quickly. Then, Axel asks if my brother can get him and his friends cheap tickets to a match.

I'm not disappointed. Not even surprised, really.

I make up an excuse about my friends waving me over, then head back over to the table. They're all discussing Paris Fashion Week, set to take place at the end of September, which we usually travel to.

I sip my drink and glance around, not really participating in the conversation until Emilia addresses me directly and asks if I'm allowed to bring guests to the game with me.

Her family is rich. She could buy tickets to every Kluvberg match if she wanted. Travel to the away games even. It's the access she's after, same as with all of my friends. I'm a door into places they couldn't be part of otherwise.

"No," I answer. "It's part of my internship. It's work, not a gala I get a plus-one to."

"I can't believe your *job* is to look at those guys," Mia says.

I take a sip of my drink, wishing I'd never brought the assignment up. "It's not my job. I'm not even getting paid."

"It's not like you need the money, though," Clara says.

My smile tightens. Turns fake. I'm so sick of all roads leading back to my last name. Money means more when it's connected to fame. Because everyone knows you have it.

Across the table, Andrea suddenly sits up straighter. "Some of your non-jobs just arrived."

My head snaps to the left, in the direction of the door.

Five FC Kluvberg players are entering the club.

I'm not the only one looking. Everyone's attention immediately swivels their way. It's not uncommon to see footballers out and about, especially in places like this. Most of the guys on the team are young, single, hot, and rich. They're recognizable, too, since photos of the team are plastered all over the city. They also move with the confidence of a pack of predators. The sight is compelling even if you don't care about sports.

Quickly, I scan the group of guys.

I don't realize what—who—I'm looking for until I experience the strange disappointment of discovering Will isn't with them.

They're coming this way, several of them smiling at me. Nice guys, many of whom have been on the team for several seasons. Simply being friendly or feeling some obligation to acknowledge me because of Adler.

Otto speaks first. "Hey, Sophia."

I smile back at him. He's played for Kluvberg for a few years now, working his way up to starting goaltender. He views Adler as a mentor, imitating him off the field too. Acting like a second older brother.

"Hey. Nice saves today."

Otto makes a face. "Aside from the one I missed."

I'm grateful when the group of footballers moves on a minute later.

The rest of my friends are disappointed. Andrea declares it's time to dance. I finish my drink, hoping the alcohol will be enough to numb the pain in my feet, announcing I'm heading to the restroom first. I make it down the hallway, but before heading inside, I lean back against the wall, pull out my phone, and type out a new text.

Send it and then walk into the bathroom.

His play.

CHAPTER ELEVEN

WILL

69 1324 5572: Viktualienmarkt. Eleven a.m.

I'm early. I show up early to something for the first time in...I don't even know the last time it happened.

I'm often on time. Occasionally late. Early? That doesn't really happen.

Boredom is a factor. I've never liked recovery days. No matter how sore my body is, I'd rather be moving than sitting around. Win or lose, my head's filled with thoughts of the game. Ways I can improve, even if it was a victory.

I'm my own worst critic because it's a role no one else ever took on.

My dad wasn't around. My mom was busy. My brother wasn't athletic. My coaches...they told my teammates to pass me the ball.

No one else cares about your career more than you.

A lesson I learned the hard way. The last man standing of the people I spent years working with—and for—in Seattle is Shawn, and he has a financial stake in my success. I've made him a lot of money from ads and photo shoots in addition to my being one of the highest-paid players in the league, all of which he received a cut of.

I turn in a slow circle, surveying the open square. The ground is made up of stones that have been perfectly placed. There's a giant, gorgeous cathedral that's just *there*, between a closed supermarket and a building that looks like apartments. I'm not used to a building that looks thousands of years old— that *is* thousands of years old—being casually present. A place you walk past to buy eggs or to catch a bus, the colorful, historical architecture as common as a coffee shop.

"Hi."

I spin, my breath doing a funny catch in my throat when I see her.

I've given my number to exactly one person outside the Kluvberg organization. I figured it had to be her when I saw the message from a German number this morning. But it hits differently, seeing Sophia standing in front of me.

She's wearing a yellow sundress, which sounds like something a grandma might be dressed in. But it looks sexy as hell, the short hemline showing off her long legs and the neckline teasing at the curve of her breasts. Her blonde hair is down and loose, wavy strands blowing around in the slight breeze.

"So," she says, adjusting her sunglasses.

I realize I never responded to her greeting. That I haven't said anything. I've just been standing here and staring at her.

I stuff my hands into the pockets of my shorts, feeling weirdly off balance.

Nothing's familiar. I'm in a strange place with a strange woman, having no idea what will take place next. That hasn't happened in a long time.

I'm not sure it's *ever* happened, actually.

"So," I repeat.

"So, you're a football player."

I snort. "Yep. And you're a...sports photographer?"

She glances toward the nearby cathedral. "Just a photographer. I'm doing an internship with a local newspaper, and..." She shakes her head, meeting my gaze again. Or rather, it looks like she does.

I can't tell past the barrier of her sunglasses.

"It's kind of a long story, but it ends with me getting assigned to cover Kluvberg for a few weeks. Interest in the team is especially high at the moment, and it's cheaper for me to take photos than for the paper to buy them elsewhere to run with stories."

"Why didn't you say no?"

"It's complicated."

I shrug. "Okay."

"So...you scored a goal," she tells me.

I shrug again. "Direct kicks don't really count. I can do those in my sleep."

Just getting the ball past the goalie isn't the same challenge as active play. It was like making the shot during my first practice with the team. Nice to know I've still got it, but not entirely satisfying.

Sophia slides her sunglasses down her nose to study me. "I can't tell if you're being weirdly modest or you seriously think scoring a goal in your first game isn't impressive."

I smirk. "I'm impressive, huh?"

She pushes her sunglasses back into place. "Cool. You're cured. Come on. I need some coffee."

I follow Sophia down the street and into a small storefront I would have walked by had I been exploring by myself. It's so tiny inside; there's not even any seating. Just a counter that's mostly covered by an espresso machine.

"Can you order me an iced coffee?" I ask Sophia.

"No," she replies. "It's not on the menu."

"What do you mean, it's not on the menu?"

She sighs. "Saylor complains about the same thing. It's not common here."

"*What's* not common here? *Ice?*"

"I'll order you an Eiskaffee." Without explaining what the hell that is, Sophia spews off a rapid flurry of German.

The woman behind the counter replies, and then Sophia holds out a hand toward me.

"Aren't you rich?" I ask, flipping open my wallet and handing her my credit card.

"My parents are rich. My brother is rich. Me? No, I'm not rich. And I know how much you make. You can afford to buy your tour guide a coffee."

I lean an elbow on the counter. "You looked up my salary?"

"One of my bosses mentioned it."

Sophia hands me a drink that looks kind of like a sundae. The plastic cup is cool at least, but the drink itself looks to be half foam, topped with some whipped cream. Hers is a white paper cup with a black lid.

"What did you get?"

"Just black. Late night."

Not a *fun* night, I notice.

She doesn't look hungover. And I'm not—for the first time

after a game since middle school, maybe. Games were followed by parties in high school and college and after signing my first pro contract.

Last night, I went straight home. I was filled with mixed feelings after the game. Relief I'd gotten some playing time and reconciling how different my career here might look in comparison to what I was used to. One goal off a direct kick and the score ending in a draw—it was not exactly the breakout, headline-making performance I had been hoping for.

I try a sip of the drink Sophia got me as we step outside. It's not terrible. Sweeter than I'd normally order, but chilled and somewhat refreshing.

"You like museums?" she asks me as the pavement we're walking on transitions to cobblestones. Based on what little I know about Kluvberg, it means we're headed into the older section of the city.

I shake my head. "Not really."

"Great," she says. "Let's go."

I smirk before following her across the square.

Sophia points out a few impressive-looking buildings as we walk along, acting exactly like the tour guide I requested. But I'm having a hard time focusing on the scenery with her walking just a foot away. And not just checking her out, although I've definitely glanced lower than I should have a few times. I want to talk to her—and not about two-thousand-year-old cathedrals.

I'm curious about a lot. Dying to know one thing in particular. "Why'd you text me?"

I figured any chance of her using my number disappeared as soon as she found out I was a soccer player.

Her response is unsatisfying. She glances away first, so I can only see her profile. "Did you not want me to?"

"I gave you my number, remember?"

"Yeah, but that was before you knew who I was," Sophia says, pausing to toss her coffee cup into a trash can.

"I don't know who you are."

"You know what I mean. You didn't know my last name at that scrimmage, just like I had no clue you were on the team."

"Yeah, I figured that out when you didn't ask for my autograph."

She rolls her eyes, and I smirk.

"What does that have to do with anything? Beck is on the team, and you talk to him."

"You're comparing yourself to my *brother*?"

"Oh, you two are related?" I fake some surprise.

Another eye roll.

"It can have nothing to do with us," I tell her.

"What do you mean?"

"I mean, I don't give a fuck who your brother is. And I don't give a fuck if you hate soccer. Just like you obviously don't give a fuck that I hate museums, so..."

I catch a smile as I follow Sophia over an arched bridge toward another large, majestic building with a sign in German in front. I spot *das Museum* among the unfamiliar words and surmise this is the museum we're visiting.

I focus on Sophia as we enter what turns out to be a massive lobby. It's startling, both the temperature shift from warm to cool and also the sunshine and activity outside to muted voices and lots of white. The floor is white, the walls are white, and there's nothing to distract from any of it. It's like standing in the center of a blizzard.

Sophia exchanges rapid German with the woman sitting behind a white desk. I glance around at nothing, basically, then stare at her while she speaks. Every time I hear German, it's a harsh cacophony of syllables that sound like they're fighting for space. Sophia manages to make the language sound melodic, the flow of words much faster than when she speaks English.

The conversation ends, and she glances at me. "Come on. Galleries are this way."

"This place reminds me of my apartment," I say, glancing around as we walk toward the opening on the far side of the lobby.

"White walls?"

"No furniture."

She glances at me, one eyebrow raised. "You don't have *any* furniture?"

"Place came unfurnished. I bought a mattress, but that's it so far."

"Why haven't you bought anything else?"

I rub the back of my neck. "This wasn't exactly my idea."

"I know. You already said you don't like museums."

I laugh, shaking my head. "I mean Kluvberg. Coming here, playing here. Buying furniture seemed like...accepting it."

There's no way Sophia doesn't know how I ended up playing here. She works for a local paper. Her brother is Adler Beck. But she hasn't said a word about the scandal that made this move necessary. And she still doesn't mention it now.

She just says, "You should buy some stuff," before we enter the first gallery.

The paintings in here are all colorful and vibrant, which is a welcome change after the minimalist lobby. I'm still mostly studying Sophia, though.

After she catches me twice, I make an attempt to look at the artwork.

"Do you paint?" I ask her.

"No, I just take photographs."

There's a dismissiveness to her tone I'm surprised to hear. Like it's frivolous or trivial.

"You don't think that's art?"

"No, of course it is. But anyone can point a camera and click a button, right?"

"Anyone can slap some paint on a canvas too. I mean, what even *is* this?" I nod toward the nearest painting.

A middle-aged woman standing near us shoots me a nasty look that makes me think she understands English and doesn't appreciate my disdainful tone.

"It's a haystack," Sophia tells me. Her lips are pressed together, but I think it's to hide her amusement, not because she's also annoyed.

"Huh." The longer I look, the more I can see the distinction between the brown and gold shades. The shifting texture of the strokes.

I stare at it for a while longer, long enough that Sophia is smirking when I glance away.

"What?"

"Nothing. It just doesn't look like you're about to die of boredom."

"If I do keel over, can I count on you to call 911?"

"It's 110 or 112 here, actually."

Another reminder that I'm a foreigner. But here, standing next to her, it doesn't bother me as much that I'm so far from familiarity.

"I knew you'd be a great tour guide," I tell her as we move on to the next painting. This one is a sunset past what looks like fishing docks, piles of gray fish blocking some of the pink-and-orange water. "So, is pointing a camera and clicking a button your favorite part of being a photographer?"

"No."

"What is then?"

"It's hard to explain."

"So, you stopped trying to?"

Sophia looks at me—*really* looks at me—the tiniest glimmer of surprise or respect appearing. I'm not sure anyone has ever stared at me this way before. I'm certain I don't want her to stop. She glances away, refocusing on the art far too soon.

"Yeah, I guess I did."

"I think you should keep at it."

One corner of her mouth quirks. "I think you should buy some furniture."

I smile, then glance back at the haystack. Feeling a little less lost.

CHAPTER TWELVE

SOPHIA

I inhale deeply. The early morning air tastes crisp and clean. It rained overnight, so each breath carries an undertone of damp earthiness. Sunshine filters through the canopy of leaves overhead, decorating the dirt path with patches of golden light.

I pause, pulling my phone out of my pocket and using it to snap a photo, aimed skyward. Admiring the glow of light through the leaves.

Walking here is the one form of exercise I actually enjoy. Not only is the national park, located just outside of the city limits, a beautiful place to exercise away from the hustle and bustle of traffic and commotion, but it's also one of my favorite places to photograph. It's where the idea of studying photography first occurred to me, wanting to capture the natural beauty of this place.

Since I'm out walking with Saylor, it hasn't been the most relaxing pace.

The times I've come here with Adler have been the same way. It's like professional athletes only have one speed.

Not only am I struggling to keep up with her, but I'm also

hindered by taking photos. I've never brought my camera here since it cost several thousand euros and isn't exactly lightweight. My phone is much more convenient in this circumstance. And these pictures are just for me.

When I catch up with Saylor, she smiles. "Are trees more fun to photograph than footballers?"

I roll my eyes. "Don't tell Adler because I don't want him thinking I've developed an interest in football, but photographing the game wasn't as bad as I'd thought it would be."

Saylor laughs. "Your secret is safe with me."

For the past half hour, I've debated confiding in her about another one.

I have no newfound interest in football...aside from a growing fascination with a football player. One that's refused to fizzle, no matter what I tell myself.

Texting Will Aster was an impulsive, vodka-influenced decision. I'd been wanting to see the new Bavarian art exhibition at the local museum, and it's something I knew none of my friends would want to go to. Something I doubted Will would want to do, and I was right. But he didn't leave when I told him where we were going. Or after the first few rooms of the museum. He spent his one day off walking through countless galleries with me.

I hadn't expected him to show up. I definitely hadn't expected for us to spend hours together. Or for him to not ask me a single question about football or Adler.

Saylor is still setting a brutal pace. She's on maternity leave, probably averaging a few hours of sleep a night, and she's moving twice as fast as me.

"Did you decide what you're submitting for the EPAs?" she asks me.

My stomach twists. "No, I'm not sure yet."

The European Photography Awards—or EPAs, as they're more commonly referred to—is the most competitive international photography competition. The photography world's version of the World Cup. Hundreds of thousands of entries, judged by the most respected names in the industry. One winner per category. Submitting to the Sports one never occurred to me until I was looking through the photos I took after the game. They might be my best options because everything else I've taken seems lackluster.

I have a minuscule chance at winning in any category. But I can't help but feel like what I submit really matters. Just like with the possible staff position at *Neues Kluvberg*, it's a rare opportunity to prove photography is something worth pursuing. Not a passing fascination, but an actual career. Me excelling at what I'm meant to do, the same way my family shines on a football field.

"What about the photos you've been taking for your internship?" Saylor questions. "Are any of those options?"

"Maybe. I've got a lot of options. But none that seem EPA-worthy."

There are many photos I could submit, but none that I really *want* to. None that seem original enough or fresh enough or exciting enough.

"You still have some time to decide, right?"

"Yeah."

Submissions aren't due for another six weeks. But it's not like I'll be going on another safari in that stretch of time. There won't be any special opportunities to photograph anything different. Just chances to shoot various versions of what I already have as options. That shouldn't matter, though. What makes the best photographers *the best* photographers is their ability to make the mundane memorable. The ordinary extraordinary. If that's a talent I possess, it hasn't appeared yet.

"Well, I can't wait to see what you end up sending in," Saylor tells me. "I wish I had any of your artistic talent. All of the other mothers in my mom group are insanely jealous of the newborn photos you took. They're all interested in hiring you, so just let me know if you want me to give them your info."

"Let me get through last semester first," I say.

But what I really mean is, *Let me see if I get a staff position first.* That'll give me the freedom to not have to rely on free-lancing.

Any compliments on my photography mean something since I don't have a ton of confidence in my work. But I'm not hoping to launch a career in baby portraits.

Or football, despite enjoying sports photography more than I was expecting to. My photos from the first game were decent. Alex and Harry seemed very impressed, although that could have just been their gratefulness because I'd agreed to do it. Either way, hopefully, it'll mean a staff position will be mine.

"Get through?" Saylor raises an eyebrow. "That doesn't sound like the queen of the clubs."

I roll my eyes. She's never let me forget I invited her to go clubbing the first time we met.

Before she and Adler became boring parents, we would go out often. Saylor's the sister I always wanted. And I do love going out to bars. Getting dressed up and meeting new people. I'm young and single, and I've tried to enjoy this phase of my life. But lately, it's felt repetitive. I was bored out with Maria, until I saw Will standing a little ways down the bar. Just like I was bored at Queen Victoria, going through the motions until my feet hurt so badly that I had to leave.

"Lately, it's just felt like...I don't know. Like a lot of the same. Same people, same places, same routine."

"Then, do something different," Saylor suggests.

Solid advice.

I tried that. I texted Will Aster, and now I keep thinking about him.

And again, I consider telling Saylor about it. She's seen the craziness of my family up close. Willingly married into it. She's met some of my exes and gotten to know them better than my parents and Adler. But if I tell her about Will, it will require her keeping it from Adler, and I'm not sure I should ask her to do that. She's usually in support of any crazy ideas I have. Hanging out with a bad boy who has an infamous reputation is something I could see her cautiously encouraging. But he plays with Adler, meaning his choices affect my brother's career, and that adds a different dynamic. Football is the one thing Saylor takes very seriously.

I'm not even sure how I would describe what being around Will feels like. *Different* doesn't really cover it.

So, I just say a vague, "Yeah, maybe..."

"You still seeing that guy from the bar? Noah?"

Saylor's the only family member I've continued telling about guys. She gives good advice and jokes she's living vicariously through me now that she's a boring married woman.

I'm not sure anyone could call Saylor *boring* with a straight face.

"No, I'm not," I answer. "He took me to Kluvberg's last friendly match."

Saylor groans. "No, he didn't."

"Yes, he did," I respond.

I've never understood why me not liking football is such a difficult concept for people to understand. It seems logical to me. Spend enough forced time around anything, and you start to resent it.

Strangely, the one person I've met who immediately surmised how I felt about football was a *football player*. It stood out to me at the time, mostly because of Noah's willful oblivion. But it's even more surprising now that I know Will plays football. That he *loves* football. I have a dozen photos of the expression on his face when he got subbed in to play.

And...I'm thinking about him. Again.

"Plenty of other guys out there," Saylor says. She doesn't sound even the least bit out of breath while my calves are burning as we head uphill.

"I'm thinking about a dating hiatus. I'm focusing on me for now, not guys."

"Even better," she tells me. "Just enjoy the end of college. It'll be over before you know it."

I nod.

It's the truth; I am focusing on me. But I picture Will frowning at the haystack painting, and it sounds a little like a lie.

CHAPTER THIRTEEN

WILL

I take a step back. Tilt my head, the chemical scent of paint burning my nose. "I hate it," I decide.

Sophia snorts.

I glance over at her. She's studying the same spot on the wall that I am, arms crossed.

"What do you think?" I ask.

"It's terrible," she says cheerfully.

"This was your idea," I remind her. "*Will, your apartment is boring. Will, your apartment needs color. Will, let's paint the bedroom.*"

"Your imitation of a German accent is even worse than your German," she tells me. "And *you* picked the color."

I grin, then set the paintbrush down on the tray and cover the container.

I texted her last night, impulsively, asking if she had suggestions on where to get furniture from. After my goal last weekend, some of the guys on the team have warmed up to me a little. But after the day we spent together, Sophia still feels like the closest I have to a friend in this city. She replied, saying she needed to see my place first.

Ten minutes after arriving at my apartment, Sophia told me exactly what I just recited. So, we picked up the paint when we went out to get pizza, and now, I'm stuck with a blue splotch on a white wall.

"You hungry?" I ask.

We decided to test out the paint before eating, which was probably a mistake. Maybe it'll look better on a full stomach.

"Starving," she replies.

"Well, at least now, we don't need to worry about painting the rest of the room," I tell her, taking a seat on the mattress, which is still the only furniture I have.

Sophia kicks her shoes off and takes a seat cross-legged on the bed. She's wearing another dress, and I avert my eyes as the hemline creeps higher up her thighs.

"I can't believe you've been living like this," she says, taking a slice of pizza and glancing around the empty bedroom.

My suitcases are piled in one corner since this place doesn't even have a closet. Normally, there's also dirty laundry flung across the floor, but I cleaned up a little before she got here. It makes the place look even emptier.

I shrug before standing and heading into the kitchen. "I don't need a lot of shit. Beer?"

"Yeah, sure."

I return with two cold bottles, passing her one before sinking back down onto the mattress. My sore muscles protest every movement.

"So, you have nothing in your fridge, except beer, and no furniture, except a mattress?"

I smirk before taking a long pull of beer. "Pretty much. I

grab takeout on my way home from practice, and all I really need is a place to sleep."

"Do you have a car?"

"No. I've been taking the S-Bahn around. Thought about shipping my bike over here, but..." But I didn't—for the same reason I didn't bring anything, except clothes.

Everything else I own is in a storage locker in Seattle, waiting to be dealt with at some point. Hopefully moved to a different US city after an incredible season here that convinces an American team to take a chance on me.

"Bike? As in a motorcycle?"

"Uh-huh." I sip more beer.

God, it's good. Paired with the hot pizza, it tastes like the best meal I've had in weeks. Maybe it's that I have company, that I'm not lost in a swirl of unpleasant thoughts, wondering if I totally fucked up the rest of my life.

"That's hot," Sophia tells me. "Guessing it worked well for you?"

"Actually, I hardly rode it. Seattle gets a lot of rain, and motorcycles are a lot less sexy when you're drenched and worrying about hydroplaning."

"It doesn't rain that much here."

I shrug, then take a bite of pizza. Chew and swallow. "Would've been expensive to ship all the way here."

"I thought you were rich."

"*You* said I was rich. I've done all right."

I've made more money than I ever dreamed I would, especially considering I made most of that money playing soccer and I would have paid *to* play. But part of me will always be that kid who grew up with a fridge that looks a lot like the one in my kitchen right now—and not by choice. We were never starving, but there was never excess. I've been financially responsible to the point of frugality, never splurging on the diamond-studded watches or luxurious vacations or expensive liquor that my teammates often would. It still makes me uncomfortable, honestly, being around extravagant displays of wealth.

"Are you hoping to go back to Seattle?" Sophia asks. "Is that why you left all your stuff?"

I shake my head. "No. I never want to go back to Seattle. Too much...too much happened there. If this season goes well enough, I'm hoping to get a contract with a different American team."

I really don't want to discuss Cassandra. If we keep hanging out—which I'm hoping we will because setting aside my attraction to her, Sophia happens to be the one person I've met in Kluvberg who I enjoy spending time around—I'm guessing what happened will come up eventually. Maybe I'll even tell her the whole story. But I'd rather just not discuss it.

I'm relieved when all Sophia says is, "Do you still talk to your teammates from there?"

"Not really. We're not teammates anymore." I feel a pang of guilt, thinking of all the read messages on my phone with no response.

A bunch of the guys texted after my signing to Kluvberg was announced, congratulating me on finding another club. I didn't answer a single one. It was all too raw, especially considering none of them had reached out to me after the scandal broke. I'd put them all in a shitty position, getting blacklisted from the organization they were all contractually a part of. But the congratulations felt patronizing, like I should be grateful any team wanted me when all I'd done wrong was get wasted and have sex with a willing woman—something I'd witnessed them all do many times.

"They haven't won a single game since I left," I tell her.

I have a score alert set on my phone so I don't have to keep checking the team's site. And I get more satisfaction from it than I probably should, watching the record become more and more lopsided. Just like I probably shouldn't have admitted that to Sophia. But I'm not trying to impress her. Not trying to act like I'm not a cautionary tale about poor decision-making. I'm bitter, and I enjoy watching my former team struggle without me.

I sip more beer, surprised to realize it's already almost empty. Maybe that's why I'm willingly telling Sophia stuff I'd normally refuse to discuss. I haven't been drinking much lately, so my tolerance isn't what it used to be. Better for my body and my head. But also dangerous when there's a gorgeous woman who happens to be Adler Beck's little sister on my bed.

"Did you grow up in Seattle?" Sophia asks.

She seems genuinely interested in getting to know me. *Me*, Will, not the professional athlete. And I'm not sure what to make of it. I don't have many friends. I don't have *any* friends who are women. Chicks strike up conversation with me because they want to fuck me. They shower me with compliments, hoping it leads to my cock ending up in their mouth or their pussy. They don't ask about my childhood. Even if they did, I wouldn't answer. It's not my favorite topic, to say the least.

"Nah, Boston."

"I've only ever been to Georgia." Sophia leans forward, grabbing another slice of pizza. "That's where Saylor—Adler's wife—is from. They had a second wedding ceremony in her hometown."

"Are you close with her?" I'm curious about Sophia's family's dynamic, so different from mine. Hers is rich, famous, whole.

Sophia nods. "She's like a sister."

I get up and grab two more beers, concerned she's going to ask about my family next. I'd need to be way drunker than I am now to willingly wade into that mess. If she thinks my relationship with my former teammates is dysfunctional...

"What about you?" I ask once I've cracked a new bottle open.

Sophia raises an eyebrow. "What about me? Anything you want to know, you could just look up online."

"Well, I didn't. Where did you grow up?"

"Here. Close to Kluvberg. My parents have an estate outside the city."

An *estate. Jesus.*

"My dad played for FC Kluvberg. My mom played for the nearest women's team. The same one Saylor is on now." She studies me closely as she takes another bite of pizza, like she's testing my reaction to that information.

"I heard they played," I tell her. "I didn't know where."

"I almost went to university somewhere else. You know, just to...get away from it all. The attention's not just here, especially since Adler went through his fuckboy phase."

I cover my smile with my beer, imagining my stoic captain's reaction to his little sister talking about his *fuckboy phase.* "Why didn't you?"

"I don't know. I like Kluvberg. It's home. All my friends were staying here. There was nowhere else I really wanted to go. So...I stayed."

"Photographers work all over the world. You could still go."

"I've thought about it. I'm in my last semester before I graduate. But I'm hoping to get a position at the paper I'm interning at right now. If I do, I'll stay."

"Even though you'll still have to deal with the attention?"

Sophia picks at the damp label on her bottle. "I don't know if it's the attention I hate. I hate how it makes me an outsider in my own family, I guess. Like there's some secret club I'm not a part of. A secret club I don't want to be a part of. I never would have been as famous as Adler is since the women's league doesn't receive the same attention as the men's. But I could have played, and people always want to know why I didn't. It's like I had this identity forced on me, and I'm forever getting judged for not accepting it. And it's my *name*. Not something I can easily separate from. When I go to the bank or the post office or meet with a professor, it always comes up. So, I either have to lie, then wonder if they look up pictures of me afterward and realize I did, or accept it and talk about it. It's just..." She sighs. "It's exhausting."

"Is that why you started taking photos? Because someone else is the center of attention?"

Sophia's eyebrows rise before she takes a drink from her beer. Somehow, she manages to make sitting cross-legged on a mattress, eating greasy pizza, look classy. "I never thought of it that way. But, yeah, maybe. It took me a while to decide what to study at university. I'd gotten a Polaroid camera for my tenth birthday and loved it. I don't—I don't do great with change. So, I guess I like the idea of knowing a moment is captured forever, that you can always look back at it."

"That is cool," I agree.

We continue talking, finishing the pizza and our second beers. Sophia tells me more about her university classes and stories from her childhood, casually dropping names of legends that I would die to be in the same room as. But I understand Sophia's feelings more now. For her, that would be like me meeting a famous chef or Picasso. You can understand why someone is revered for their accomplishments, but not appreciate them the same way someone else might.

I'm shocked when I check my phone and see that it's already after midnight. Clocks are another thing my apartment is missing. I have practice at eight tomorrow, and I'll probably have a hangover from the beers I blew through. But I don't regret anything about tonight.

I needed this—a night to relax and do a few things I shouldn't. It's the closest to normal I've felt since arriving here, aside from the time spent playing soccer.

Sophia looks equally surprised when I tell her the hour.

"Did you drive?" I ask.

We walked to get the paint and the pizza, and I hadn't thought to ask when she first showed up. I was too stunned that she actually did.

"No." She covers her mouth as she yawns. "I only live a few blocks away."

That's...knowledge I didn't need. I'm not spending time with Sophia because it's convenient, but I don't want to know she's basically just down the block. It's temptation, which I'm terrible about ignoring. Especially where she's concerned.

"I'll walk you home."

Sophia groans, sprawling back on the bed. Her blonde hair spreads like a halo around her as she yawns. "I wish I'd driven," she mumbles. "I don't feel like walking."

"Then, just stay here. I have practice at eight, so I'll be up early. As long as you don't care about that..."

Her head rolls to the side. Blue eyes pin me into place. "You're asking me to spend the night in your bed?"

"To sleep, yeah."

I stand and walk over to my suitcase, pulling out a T-shirt, boxers, and a pair of pajama pants I haven't worn since I arrived. Supposedly, my apartment building does have air-conditioning, but it doesn't work that well. I usually end up opening all the windows at night, the air outside cooler than inside. But if Sophia stays, sleeping naked like I typically do is not an option.

I toss the T-shirt and boxers on the bed beside her. "Let me know what you decide," I say before heading into the bathroom to change and get ready for bed.

I'm still a little buzzed, but it's turning into lethargy. My muscles feel like dead weight I'm dragging along, my thoughts and worries moving much slower than usual.

When I step out of the bathroom, Sophia's wearing my clothes. The shirt dwarfs her, but she's tall enough that the hem doesn't totally cover the boxer briefs.

"Do you have a spare toothbrush?" Sophia asks, brushing past me to head into the open bathroom.

"Yeah." I clear my throat. "Under the sink."

I head for the bed, telling my trodden ego it's a good thing she didn't look the least bit affected by the sight of me shirtless.

Inviting her to stay was an impulsive decision, which I make a lot of. But I've never just *accidentally* invited a woman to sleep in the same bed as me. The only person I've ever shared a bed with is Tripp, and that was because our bedroom was too small for two beds. When I hit puberty, our mom turned the dining room into Tripp's bedroom. Not like we ever sat down for any family meals anyway.

I should call my baby brother soon. Should call my mom,

too, but that's an even harder conversation to have. I haven't been in the right mental place to speak to either of them. Tripp, because he'll worry if I sound too pessimistic. My mom, because I'll probably end up saying something I'll regret. Better for both of us if I say nothing at all.

Sophia opens the bathroom door and turns out the light. I can't see anything as my eyes adjust to the dark, just hear the soft footsteps approaching the bed. Feel the unfamiliar dip of the mattress as she slips under the covers beside me.

"A gentleman would have offered to sleep on the floor," she tells me.

"We are on the floor," I reply.

"A gentleman would have given me the bed."

"I knew what you meant. I'm more confused about how I somehow gave you the impression that I'm a gentleman."

Sophia snorts.

We lie in silence, the only sound the distant street noise filtering in through the open living room window. It grows quieter and quieter, the later it gets.

I can tell Sophia hasn't fallen asleep. Every few minutes, she shifts, tugging the sheets with her a tiny bit. Every time, my entire body reacts, the foreign movement beside me jolting me to high alert.

"What's wrong?" I finally ask.

"I can't fall asleep."

"Why not?"

"If I knew that, I'd be asleep."

I smile into the darkness. "Well, what do you normally do when you can't fall asleep? Count sheep?"

"No."

"Drink tea? Breathing techniques? Listen to music? Shot of vodka?"

"I make myself come."

I choke a little. On spit, I guess. That wasn't at all what I had expected her to say.

She exhales. "Never mind. Forget I said that."

That'll be fucking impossible.

"Go for it," I tell her.

"What?" She scoffs. "No way. Watch porn like a normal guy if you need some live entertainment."

"I can't see shit." Not totally true. I can see shapes. Shadows.

Her touching herself under the covers, I wouldn't get to see. But it'd be one of the hotter things I'd experienced and technically wouldn't be breaking my *no women and no booze* vow to Shawn. I've rationalized not sticking to sobriety is fine as long as I'm at home.

"I don't care," Sophia replies. "I'm not touching myself in front of you. It's too weird."

"Want me to do it?"

What the fuck are you saying? I know what I'm *doing*. I'm dying to do something fun. And getting her off but denying myself feels like another loophole.

"How drunk are you?"

"I'm a little buzzed," I reply. "Went through a sober spell, so my tolerance is absolute shit."

"You were right. It does get you into trouble."

I smile at her reference to our first conversation. "Night, Sophia."

There's a long pause, and then she asks, "Mouth or fingers?"

"Fingers," I respond. "I don't do oral."

"How generous," she drawls.

"Hey, I offered to help you sleep, remember?" I say, rolling toward her. "That was charitable."

"You sure are—"

She stops talking when my hand lands on her thigh. As soon as she asked the question, I knew this was going to happen.

The oversize fabric she's wearing—my clothes—is so easy to slip a hand under.

I catch the motion as her head turns toward me, hear the rustle of cotton as she spreads her legs beneath the sheets. I wish I could see her, and it's also surprisingly sexy that I can't. That this is happening when it's dark and quiet, taking place like a secret with no distractions around us.

My fingers move higher and higher, drawn toward the center of heat like a magnet pull.

She's soaked, I discover, as I run teasing circles around her entrance before moving higher to rub the swollen bundle of nerves.

Sophia gasps when I touch her clit, shattering the stillness around us.

"Does that feel good?" I whisper.

Her breathy whimper has my dick swelling. Fuck, she's so *responsive*. Wet and warm and rocking into my touch like she's desperate for it. Her thigh is quivering against my wrist, and I realize she's close. That she was already turned on before I touched her. I trail my fingers lower, along sensitive skin, until I reach her pulsing pussy.

There's a weird hum of nerves buzzing beneath my skin. I've touched a lot of women a lot more intimately than this. Most of them, I didn't even know their last name.

I forgot—or maybe I've never experienced—what it's like to

touch someone and *care*. Notice how they react. Observe every response.

Even in the darkness, I can't focus on only the sensation. I'm hyperaware it's Sophia reacting.

I press a finger into her pussy, unable to contain the groan when I feel her cunt clench around me.

She's so wet that she's drenching my hand, so wet that I can smell her arousal, mixing with the floral scent of her shampoo and the lavender laundry detergent I accidentally purchased because I just assumed the packaging here was purple. But she's so tight; it's still a struggle to fuck her with my fingers.

I'm fully hard now, and there's also something erotic about ignoring the arousal and focusing on her pleasure. Of knowing my gratification will be delayed.

I can tell the second she's coming, the contractions strangling my fingers the way I wish they were squeezing my cock. Fuck, I miss sex. I went through a self-pity spiral after everything went down in Seattle, but I haven't been with a woman since I got to Germany. Not only because of Shawn's rules or fear that history will repeat itself somehow, but also because I'm trying to be different. Be better.

Aside from the muffled blare of a horn, Sophia's heavy breathing is the only sound in the room. I pull my hand free from the boxer's band, sucking on the two fingers I just had inside of her. Sweet and a little salty. It sort of makes me wish I *had* offered my tongue.

She moves beside me, tugging the sheets up higher and flopping one hand above her head. "I can't believe you did that." Her tone is breathless and a little bit awed, and fuck if I don't find it immensely satisfying. That'd better have been the best she's ever had.

"You're welcome," I say, acting like it was no big deal. Because it shouldn't be. I've gone further with strangers on a club dance floor. I just...touched her. Basically the same as holding her hand or something.

The same as holding her hand? *I'm an idiot.*

I scowl at the darkness, wishing I'd kept my mouth shut and my hands to myself.

"I'm grabbing some water," I say. "Do you want anything?"

"No, I'm good. Thanks."

I roll out of bed, padding into the kitchen to grab a bottle of water out of the fridge. I chug most of it, then head into the bathroom to take a piss, which is hard as fuck to do while I'm... well, hard as fuck. I think of depressing shit—my career is over; my apartment is empty with an ugly wall—in an attempt to get rid of my erection. It sort of works. At least it's dark enough that Sophia can't tell as I return to bed.

She says nothing until I'm lying back down beside her.

"Is it weird? Or do you always *go get water* after?"

I chuckle at the emphasis. "It's not weird. Go to sleep now that you've gotten your sleep, uh, aid."

Sophia scoffs. Then asks, "What about you?"

"I'm good."

If she touches me, I'll end up fucking her. And I absolutely cannot fuck her. That would not be crossing the line; that would be obliterating it. Had I known who Cassandra Owens was that night, I never would have touched her. I know who Sophia Beck is, and I still touched her. I've already done a fantastic job of intentionally blowing up my soccer career. If the rest gets destroyed, it won't be from self-sabotage.

"That's a first," she tells me.

I scowl into the darkness, thoroughly ticked off at the

thought of Sophia sucking some faceless guy's dick. Whoever he was—or will be—he's not good enough for her.

"Night, Sophia."

I roll over, punch the pillow, and try to fall asleep. At some point, I actually do.

CHAPTER FOURTEEN

WILL

I have to hide my shock when Sophia pulls up outside my apartment building in a sleek black coupe. The rearing horse insignia on the hood is impossible to miss.

It says a lot about how attracted I am to Sophia that I don't immediately focus on the sleek interior of the expensive car when I climb inside.

She's wearing a cropped tank top and a pair of high-waisted shorts today, her long blonde hair pulled up in a ponytail. The silky strands slide across her shoulder as she leans over to tap something on the massive screen that takes up most of the dashboard.

I imagine touching her hair. Tangling my fingers in those silky strands. Tugging.

She's Adler Beck's sister, I remind myself. Fucking ridiculous how many times I've had to tell myself that. Around the same number of times I've jerked off to thoughts of her coming on my fingers in my bed.

"Nice ride," I say, banning all images of her riding *me* from my mind.

"Well, it's no motorcycle," she replies, shifting back into drive.

"You got a thing for Ferraris?"

"Not really. It was a gift."

"A *gift*?"

This car must be worth a hundred thousand dollars. At least. What the hell kind of gift is that?

"Adler did some car commercials a few years ago. He gave this one to me since he already had one."

I knew there was a pay discrepancy between American and European players. And sponsorship opportunities. But I didn't realize how huge until I moved here.

"Damn. I couldn't even book a Ford ad. They gave it to some football player."

"You *are* a football player," Sophia says.

"American football. He was a big-shot quarterback who went to school in Michigan. They liked the Detroit connection."

"American *foot*ball, which is played with *hands*."

"I'm not arguing it makes sense, just reminding you that's what it's called," I tell her, my grip tightening on the door as she takes a turn.

Sophia drives like she's in a Formula One race or something.

If we were in a car with less horsepower, I'm almost positive we would have been in several accidents by now.

We're headed to look at furniture for my place. She texted me, asking if I had bought anything yet, and I admitted that I still hadn't. So, she offered to go with me, and I immediately took her up on it because I am sick of staring at no furniture. At least the blue splotch on the wall in my bedroom makes me think of her. Makes me smile.

"You can drive it home, if you want."

"Thanks, but no thanks. Everyone is driving like lunatics. Including you. No offense."

Sophia smirks, the air flying in the open window blowing her hair all around.

"I kinda hate this car," she tells me. "I don't care if you crash it."

"*I'd* care," I reply. "Why do you hate this car?"

"I don't feel like I earned it."

I tap my fingers on the door, admiring the smooth texture. "You don't earn gifts."

"What's the best gift you've ever been given?"

My fingers keep up their restless tapping.

I can't think of anything, which is embarrassing. I got gifts as a kid—trucks and books and puzzles. Nothing that stood out. And it didn't take me long to figure out they had been bought with money my dad hadn't earned, which I felt guilty about. Buddies and teammates would always get me joke stuff, like condoms or weird candy. Tripp buys me ties or other practical gifts now. I think, for my last birthday, he got me a blender. My mom sends me a check every year, even though I stopped cashing them when I turned twenty-two and started earning my own money. I've never had a girlfriend, so the only "presents" I've received from women have been in the form of sexual favors.

"A soccer ball, I guess," I finally answer, following a noticeable pause.

It wasn't even a gift. I borrowed—stole—it from a neighbor's yard.

"You really love football that much?"

"It's my whole life," I answer.

I'm not being dramatic in the least. It's always been my

guiding light. My North Star. Without it, I don't know who Will Aster is, and I'm terrified to find out.

"You asked why I agreed to photograph the team...I love photography. And I'm worried I'll fail at it and everyone will know. That I'll be famous for only being famous because of my family. The paper I'm interning for...well, my boss suggested photographing the team might mean I'm more likely to be offered a staff position at the end of my internship. The sooner I make money, the sooner I can stop relying on my family's. The sooner I can prove to them that photography isn't pointless. Or that me pursuing photography isn't pointless."

"That's what they think?"

She shrugs. "My parents think I'm flighty and spontaneous. That I flip through guys and spend most of my time partying. That photography is something I do for fun and decided to try and make a living at it."

"My family thinks soccer is a waste of time. Hasn't stopped me from making a career out of it."

I can feel Sophia's eyes on me. Mine stay focused on the road—where hers *should* be. It's the first time I've mentioned my family to her, something she obviously noticed.

Finally, she looks away. "Did you see the links I sent earlier?"

"See? Yeah. Look at them? No. I'd rather see stuff in person."

She scoffs. "You're welcome for sending them."

"*Thank you* for shopping with me. This'll be quick, I promise. I only need a few things."

"For your *empty* apartment?"

"I'm decisive. I know what I like. When I see something I want, I go for it."

Fuck, that came out more sexual than I'd meant it to.

Things aren't weird between us, like I promised her. We both got up early the morning after she spent the night. I walked her home, then hopped on the nearest transit line to get to the practice facility. We texted a few times throughout the week, she offered to do this with me, and here we are. The sexual tension isn't suffocating, but there's a noticeable charge in the air. To me, at least. Based on how wet she was when I touched her and how quickly she came, I think it's there for her too.

Sophia pulls into a massive parking lot that's about half full, and we climb out of her car to head toward the automatic doors that lead inside what is essentially a huge warehouse. There are fake rooms set up toward the front of the store, three walls containing pretend bathrooms and kitchens and bedrooms. Past the browsing area are towering rows of shelves that must stock the furniture on display and a line of cash registers to check out. I grab one of the clipboards and pencils provided to keep track of whatever I decide to get.

I've never shopped for furniture before. I went from living at my mom's to college to playing in Seattle. The house I rented with a few teammates came partially furnished, and the other guys all had stuff to fill in the gaps. Living alone in an empty place is new to me.

Sophia pauses in front of one of the bedroom setups. "Do you like this bed?"

I assess the white wooden frame. "No."

She looks affronted. "Why not?"

"I just don't. It's white."

"What's wrong with white?"

"*Everything's* white. I don't need more of it."

"It goes with everything," Sophia argues. But she's already moving on to the next setup.

This bed frame is black metal.

"I like this one."

Sophia gives it a cursory glance. "Let's keep looking," she suggests.

I smile. "Oh, right. I forgot that we're shopping for *your* apartment."

"You asked for my help."

Sophia is used to getting her way, I'm sure. To guys who set aside their own opinions to get in her good graces. Whoever brought her to the friendly match where we met, I'm sure it was an attempt to impress Sophia, not annoy her. I'm not that guy, the one who bullshits to get a woman in bed, and I wouldn't be even if I thought I had a chance at hooking up with her.

"No. You *generously* offered your help, remember?"

She scoffs. "Fine. I'll just stand here and stay quiet."

I grin. "Yeah, right."

Sophia just rolls her eyes. She stays stubbornly silent for the next couple of showrooms, but eventually can't resist chiming in on a few furniture pieces. We bicker like an old married couple as we peruse the rest of the store. I pick out what I want, but it's entertaining to hear her running commentary on which pieces "fit with my place" and which ones "suffocate the space." Whatever the hell that means.

We're looking at a bathroom—the one room I don't need anything for since I stole towels from the practice facility—when there's some German spoken behind me. I still can't understand a word of it, but at least I can recognize it *is* German by now. I turn to see a woman with light-brown hair. She's wearing a yellow shirt and a name tag that reads *Lina*, so she must work here. We've already been in the store for a while, so I'm surprised to see her. Whenever I went shopping back home, employees started asking what they could help with from the second I stepped in the door.

She smiles, very obviously checking me out. The interest on her face is flattering. And familiar, honestly. It's also a little weird.

We're not in a crowded bar, which is where I'm most used to this kind of attention. And from the outside, it looks like Sophia and I are a couple, I think, which makes it extra strange. I don't find encouraging or participating in cheating to be sexy. Aside from the ways it affected my soccer career, that's what made me most furious about Cassandra's lies.

"You work here?" I ask.

"Yes," she replies, switching to English.

"You guys deliver?"

They'd better because there's no way I'm fitting even one box into the back of Sophia's sick ride.

"We do."

"Great." I hand her the list with all the stock numbers. "I'll take all that, please. Where do I check out?"

"Right this way, sir." Lina heads for the registers.

I wink at Sophia before I follow her. "Told you I'm decisive."

This would've been an even faster trip, if I didn't enjoy arguing with her so much. That, I don't mention.

CHAPTER FIFTEEN

SOPHIA

"Aha! Found it!" I hold the missing bolt aloft like it's a piece of missing treasure, then take a healthy gulp from my glass. It's my...I've lost count of how many sips, meaning I barely notice the burn of the vodka as I swallow.

"Thank fuck," Will says. They didn't include any extras, so he couldn't complete the couch without it.

Our fingers brush when he takes the bolt from me. I feel like he shocked me—literally. A zap of sensation races up my arm and through my body. Like sticking a finger in an electrical socket, except pleasurable instead of painful. And non-life-threatening. Except it's killing my confidence that I don't want him to touch me the way he did last time I was here.

I'm sitting cross-legged on Will's new living room rug, sorting through the hardware that came with the couch. He texted me yesterday, letting me know that everything we'd picked out had been delivered and thanking me for my help. Not that I had done much. It was the shortest shopping trip I'd ever been on.

And I, for a reason I'm still pondering and possibly regretting, replied, asking if he wanted help putting it all together.

It's a Friday night.

Normally, I'd be out in a bar with friends. My phone keeps buzzing with messages I'm ignoring.

Instead, I'm drinking vodka on the floor, wearing barely any makeup, with my hair knotted up in a bun because it was falling in my face and making it hard to see the paper pamphlet of instructions.

Will's installing the missing bolt, his bottom lip sucked into his mouth and his forehead furrowed with concentration. No matter what he says, he's rich. Or at least, wealthy enough to pay someone to do this for him. He could have gotten the furniture delivered fully assembled rather than spending an evening doing it himself. There's something endearing about his determination to do so.

I give up on pretending to read the instructions. He seems to have figured it all out on his own anyway.

His apartment is a sparse mess, white walls and stacks of brown boxes. My attention returns to Will, more warmth creeping along my skin, the longer I stare at him. He's not wearing a shirt again, and I can't ask him to put one on without admitting it's affecting me. Stubborn could be a synonym for my name.

But, *fuck*, he's so hot. Attractive in a way that's impossible to ignore. Seeing a photo of him shirtless was nothing in comparison to witnessing it in person. Like sniffing vodka in comparison to swallowing it. One exposure is much more potent than the other.

Will doesn't have any tan lines, so he must go shirtless at practice a lot. *Lucky teammates.* His torso is an endless expanse of golden, sun-kissed skin that shifts and bunches as his muscles move. There's something beautiful about the sight of the controlled power and savage strength, which I've seen on display when he plays. My eyes end up on his hands, which are sorting through the pile of hardware. They're huge, long fingers and wide palms. I recall what it felt like to have his right one between my thighs, and a flash of fever appears that has nothing to do with the temperature of his apartment or the amount of alcohol I've consumed.

Coming over here was a terrible idea. Yeah, I just found that bolt that I was probably responsible for losing in the first place, but my other contributions have mostly been drinking the bottle of vodka I brought over because I figured he'd just have more beer and fantasizing about what's under the shorts he's wearing.

He's a football player. He's a very experienced football player.

And I'm very *in*experienced, not that Will knows that. No one does. My friends all think I started having sex years ago.

I'm blaming that curiosity for how I can't stop objectifying him. And the vodka. Plus the way his magical fingers made me come so hard that it felt like I couldn't breathe the last time I was over here.

"Okay. Try it out."

While I've been lost in a haze of lust, Will finished building the couch. He glances at me expectantly and almost catches me checking him out. I avert my eyes to the instructions just in time.

I get to my feet and stretch, ignoring his growing smirk as I hobble over to the brand-new couch. My feet fell asleep a while ago. And, yeah, I'm tipsy. Drinking as a distraction from how damn gorgeous he is wasn't my best idea.

"You're drunk," he comments, realizing the same.

"Mmhmm." I tumble onto the couch and sink into the soft cushions, pulling my knees up into my chest and wrapping my arms around them. "It's comfy."

"You gonna help with the bookcase or nap?"

I roll onto my side so I'm facing him. "I'm helping. I'm offering moral support."

Will snorts. "Nap. Got it."

I watch as he unboxes the wood for the bookcase. "Do you even have any books?"

"Nope." He pops the *P*.

"Why did you get a bookcase, then?"

"You said it would look good in here."

"So, you listened to my opinion on that, but not the bed frame?"

He got the black metal one I hadn't liked. The one that appears charred. Better than him sleeping on the floor, I guess.

"The saleslady said it's one of their bestsellers."

Of course *Lina* said that. A woman I hated on sight for no other reason than she was looking at Will the same way I shouldn't have been. He's smirking, making me think he noticed the way she was checking him out too. It was hard *not* to notice. But he didn't flirt back with her, which I found interesting. I shouldn't have noticed, let alone been relieved about it.

"You excited for the game tomorrow?" I ask, yawning as he pages through the instructions for the bookcase.

"I'm ready," he replies, which isn't really what I was wondering. "You?"

"Ready? Yeah. Excited? No."

He half smiles, focused on ripping open another bag of bolts.

"But I don't hate it as much as I thought I would," I tell him. "The whole sports photography thing."

"Yeah?"

"Yeah. It's more exciting than I was expecting."

"Sounds like you enjoyed a soccer game, Sophia."

He sounds *so* American, between his stubborn insistence on calling the sport soccer and the way his accent alters the sound of my name. But I don't hate it. I kinda love it.

Just like I enjoyed watching football because I like watching him play. It's impossible to miss how much he loves it, that passion bleeding out in every play.

"I've gotten a few good photos of you," I tell him. "You could send them to your family or something, if you wanted to."

Yep, I'm drunk.

Drunk and fishing. Ever since he made that comment about his family not supporting his playing when we were out, buying all of this stuff, I've wondered about his relationship with them. How he's so charming and magnetic and *alone*, it seems like.

"Sure, send them to me," he says.

I abandon any subtlety. "Does your family hate soccer? Or hate that you play soccer?"

Fuck, he's rubbing off on me. Adler would lose his shit if he heard me calling his life's passion by the American term.

Will's smirk suggests he's thinking the same thing. Proud of his influence. "It's complicated. And no matter what you say, I don't think that you hate soccer. It's a field and a goal and a ball."

"I hate...I hate that it overtakes everything. That it's this *force* that consumes so much attention. That it's all anyone knows about me."

He nods. "So, tell me something *no one* knows about you."

I inhale. Exhale. Deliberate a few different responses. Then decide. "I'm a virgin."

Will chokes out a cough, very similar to the sound he made when I told him an orgasm helped me fall asleep. "What? Really?"

I shrug like it's no big deal rather than a vulnerable admission. The bravado is forced, not my normal confidence. "Fuck me and find out."

His eyes widen. A little pride mixes with embarrassment. In the short time I've known him, I've learned Will doesn't get caught off guard very easily. He's hard to faze, so it's satisfying to surprise him.

"Your turn."

Thank God I'm drunk. It makes this nonchalance much easier. The memories of the last time I told a guy that fight to the surface, just like I was worried they would.

The, *"That's so sexy,"* and, *"I'll make you feel so good,"* and, *"It'll be so special,"* all echo around in my head, making my skin feel too tight and itchy. He made my virginity feel like a prize, which was exactly what *I* was to him.

Will doesn't say any of the same things Ansel did. I knew he wouldn't. Aside from telling me he doesn't give a fuck who my brother is, he's never once mentioned Adler to me. He's not in awe of or in competition with my brother.

This is the guy that fingered me as a *favor*. Who I'm certain has had sex with a lot of women and I'd wager doesn't remember anything about most of them.

Silence. A lot of silence.

I lean down, pick up my glass from the floor, and take another swig, ignoring the feel of his eyes on me. Trying to act

132

like it won't matter to me if he doesn't share anything. Or worse, if he chooses something insignificant.

Finally, he speaks. "My mom tried to kill herself after my dad went to prison."

I instantly still, listening to Will's heavy exhale.

"The doctors who treated her know about it, I guess. But I've never told anyone, especially my brother. My mom's explanation was she forgot to eat and fainted. He was seven—not about to question things. I doubt he even remembers that day. But I..." He swallows. "I remember. I found her. I called the ambulance. Went to the hospital with her to have her stomach pumped. We've never spoken about it, just like we don't talk about my dad ever. She knew our dad was gone—locked away for years. And she tried to leave us forever. We would have ended up—I don't even know. Foster care, probably. That's not the sort of thing you just get over or forget about."

I don't feel drunk anymore. I'm still warm, the buzz of alcohol heating my veins. But I feel clearheaded. Sad.

"How old were you?"

"Ten. It was a long time ago. You asked about my family, if they hate soccer. They don't. They just...my relationship with them is complicated. That day complicated it even more. Tripp —my brother—has no clue what happened. My mom never told him. And I didn't want to be the one to tell him. I wish *I* didn't know, and I resent her for that too. I don't know who else she thought would find her. So...yeah." He shakes his head, then takes a long pull of beer. "Sorry. I should have said something else."

"No. I'm glad you told me."

His mom tried to commit suicide, and he's never told *anyone*. I can't imagine experiencing that, let alone carrying the weight of it around alone. I'm sad for his mom, that she was depressed enough to do that. And my heart breaks for the little boy who found her.

I feel innocent in other ways besides sex. My life has been easy by most measures. I complain about silly drama with my friends and the attention that comes along with my last name, but I've never gone through anything like what Will just described. I grew up with two loving parents and a protective brother, with everything I could possibly need and pretty much whatever I wanted. There were rules—curfews and allowances and expectations—but if I asked for something, I usually got it. I've never struggled for anything.

I wonder what Will's childhood was like before that happened. If he ever got to experience being a carefree kid.

"Oh." I'm not sure what else to say. If I should ask more questions or say sorry again or what. We're...friends, I guess, and I've never been friends with a guy. Not the kind where you do more than exchange small talk at bars, at least. Not this sort where you swap secrets.

"Why haven't you had sex?" he asks me.

"I just...haven't."

What happened with Ansel is another secret I've never shared with anyone. I was angry, humiliated, and felt foolish. There was no one in my life I felt comfortable sharing that with. I didn't want to discuss it with my friends. Adler would have been furious. My mom would have been sympathetic, but I know she would have been thinking I should have known better. And my dad...no way was I describing how I had gotten into that situation to him. It would have been torture for the both of us.

"And you've never told anyone?"

I shake my head. "I go out a lot. Flirt with a lot of guys. Everyone just assumes it happened a long time ago, I guess. My friends started coming to me for advice, and I was always...it was hard, being Adler Beck's sister. People always paid attention to me for that reason alone. They'd try to sell photos of me to the papers and always ask me about my home life. So, I learned to be careful with what I said. Who I said it to."

I drain my glass, then lie back down. "Is your dad around now?"

Will lets me change the subject.

"No. He got out, and we never saw him again. My dad was never great at owning up to mistakes. If you asked him, he could do no wrong. My parents weren't married. He spent more time in the garage working on a car than he ever did with me and Tripp when he lived with us. Him disappearing wasn't much of a surprise. Maybe...I think that's probably why she did it. She knew he was never coming back."

"What did he go to prison for?"

"Drug stuff, mostly. He ran a few scams as well. Laziest guy you'd ever meet. He couldn't hold down a job, no matter what."

"Is your brother still in Boston?"

"Yeah. Tripp's in his last year of dental school. He got all the brains in the family."

"Adler got all the athleticism."

"You never played?"

I shake my head, but I'm not sure he can tell since I'm lying down. "No. It was easier to just avoid the whole thing. I knew I'd never measure up to Adler. He wanted it, and he was good at it, and there was no way for me to just *try* it. But shunning it...it was hard not to feel like an outsider in my own family. To love them and not love football."

"I think you can love someone and not love what they love. Those are two different things."

I smile, but my face is snuggled into the cushions, so again, I'm not sure he can tell. "I don't think Tripp got all the brains in the family."

Will scoffs, but he's smiling as he takes a sip of his drink, the corners of his eyes crinkling.

"So, how's that *not getting in trouble* thing going for you?"

"I'm assembling a bookshelf on a Friday night. How do you think?" He leans back on one hand, glancing around his no-longer-empty apartment. "But I'm also drinking beer and—" His phone rings, cutting him off. Will glances at the screen, smiles, then tells me, "One sec," before answering. "Hey, Wyatt." A pause, then, "No, I'm not watching. Warren's still out, and Rodriguez's pitching has been shit." Will shakes his head at whatever is being said on the other end, then laughs.

I watch him, not bothering to look away, even when Will glances this way and catches me staring.

He stands and heads into the bedroom, returning with a laptop tucked under one arm. I pick up my phone and scroll through the unread messages, then toss it away without responding to anyone.

It's already after midnight. I should go home. I should have left a while ago. But I want to keep lying here, staring at Will as he talks with his friend while setting up a baseball game on his computer.

My eyelids start to feel heavier and heavier until I don't bother keeping them open any longer.

The last thing I'm aware of is the comforting weight of a blanket being dragged over me.

CHAPTER SIXTEEN

WILL

My practice jersey is so soaked with sweat that it's clinging to me. Every time I run a hand through my hair, I can feel the sticky residue coating my hand. It's not even that hot out. I'm just working—hard. Starting over is all about proving yourself.

My biggest fear has always been turning into my father.

I know we're similar in many ways. You have to be charming and likable to swindle strangers out of their savings. He turned the charm on and off, the same way I can. The same way I *do*. It's rare that I drop the barrier of confidence, which doubles as a magnet and a shield. People want to get near it, but they can't get past it.

I do a bunch of toe taps, then practice some more goal shots, shooting from different angles and aiming for different spots in the net.

By the time I stop, my breathing is labored, and my muscles ache. But it's a good burn. A satisfied, earned burn.

I'm squirting water into my mouth when I spot the figure leaning against the fence that surrounds the field. The rest of the team headed inside a while ago, after practice ended, for massages and ice baths and all the other amenities available here. Some of which we had in Seattle, most of which we didn't.

Wagner straightens, then starts to walk this way. I drink more, waiting to see what he has to say.

"It's been a while since I saw a player stay late. Practice wasn't long enough for you?"

That's a trick fucking question if I've ever heard one. "I felt like I had more to work on."

Wagner looks past me, at the field, without reacting to that response. "I had ten people tell me that signing you was a mistake. Who told me I had an excellent club and asked what I was making changes for."

"Thanks for not listening, I guess."

Another glimmer of a smile. "You're an excellent athlete, Aster. But you're playing a team sport. Shooting instead of passing, staying late to practice alone? That is not how you win."

"I'm not here to make friends. I'm just here to play socc—football. Look at my stats, if you think I can't contribute to a game."

"I didn't sign you because of your stats, Will."

I stiffen as soon as he says my first name. I can't recall the last time a coach called me anything except Aster. Hearing Will instead removes a degree of deference and adds some sincerity. Wagner is the only coach I've ever really looked up to. They might have called me by my last name, but my former coaches all placed me on a pedestal. A move that, honestly, never earned them any of *my* respect.

"If you want to start a match, show me you want to be here."

Maybe I haven't been as great about hiding my feelings as I should have been. But it's not like everyone doesn't already know why and how I ended up here. I lucked out, coming to Kluvberg, honestly. They're an impressive organization, way better than most of the other teams I could've ended up on. Coming here wasn't some big, exciting change, though. It was the best of bad options. Bad simply because I didn't have a say in any of it. And it feels like that stigma has been a dark cloud hovering overhead ever since. It's cleared some, the more time I spend around the team. Fritz is friendly toward me. And several of the other guys, including Otto, always greet me. But it still feels like I'm a long way from being a real part of the team in any meaningful way.

"I bought furniture," I tell him.

It's the first thing that pops into my head. The only proof I've accepted this as a permanent move.

Wagner studies me, and I think his reaction will be confusion. Irritation maybe. Instead, his nod looks approving. Like that's what he wanted to hear. "Good."

"Great," I respond, not sure what else to say.

By far, this is the most bizarre conversation I've ever had with a coach. I can't tell if Wagner pities me or believes in me. If his refusal to start me is a challenge or a punishment.

"See you tomorrow, Aster."

He leaves without saying anything else.

I collect the balls, drink some more water, and then head toward the practice facility. My phone buzzes in my pocket halfway to the doors.

I pull it out and answer right away when I see the name on the screen. "Hey, man."

"Hey! How's it going?"

The sound of my brother's cheerful voice puts an automatic smile on my face.

"Not bad. You?"

"Good," Tripp answers. "Just leaving class. Thought I'd try you. It's, what, four there?"

"Yeah, that sounds right. I've been practicing, lost track of time."

I've only texted with Tripp a couple of times since moving to Kluvberg. Twice more than I've been in contact with my mom. My brother and I are close, but not overly communicative. I'm definitely not, at least. Tripp is usually the one who calls me.

"Things going okay?" His tone is cautious.

After things blew up in Seattle, I made it clear my soccer career was not a topic I wanted to discuss.

"Yeah. We won our last game." The victory felt a little hollow since I didn't start and didn't score a goal. But that's just my selfish motivation talking.

"That's awesome!"

Tripp is a basketball fan. Diehard Celtics guy. But he never played sports himself. He focused on school, the opposite of me.

"Everything okay with you?"

"Yeah, pretty good. School's busy. Final year, you know."

I don't know. I barely made it through college, let alone graduate school. If not for the university's more lax grading policy when it came to student athletes, I never would have graduated. I was there to play, not for a degree.

I clear my throat. "How's Mom?"

"She's good. She switched to a new yoga studio near campus, so we've gotten brunch a couple of times."

It's a scene—a world—I can't picture. I've never had the relationship with our mom that Tripp has, even before that fateful afternoon I found her unconscious.

As soon as I turned eighteen, I left Boston and never really looked back. My trips back home since have been brief at best. Obligatory. I love my brother and my mom; I'm just not great about showing it.

"That's good."

My phone buzzes with another incoming call. It's Shawn.

I sigh. "Can I give you a call back later? My agent is calling."

"Yeah, of course. Talk soon. Bye."

"Bye," I echo, then answer Shawn's call with, "I haven't done anything."

My only questionable behavior as of late has been fantasizing about Sophia Beck.

But I haven't touched her again. Or gotten wasted in a club or had sex with a random woman, which is what Shawn is most concerned about, I'm sure.

"That's not why I'm calling." There's a somber note to his voice that immediately has me on high alert.

"What is it?"

"Cassandra Owens did a magazine interview. It's coming out next week."

"So?" I ask with a bravado I don't feel. Foreboding creeps across my skin, cooling the coat of sweat.

"I got an early copy through a friend of a friend of a friend. And...it's bad, Will. She's claiming you had an affair lasting a few months."

"She's *what*? Why the fuck would she say that?"

Shawn sighs. "Mark Owens is rumored to be filing for divorce."

Great. I can add homewrecker to my resume.

"So, she's using me as a *fuck you* to her asshole husband?"

Another heavy sigh. "Most likely."

I pinch the bridge of my nose. "Can I sue her? Isn't this defamation? She's *lying*."

"I already sent the article to the legal team. They're reviewing it now. But my guess is, we can't sue for defamation without proof she's lying. Which we don't have. It's her word against yours at this point."

"What about the interview? Does she mention dates? Places?"

"Good idea, and I already looked. She's very careful not to mention any details. Lots of flowery descriptions about your secret meetings, no mention of when or where they took place. Probably for the exact reason you want them. But..." He sighs. "It's compelling stuff. I doubt anyone, except us, will be asking those questions."

He believes me, I realize. Something I wasn't sure of before.

As soon as the photos started coming out, I told Shawn I'd had no clue who the brunette in them was when we went into that restroom together. Owens had a financial interest in the team. He wasn't showing up for practices with a whistle and his wife by his side. I didn't get why people didn't think me having no idea who Cassandra Owens was, was a possibility. Still don't. Aside from the fact that me sneaking around with my club owner's wife is a much more scandalous story than me having sex in a bar restroom with a stranger.

"Look, I know this is the last thing you want. But you come out of this looking okay. She's actually very complimentary of you. *He's a hot sex god. He treated me well. He was the bright spot in a dark time.* Blah, blah. It'll be a softer landing than the first story. More details, but the same people involved. Nothing *that* juicy."

Shawn's taking this better than I would have expected. Better than I am.

I can feel a vein pulsing in my temple. The last time this story broke was one of the worst days of my life.

Everything that seemed certain—my team, my friends, my future, where I lived—crumbled around me. But this will be worse, I realize. Waking up and coming to this field for practice and knowing that all the guys I'm fighting for some respect from will know—will *think* they know—that I had an affair with a married woman lasting months. That any progress I've made with them will likely get erased. That the approving nod Wagner just gave me will revert to a disapproving frown. *Sophia* will see it. Some of her photos might accompany the articles that will get published about it here.

"I want to put out a statement," I decide.

"What?"

"I mean it, Shawn. You told me to keep my mouth shut and ride it out before, and I did. Not this time. Kluvberg can't release me for saying she's lying when she *is*."

A pause, then, "I'd rather not find out."

"This is way too fucking far. She twisted the truth before, acting like I knew who she was, but technically, we did have sex. I screwed up there. But this? An affair lasting months? It's complete fiction. I don't care what you say about rising above and not adding fuel to the fire and not getting involved. Silence means guilty to anyone else. At least my side of things will be out there. And she's *lying*. She got lucky that people took photos of us that night. There's not a single shred of evidence she could possibly have to support us having an affair for months. Everyone in Seattle—teammates, trainers, coaches—knew I didn't do relationships."

Shawn blows out a long breath. Instead of arguing, like I'm expecting, he agrees. "All right. We'll draft something, send it to you for approval."

"Thank you."

"Written statement is it, okay? No sound bites. *No comment* is all you say if you get asked about it after a match. Got it?"

"Yeah, I got it."

"Good. Check your email in a few hours."

I hang up. Then fling the water bottle I'm carrying as hard as I can at the cinder-block wall of the training facility. Plastic explodes, water spraying everywhere.

Predictably, it doesn't make me feel any better at all.

CHAPTER SEVENTEEN

SOPHIA

"Wow. You're soooo pretty."

I force a smile in response to the slurred compliment, leaning away when the guy takes a step forward. He's cute. Drunk, but cute. Probably a university student, based on his casual clothes.

There's not even the slightest spark of interest when he continues flirting with me, which is annoying. It piles on to the irritation I'm already experiencing.

I mutter an excuse to the guy, then head for the corner booth, where my friends are sitting. I don't even bother to wait for the approaching bartender to order another drink, which is why I originally went over there.

I've been here for three hours, and I wish I'd left a while ago.

My friends love coming to the club Adler owns because there are often Kluvberg players hanging out here. And possibly seeing Will is the main reason I agreed. Which I feel stupid about, seeing as he's not here. Seeing as he hasn't texted all week. We haven't spoken since the night we swapped secrets while he built furniture. I saw him at the game earlier, but only from a distance and through the lens of my camera.

It shouldn't matter to me. Just the end of a few unexpected yet compelling hours spent with a guy who no longer feels like a stranger. A *footballer* who I should have absolutely no feelings for.

Relief is what I should be experiencing, that things ended cleanly between us. That we'll both move on with our lives like we would've if I'd never sat in that seat.

But I'm not reassured. I'm restless.

"What happened to your drink?" Emilia asks when I reach the table.

I shrug. "They were busy."

"Too busy to help *you?*" She arches her eyebrows, incredulous.

An expression I've seen so many times before. That I grew up with money is common knowledge. People assume I'm the privileged princess of Kluvberg's royal family. The fact that I don't play football has never been relevant.

"I'm not feeling great. Going to head out," I say, grabbing my clutch off the table.

"It's barely midnight." Clara tosses her dark hair over one shoulder. "And it's been *forever* since you came out."

Maybe I'd feel less guilty about leaving if I didn't know they want me to stay in case any Kluvberg players show up.

I open my clutch, checking to make sure my phone and keys are inside. "I'll see you guys soon."

Then, I head for the door before any of them can say anything else.

Felix, the bouncer, offers me a friendly smile as I reach the exit. "Heading out?"

I nod.

"Let me get you a car."

Yeah, so there are perks to having the last name Beck. Especially here. Adler makes sure his staff is on high alert whenever I stop by.

Ten minutes later, I'm in the back of a sedan, speeding toward my neighborhood. I pull my phone out of my clutch, then open my last text chain with Will and scroll through the messages until I reach the very first one. The one that I sent, using the number I promised myself I wouldn't.

I lied to him. I still have the damn ticket he gave me sitting on the table next to my bed. Most nights, I stare at it as I'm trying to fall asleep.

"Excuse me. Do you mind taking me to Sparkassenstraße 10 instead?" I ask the driver.

"Of course not."

I second-guess the whole trip to Will's building. But I still climb out of the car and head inside, walking down the hallway until I reach his apartment door.

He answers on the second knock, his eyebrows rising subtly when he registers it's me. His gaze drags down the skimpy dress and heels I'm wearing, something flashing across his face before it settles into assurance. He leans against the doorframe. Shirtless—again—and I'm not sure if that's a good thing or not. It's an enjoyable, distracting view.

"Hey," he says.

My grip on my clutch tightens as my palms prickle. "Hey."

We stare at each other, the air itself seeming to thicken around us.

"Aren't you going to invite me in?" I finally ask when he continues to say nothing.

"No," Will replies.

"Why not?"

"Because you smell like tequila and you're wearing a dress that barely covers your ass. Because I've had a shitty fucking week, and so far, this is the highlight of it, and all that means that you coming in is a really bad idea."

I step forward, forcing him to move aside and let me in. "None of those are great reasons."

Will scoffs as he shuts the door behind me.

I toss my clutch onto the countertop. Walk over to the couch. His laptop is open, another baseball game playing on the screen. A glass, half full of either water or vodka, is on the floor. Mussed cushions make me think he was lying down before I showed up.

"You should have bought a coffee table."

His apartment looks better. A lot better than the basically empty place it was before last weekend. But it's far from a settled home.

He passes me by and takes a seat on the couch, studying me. "You're drunk."

"No." I kick off my heels before spinning to smirk at him. "Just a *little* tipsy."

"Fun night?"

"Eh." I feel awkward standing, so I walk over to him, dropping down on the opposite end of the couch. I tuck my feet up under my dress. "I got bored."

"Dancing and drinking usually put me to sleep too."

I roll my eyes and lean back. "Whatever. What are you doing?"

He points at the screen.

"I don't know anything about baseball," I tell him.

"No?" he mock gasps. "You, the massive sports fan who's been to Georgia once?"

"Shut up." But there's a weird warmth in my chest. Unlike the guys I talked to tonight, Will knows me. Knows I'm not athletic and I've been to the States one time. And I like that he knows those things about me—remembered those things about me—way more than I should.

He smiles, but it fades quickly. He's staring at me so intently; it *burns*. I feel stripped and raw under his close scrutiny.

"What are you doing here, Sophia?"

"I told you, I got bored."

"You got bored out at a club, so you came to my apartment to watch baseball?"

"Yes." I rub one of the red marks my heels left. "Why was your week shitty?"

Will looks away, at the computer screen. "I don't want to talk about it."

I should go. He's all but asking me to. But I remember that flash in his expression when he opened the door, similar to the flush that feels like it's spreading across my skin right now. I look away, at his empty bookshelf.

He inhales. "Sorry. How was your week?"

"It was..." Complaining about my classes or sharing my stress about deciding which photo to submit to the EPAs sounds silly. Mentioning a low point was never hearing from him is even more off-limits. It's bad enough—desperate enough—that I showed up here. I don't chase guys. They've always pursued me. "It was fine."

"You're lying."

I glance at him. "I don't want to talk about it."

149

Something twists in Will's expression when I parrot the same line he told me back to him.

"I'll go. Enjoy your baseball."

He reaches for me as I stand, and the combination of me moving and him pulling ends with me half sprawled in his lap. I scramble to straighten, then freeze when I feel his reaction.

"Sophia." Will mutters my name like a curse.

He's looking at me with so much heat and intensity that I forget how to breathe for a few seconds. My stomach flips repeatedly, tumbling around like it's inside a washing machine.

Then, I circle my hips slowly, feeling him swell even more. I might not be as experienced as he is, but I know what an erection feels like.

The air surrounding us manages to thicken even more, contracting tight and turning tangible. Pulling us closer together, it feels like.

"Do you like my dress?" I ask, deliberately rocking into him again.

His head tilts back, the tendons of his neck straining against tan skin. He looks pained, but I think it's a good thing. That he wants this, not that he's trying to get me off his lap without hurting my feelings.

"It's short."

"Yeah, that's the point. The shorter it is, the easier it is for guys to imagine what's under it."

A muscle in Will's jaw flexes.

Usually, I have no issue flirting with guys. There's a script. He compliments me, and I ask a few questions and gush over his answers. He offers to get me a drink or asks me to dance, and then we end up making out in the dark corner of a booth. Sometimes, they'll ask me out, and sometimes, I'll accept. But always, there's a stoplight in my head that moves from green to yellow and then eventually hits red. A point where I want to stop.

I haven't hit that with Will yet, and I'm starting to wonder if I will. I came here. I sought him out, which is something I'd never done before.

Even with Ansel, part of the appeal was him chasing me. I misread his intentions, but I liked how he was the one initiating everything.

Will's different. He's a worthy competitor. He's seen past the shiny, poised exterior and all the insecurities buried beneath. He won't be fooled by false confidence. I feel vulnerable in front of him, but I also want him to see. I relish having his eyes on me.

"Is it working?" I ask. "Are you imagining what's under it?"

I'm imagining what's under his shorts. He feels *huge*.

I shift, trying to better assess the size. To figure out if he's really as big as I think.

Will's hands land on my hips, holding me still. His palms are huge, too, spanning half of my back.

The naked hunger in his gaze sends bolts of heat racing down my spine.

"This isn't a game, Sophia."

"You're the player," I remind him.

His jaw tightens again at the taunt, but the carnal ferocity in his eyes flames brighter.

He's an athlete. He's competitive. This isn't a game, but I want to play with him. I want to push him—until he pushes back. I need this to happen between us before I can revert back to what life looked like before we met. I need to know he wants me. Not because I'm so vain that I think he must be attracted to me, but because I need some outlet for the burning desire I feel toward him.

"*Lots* of guys were looking earlier. I danced with some of them. One asked me to go home with him. Should I have gone home with him, Will?"

I'm worried his jaw might crack; it's clenched so tight.

"I pretended it was you all night. You I was dancing with. You I was talking to. And then they'd say something I knew you wouldn't, and I couldn't keep pretending."

I lift a hand, finally doing something I've fantasized about since the first time I saw him. His eyes half close when I run my fingers through his short, dark hair, a deep rumble vibrating through his chest. I rock my hips into his again, and his eyes snap open.

"Like what?" His voice is a low rasp, like tires crunching gravel.

"One of them asked, '*Willst du tanzen?*' You've never asked me to dance. One told me, '*Du siehst umwerfend aus.*' You've never told me I look beautiful. Another asked, '*Darf ich dich küssen?*' You've never asked if you could kiss me."

I can see the struggle on his face, and part of me feels bad for the torment. The rest of me doesn't feel bad at all. My grip in his thick hair tightens, and I imagine tugging at the strands while he thrusts deep inside of me. I want it to happen.

So, *so* badly.

I'm getting tossed before I realize it, landing on my back on top of the soft cushions. My heart races from a heady cocktail of arousal and adrenaline as his hands slide up my thighs, slowly pushing my dress higher.

"Fuck, you're trouble." He sounds mad about it. But also amused.

My breathing has turned embarrassingly fast. I wish I were still on his lap, rubbing against his cock. But he's touching me, voluntarily, which has me praying this isn't about to end.

"I play soccer; I don't dance."

His hands finally reach the curve of my hips, this time beneath my dress. His fingers hook the scraps of lace circling my waist, yanking my thong down with one quick jerk.

"You're not beautiful; you're the most goddamn gorgeous woman I've ever seen."

I'm unraveling. From what he's saying; from how he sounds saying it; from the possessive way he spreads my thighs so he can look at my pussy. From the anticipation of what might happen. He's seized control of the situation, and I trust him enough to let that happen.

"*Darf ich dich küssen?*" His pronunciation is terrible. But it's the first time I've ever heard Will even attempt to speak German. One of his hands slides higher, the heel of his hand applying pressure in the spot I want him most. My hips jerk. "Here?"

He smirks at the surprise I'm sure is on my face.

"I thought you don't do that."

"Just answer the question, Sophia."

"Yes."

He leans over me, the sight of his dark head hovering between my legs so erotic that I can barely think straight. I hook one knee over the back of the couch, opening myself as wide as I possibly can. The pulse between my thighs is throbbing and persistent. I can feel how wet I am. Smell it.

From the first touch of his tongue, I'm moaning. I thought nothing could feel better than his fingers inside of me, and I was so, so wrong. This—*this*—is nirvana. He sucks and licks and swirls, his mouth applying the perfect pressure at the perfect angle in the perfect spot.

I push my fingers into his hair again, fisting the short strands as I lift my hips to press my pussy even closer to his mouth.

I can feel the vibration of his chuckle. Whatever. It's not like he doesn't already know how badly I want this.

The inferno of pleasure builds higher and higher inside of me, stoked by each swipe of his tongue. Already ablaze, and more accelerant keeps getting added. I detonate without warning, shouting his name as the waves of release roll through me. It lasts for a lot longer than when I touch myself and is even stronger than the last time he touched me. If I wasn't already lying down, I don't think I'd be able to stand. My muscles feel loose and shaky, like I just ran a marathon. I'm certainly breathing like I did.

"Oh my *God*."

Will smirks as he sits up, his tongue running across his glossy lower lip. He reaches for the waistband of his shorts. I watch in fascination as he tugs them down harshly, releasing his cock.

I can't contain the small gasp when I catch the first glimpse of him naked. It bursts out of me, an involuntary reaction.

My muscles freeze in place as I watch when it bobs out to slap his stomach. As he fists the long length and gives it a few lazy tugs.

I'm hypnotized by the sight. By the fast jerks and the growing size. The way the skin is stretched so tight that it looks shiny and the swollen, glistening tip.

I've gone this far with guys. Will's isn't the first penis I've ever seen. But this feels like a first, like something entirely different from anything I've ever experienced before. It's indescribably intimate, seeing *him* like this. How it's happening on the couch I helped him pick out.

He's not watching his hand stroke himself, the way I am. He's focused on me, still sprawled on the cushions.

"Is this what you wanted, Sophia, when you were rubbing your pussy all over my lap? You wanted to see how hard I was for you?"

Someone sucked all the oxygen out of his apartment, I decide. It's the best explanation for how my lungs can't seem to pull in any air. I'm transfixed and turned on and so overwhelmed that my body forgot how inhaling works.

"Take off your dress."

I blink at him, too mesmerized by the sight of him to react right away. I've never seen Will act this *dominant*. He's always assured, but never this authoritative.

"You wanted me to picture you naked? Show me the real thing. *Take off your dress*, Sophia."

There's no room for arguing in the demand, and I don't want to. I sit up and tug my dress over my head. He already took care of my thong, but I unhook my bra too, revealing my breasts before lying back down.

"Fuck," Will curses. "Fuck, fuck, *fuck*."

He's rubbing himself harder now, rapid tugs that almost look painful. More moisture keeps appearing at the tip, which he uses as lubricant, swiping the flared head every few strokes as his eyes rove over my naked body.

I've never seen a guy pleasure himself before, and it's way hotter than I would have thought. Not the least bit awkward or strange or uncomfortable.

"Spread your legs," he says roughly. "So I can see—*fuck*."

I obeyed instantly this time.

His eyebrows pull tight together, until they look like one slash of black. And then he's coming, spurts of white cum landing on my stomach as Will groans loudly. He runs his free hand through his hair and then releases his dick, which is still a startling size, the muscles in his shoulders shifting and rippling in tandem.

He stands and disappears into the bathroom, emerging a few seconds later with a white towel in hand. He wipes my stomach gently, cleaning the evidence of his release off of my skin.

The logo embroidered on the towel makes me smile. "You took towels from the team?"

"Uh-huh. I'll return them once I buy some more."

"Not sure they'll want them back now."

It's shockingly natural, talking with him like this after what just happened.

He smirks before tossing the towel toward the bathroom. He grabs his shorts, stepping back into them and covering up the dick I wasn't done looking at, honestly.

"I could have done it," I say, sitting up and reaching for my dress. Remaining naked feels strange when he isn't.

I know he understands what I'm referring to when he replies, "It's fine."

Same thing he told me last time.

Some insecurity appears. He knows I'm inexperienced. Maybe he doesn't think I'll know what to do. Be able to please him. "I've done that plenty of times before."

His lips press together into a thin line before he turns and starts walking toward the kitchen. "Want something to drink?"

I stand and head toward the bathroom. "Sure. Some water."

Will's nod is the last sight I catch before I close the door.

CHAPTER EIGHTEEN

WILL

I sip some of the vodka Sophia brought the last time she came over, barely wincing at the burn when I swallow. It feels like penance. And, yeah, I'm trying to erase the memory of what happened on this couch earlier. The more I think about it, the more I'll want it to happen again. And it *can't* happen again.

She's a virgin.

She's Adler Beck's sister.

Most importantly, she deserves better than a guy who's about to be in the midst of a media shitstorm. Shawn's putting out a statement, just like I asked. And Cassandra's interview probably would have blown up anyhow, based on the attention the first story about us received. But me calling her a liar this time will be like pouring gasoline on a roaring bonfire.

The bedroom door opens, and Sophia steps out. She's no longer wearing the sexy dress at least, but the sight of her in my clothes isn't much better.

"Your water is on the floor," I tell her.

She was right; I should've bought a coffee table. Decisiveness can have the downside of forgetting things.

"Thanks." She picks up the glass and takes a seat on the opposite end of the couch.

We sip in silence at our respective clear liquids.

Turning on music while she was changing would have been a good idea. Or a baseball game. The silence between us isn't uncomfortable exactly, but it's noticeable. I feel like I should say something, but I'm not sure what to tell her.

I drink more vodka, hating that Cassandra has followed me here. Hating her for dragging this drama out to suit her own purposes. Hating myself for how I let her gain an advantage over me in the first place.

Finally, I speak. "You heard how I ended up here?"

Sophia doesn't reply right away. "I saw a few headlines."

A diplomatic answer that also sounds like she's maybe giving me the benefit of the doubt. More than most people I'd known for years bothered to do.

"I went out to a bar with some teammates, which I did a lot. Got drunk, which I also did a lot. We'd play hard. Party harder. There were usually women around." I clear my throat, tightening my grip on the glass I'm holding. "One night, this woman approached me and said her name was Katie. She flirted with me. We did shots, I think. Honestly, most of the night is a blur. Someone took photos that made it pretty obvious what happened between us later. They recognized me. The photos got shared on social media. And then someone recognized her, and it all snowballed from there. Covers of magazines, conversations on talk shows...voided contracts. Her name was actually Cassandra Owens, and she was married to the guy who owned my old team. His fancy lawyers found a loophole in my contract, and no other team wanted to touch me with a ten-foot pole."

I take another swig of vodka.

"She lied to you?" Sophia sounds horrified.

"If I'd known she was married, let alone who she was married to, I never would have touched her. Which she knew, I guess. Or wasn't willing to risk. So, yeah, she lied to me."

"Why didn't you say that when the story came out?"

"I thought the whole thing would blow over. People hook up in bars every night. I was the star of a team that most people had never heard of. Soccer isn't as popular in the States as it is here. She married a rich man twice her age. Nothing about it seemed that special. By the time I realized it wouldn't go away quickly or quietly, the press had already written the narrative. I had a... reputation. Drinking. Girls. Fighting. No one had a hard time believing I'd decided to hook up with the owner's wife. No one ever even asked me if I had. People only care about the truth if it's juicier than the story, and it rarely is. I got released a couple of days after it happened. Anything I said after getting cut would have been written off as bitterness. I needed the story to die down as fast as possible, not give it new life while my agent was scrambling to find me another team to play for."

I rub an old scar on my third knuckle.

"Now, she's saying we had an affair. She did an interview that's coming out soon. My agent got ahold of an early copy. I found out on Monday, and it's why my week was so shitty."

Sophia inhales sharply. "How can she do that? Just *lie* about something like that?"

"People lie all the time. The more compelling it is, the better. More people read about it. More people talk about it. More people believe it. And I never challenged her version of events before, how she conveniently forgot to say I hadn't known who she was. There are rumors she and her husband are getting divorced, so she's probably trying to embarrass him even more."

"So, you're still not going to do anything?"

"I'm going to do *something*. I'm putting out a statement, saying she's lying. But that won't do much. Her side of the story is what people would rather think happened, so it's what they'll believe. I'll just look like the guy who had an affair and is now lying about it. Oldest fucking story in the book."

Sophia's silent, and I'm still too cowardly to look over at her.

"I'm sorry, Will."

Her sympathy burns like rubbing alcohol poured on an open wound. I don't want it, and I definitely don't deserve it.

"I'm not the *happy ending, serious relationship* guy, Sophia," I tell her.

Something she knows. Something I don't need to say. But it seems important after what happened between us earlier. I had been so...unprepared, which had never happened before. I wasn't expecting her to show up here. I definitely wasn't expecting things to go where they did. I definitely hadn't anticipated that giving a shit about a girl would feel like this—a rusty saw separating my chest.

"You're a *casual sex* kind of guy," she says softly.

Our conversation in the busy bar that night feels a million miles away from the two of us tucked away from the world on this blue couch, which I picked out because it was the same color as her eyes. Aside from saving my soccer career, she's the one thing I care about in this country.

"I'm a guy who's trying to fix some mistakes, not repeat them."

"You're comparing me to *her*?"

"No. I'm comparing me to *me*. It was a miracle Kluvberg picked me up. It won't happen again if I get released from here."

"You said you didn't give a fuck who my brother was."

The saw is back, slicing away.

"I don't. You're your own person, and you should never feel diminished to less. But..." I exhale. I'm dancing around the truth, and we both know it. "The season's gone pretty shitty so far. I'm averaging fifteen minutes a game. I haven't started once. I've scored one goal. The guys tolerate me, but I'm not part of the team. If Beck found out what happened between us earlier, do you think he'd pass to me at the next match? Do you think he'd mention to Wagner that I should be out on the field more?"

Right now, I despise Cassandra Owens more than I ever have before. If I'd known she would end my career in Seattle—if I'd known who she was, period—I would never have touched her. But I had no fucking clue that night would collapse my career.

I know exactly how sleeping with Sophia *Beck* could blow up what little remains. And it's more than that. She deserves a *good* guy.

I've never committed murder. Never purposefully swindled people out of their savings the way my dad liked to.

But I'm not a good guy. I'm selfish and reckless, and I've made no shortage of mistakes. Many of which I'm still paying for.

"I can't control who my brother is, Will." Her tone is annoyed, and she has every reason to be.

She's lumping me in with every other guy who's pursued her solely because of her last name. Like that asshole who took her to that scrimmage the first time we met without bothering to find out she'd rather spend an afternoon at an art museum.

It pisses me off. I'm not scared of or awed by Adler Beck. Sophia is her own person and has the right to make her own choices.

But the possibility of losing soccer terrifies me. And the chances of a third team taking a risk on me after I was released by two? Minuscule, if that.

"I know."

Sophia stands. "Can you be a gentleman tonight? I'm too exhausted to get dressed and go home."

She doesn't want me to sleep in bed with her. She's taking this as a rejection, which is the last thing I want. I'm the one who fucked this up for myself. Fucked everything up for myself.

"I—yeah, of course."

"Great. Good night." Her voice is curt as she turns and heads into my bedroom, shutting the door behind her. *The End* is what that slam sounds like. She has too much pride to ask me to reconsider.

I doubt our friendship will survive this. I'm positive she'll leave in the morning and I'll never hear from her again.

I let out a long breath, slouching on the couch and tilting my head back to stare at the ceiling.

Soccer.

I chose soccer. I've *always* chosen soccer when given the chance.

My career is all I care about, and it's hanging on by a fucking thread right now. If Cassandra Owens had given me the choice, I would still be in Seattle. I would have never come to Kluvberg. Never met Sophia.

I glance at the shut door, something slippery and unpleasant and ugly coiling in my stomach. I imagine Sophia sleeping in another guy's bed. Wearing another guy's clothes. Letting another guy make her come.

Anger flares, just like it did earlier when she mentioned her handjob experience.

I chose soccer. That's always been the obvious decision.

And I realize, for the first time, I'm worried I made the wrong choice.

CHAPTER NINETEEN

SOPHIA

"These are all excellent, Sophia. Any one of them would be great choices for your submission," Professor Graf tells me.

I gnaw on my bottom lip as I gather the photographs up, stuffing them back into the envelope I brought. Excellent, great —they sound like synonyms for fine.

Decent.

Okay.

Mediocre.

I'm aiming for shocking. Breathtaking. Startling.

But I can't seem to take that photo.

Professor Graf aims a kind smile my way. She's my favorite professor, a large part of the reason why I committed to applied arts for university.

"You have to go with your gut, Sophia. Don't worry about how it'll be judged. All you can control is what you put out into the world, not how others perceive it. That's the beauty of art. It looks different to everyone. You are the only one who decides what you share."

She sounds so wise. So aspirational. So *unhelpful* because I really just wanted her to tell me which of the five photos I'd brought was the one I should submit to the European Photography Awards.

And now, I'm worried her not choosing is her way of telling me what I already know—none of them are good enough.

I thank Professor Graf and then leave her office, lost in my own thoughts as I walk down the street toward where I parked my car.

Photography sounds so easy when you describe it. Point and shoot. A millisecond captured in stunning detail, just from one click of a button. It's so easy; it's hard. Anyone can do it, so why bother trying?

It's moments like this when I wonder if I should relegate photography to just a hobby. If it was a mistake to try to pursue it as a career in the first place. Photography felt like something totally different from the rest of my family. But even that's managed to get snarled up in football. It's no longer an escape I can claim wholly as my own.

I need to stop looking for an escape, I know. I've chosen to stay in Kluvberg, knowing it's the epicenter of interest in my family. I've accepted the attention will be there, no matter what I do. And I feel increasingly guilty complaining about it. A girl in one of my classes this morning was talking about how she wasn't able to find an internship anywhere in the city. Will overcame a challenging childhood to become a soccer star, only to have it taken away by one lie and a mistake.

I'm one semester from graduating. Weeks into an assignment that's resulted in me attending more Kluvberg games than I have in years, not to mention a bruised ego and what feels suspiciously like a cracked heart. Now is not the time to second-guess how I got here. It's time to fight for the career I want to have. Submitting the perfect photo to the EPAs is a major part of that. I need it to be one I'm proud of, like Professor Graf said.

I decide to stop into a coffee shop, needing a pick-me-up before driving home.

My phone vibrates in my pocket right before I reach the door. I pull it out quickly, deflating slightly when I see Saylor's name on the screen. Will's never called me before, only texted, so it was dumb to even...

I blow out a breath, then answer. "Hey!"

"Hey!" Saylor's voice is just as chipper as mine is. Unlike mine, I don't think her upbeat tone is forced. "How are you?"

"Great. Just headed to get a coffee."

"That sounds lovely. Treat yourself, girl!"

I smile. "What's up?"

"Just seeing if you're free for dinner tomorrow night. I know last month's get-together was...chaotic, but Gigi is sleeping better now. We won't be zombie hosts, I promise."

My laugh is automatic. So is the urge to say no.

I don't want to spend the evening around two happy couples. Don't want to justify my decisions to my parents or listen to more of Adler's well-meaning but overprotective comments.

My brother has no idea what happened with Ansel, so it's not fair for me to resent him for it. But part of me always has. And it's worse this time, knowing that Will was right last weekend. Adler would freak out if he knew anything had happened between us. He would allow it to affect Will's career. I'm mad at Will for caring about it so much—for caring about football more than he cares about me—but I'm mad at Adler too.

He was navigating high expectations and a bright spotlight

that took over his teenage years. It's understandable he never noticed mine were spent determining which girls actually wanted to be friends with me or which ones wanted him or crying over a guy who pursued me so he could film himself fucking Adler Beck's sister. Telling Will I was a virgin dredged up a lot I'd spent years trying to forget.

Add in a crying baby, and it sounds like a headache of an evening.

But I love my family. These semi-regular dinners are the only time we all get together.

"Is it okay if I bring a date?" I ask impulsively.

Noah has been texting me recently, asking if I'm less busy. I doubt there will be any new spark that wasn't there before, but meeting my family will be a dream come true for him. Practically a Good Samaritan act.

And his fanboying will hopefully keep my family occupied. Prevent them from asking me about the EPAs or how photographing for Kluvberg has gone. Two topics I really don't feel like discussing.

"You met a new guy?" Saylor's voice is high and excited.

"Sort of." No need for Saylor to know he's the guy who brought me to a Kluvberg scrimmage.

I never confided in her about anything related to Will while it was happening, so it seems pointless to say anything now that it's over.

I haven't seen or spoken to him since I snuck out of his apartment early the morning after we hooked up. He texted me five minutes after I left, which makes me think he was only pretending to be sleeping on the couch, telling me to message him when I was home safely.

A petty part of me wanted to ignore the text, but I didn't. He liked the message and has sent nothing since.

"Of course you should bring him. I can't wait to meet him!"

Maybe mentioning Noah was a mistake. But I've come this far. Too far to turn back now.

"Crap, Gigi just woke up. I'll see you tomorrow night!"

Saylor hangs up before I can say another word.

CHAPTER TWENTY

WILL

Beck is waiting at my locker when I return from my session with one of the trainers. Arms crossed, wearing his default expression—serious.

"Are you busy tonight?" he asks me.

I raise both eyebrows, tossing the towel I'm holding over one shoulder. "Are you asking me out?"

He glowers. "I'm inviting you over for dinner. My—" He grimaces. "My wife would like to meet you."

I nod. Smirk. "Your wife, huh? Yeah, I get that a lot."

If you can't beat the *I sleep with other men's wives* allegations, might as well make fun of them, right? As expected, the statement Shawn put out on my behalf did little—if anything—to convince anyone I hadn't had an affair with Cassandra Owens. All week, I've watched what little progress I made here unravel. And I haven't spoken to Sophia—the one bright spot—in a week. I'm in a shitty mood, the sort where I don't really think about what's spewing out of my mouth.

Beck's hard stare is entirely unamused. "You're awfully arrogant for a striker who hasn't started a single match."

My smile disappears. "Was that your call?"

"Wagner is the coach."

Not what I asked, I note.

"I'm ready. I can help win."

We're four games into the season. One win, one loss, two draws. I averaged about fifteen minutes of playing time in each. Came close to scoring a couple of times. But my current goal tally is only one, and I can't remember the last time that was the case.

It's like I'm playing with a handicap. I'm healthy, and I'm raring to go every time I step out on the field. But I'm playing in a stadium that's four times the size of what I'm used to, getting shouted at in a foreign language. Playing with strangers who have mostly treated me with polite indifference.

Since the new wave of stories broke, it's been more indifferent than polite. I caught a few lip curls. Some disgusted looks. They all think I'm an asshole. *More* of an asshole. If they read my statement, they didn't believe it.

Whatever.

I'm not here to make friends, just like I told Wagner. I'm here to play soccer, and Adler Beck is my best hope of making that happen. Of integrating into the squad, like Wagner told me to. This invitation is a decent start, I hope.

"Six sharp, Aster."

Germans are extremely punctual, I've learned.

Beck rattles off an address, then walks away.

———

At five fifty-six, I step out of the elevator and ring the doorbell for the penthouse. Beck is the one who answers the door, the stern expression on his face seriously undermined by the smiling, waving baby he's holding.

"I didn't know you had a kid," I say.

"Come on in," Beck tells me, stepping aside so I can enter the apartment.

The entryway alone is about the same size as my one-bedroom. This is the guy who was gifted so many Ferraris that he gave one to his sister, I guess. I don't know why I'm surprised by the obvious wealth.

I glance around, taking in the sight of the sleek furnishings. It's obvious everything is expensive, but it's not a museum either. There's a stroller parked to the right of the door. A couple of pairs of sneakers tucked beneath the bench. A smudge of dirt on the rug. A watercolor painting of a soccer field prominently displayed above a table stacked with mail.

"This way," he says, interrupting my perusal.

I follow Beck into a living room. A couple that looks to be in their early fifties is already seated on one of the leather couches. I'm assuming these are his parents. Which means...these are Sophia's parents.

"Hello." I give them a friendly smile that the woman returns.

Mr. Beck looks like his son, right down to the scowl on his face.

He holds out a hand. "Hans Beck."

"Will Aster." I shake it, then offer my palm to Mrs. Beck as well. I have no clue if that's the proper greeting or not.

She takes it. "Erika."

"Nice to meet you both." I glance at Beck. "You didn't mention your parents would be here. Real family affair, huh?"

Before he can reply, a woman's voice calls my name.

"Will!"

I turn to see that a blonde woman who must be Saylor Scott has entered the room. And she might be the first person who's looked genuinely thrilled to meet me since I arrived in Germany.

She's smiling widely, her golden hair as bright as the sunny presence she brings along. She holds out a hand, which I shake. "It's *so* nice to meet you."

I grin at her enthusiasm. She has a slight Southern accent that's a welcome change to hear. I wonder how much German she knows. Maybe she can recommend a tutor to me.

"Nice to meet you too. Heard a lot."

"Bad things?" She smirks, and I relax even more. I knew I'd like her.

"Nah. Good buddy of mine went to Lancaster. Kyle Andrews."

Saylor's eyes widen. "No way. You know Kyle?"

"Yeah, he grew up a few streets over from me in Dorchester. Couple of years older, so we were never that tight, but it was a close-knit neighborhood."

"That's crazy. I haven't talked to Kyle since graduation but—"

The doorbell rings.

"I guess I'll get it," Beck says when Saylor doesn't move.

She glances at him and grins, holding her hands out for their baby. Beck smiles back, his expression happy for the first time since I've met the guy. No scowl in sight. Having met Saylor, I have no idea how they ended up together. But I know asking won't win me any brownie points with my captain, so I keep my mouth shut.

The baby starts crying when Beck leaves the room. Saylor

bounces and shushes he or she—I'm guessing she because her pants are pink—until the baby settles.

"Sorry about that," Saylor says. "We should be good for at least fifteen minutes. Where did you go to college? Not Lancaster, right?"

"No. I went to..." My voice trails as I register a familiar female one.

A few seconds later, Sophia appears in the doorway. She smiles when she sees her parents. Stills when she spots me.

Based on her expression, Sophia is as stunned to see me as I'm surprised to see her. Beck invited his *entire* family tonight, I guess. Plus me. And plus...

My surprise curdles into annoyance when I spot the guy standing behind Sophia.

She brought a fucking date.

Last weekend, she was naked on my couch, and this weekend, she's bringing some guy to meet her family.

It stings.

I stare at her, working hard to hide my annoyance, and she stares back. Her face has smoothed, her expression as carefully blank as I'm hoping mine is.

Her mom stands to give Sophia a hug, which jolts her into movement. She kisses her dad's cheek. Hugs Saylor as well.

Then...she's standing right in front of me.

I hold out a hand, greeting her the same way I did the rest of her family. I'm certain she doesn't want them knowing we're acquainted, and that's in my best interest as well. "Will Aster."

This is how we should be meeting for the first time. Not me being an asshole and telling her that she was in my seat. Mentioning my wayward dick.

"Sophia Beck."

A stupid thrill races through me when her smaller palm brushes against mine. When our eyes connect along with our hands.

This *isn't* the first time we're meeting.

I know Sophia Beck. Know her a hell of a lot better than the guy she's here with, I'd bet.

"I'm Noah," the asshole Sophia showed up with says, working his way around the room as well.

Sophia steps away. I shove my hands into my pockets.

Beck and Hans are just as stone-faced as they greet Noah as when I showed up, so I take it less personally.

Actually, I appreciate it.

No way this guy is good enough for Sophia. He's good-looking, I guess, with longish blond hair and a friendly smile that's slowly dimming. He's the shortest guy here, but he's on the tall side compared to the general population. I'm certain he doesn't play football. His frame is too lanky, lacking the definition training requires. And he seems shocked to be here. Starstruck, glancing around the room. Erika attempts to ask him a few questions, and he stumbles through the answers, looking back and forth between Hans and Adler with an awestruck expression. If he knows who I am, he doesn't appear to care, and that irritates me too.

The socializing before dinner is awkward, which bodes poorly for the meal itself. Thank God Saylor is here. Conversation between us flows easily while everyone else feigns interest in the places and people we have in common or holds side conversations.

I should be happy for Sophia. Hoping it works out between her and Noah.

I'm not. I'm pissed. Jealous.

I excuse myself to use the bathroom before dinner, then end up in the kitchen, trying to find my way back to the dining room. This place is huge, the layout similar to a labyrinth.

Sophia is standing at the kitchen island, pouring more wine into her glass. She glances up as I enter, before I can turn around and avoid this conversation.

"What are you doing here, Will?"

"I was invited for dinner. It would have been rude not to accept."

"Right," she drawls. "And we all know just how polite you are. Mr. Manners."

I step closer. "Who's the guy, Sophia?"

"None of your business."

"Does he know you were screaming *my* name last weekend?"

She sets the bottle down so hard that I'm surprised it doesn't break. Her wineglass is so full; it's close to overflowing.

"Did you know I was coming tonight? Is that why you brought a date?"

Sophia rolls her eyes. "Get over yourself, Will. I did."

She did *not* just say that.

I can't remember the last time I was this worked up. This turned on. Electricity crackles between us, buzzing with awareness and power. Fueled by frustration. I'm mad at her, for moving on from what happened between us so easily. I'm furious with myself for being the reason. She's mad—maybe hurt—and she has every right to be.

I step even closer, caging her body between mine and the edge of the counter.

This kitchen is insane. It looks like something you'd see on a fancy cooking show. But I couldn't care less where we are. All

I'm focused on is the woman in front of me and the unfamiliar emotions she incites.

"You're *over me*, huh? Six days ago, you were coming on my tongue. How long did it take you to get off, Sophia? Less than a minute?"

She's breathing heavily, just like I am. Her heartbeat is a wild flutter just beneath her jawline as she tilts her head back to meet my gaze.

"You didn't even want it to happen," she tells me.

Is that really what she thinks? Did she not listen to a damn word I said that night?

"If I didn't want it to happen, it wouldn't have happened," I reply.

"We both know you're not known for your willpower." She snorts. "*Will*power. How ironic."

"Really? You're going to be another person who throws that in my face?"

A spasm of regret replaces her defiant expression. And I kind of hate that it appears. I wish she didn't know the full story of what happened with Cassandra. That I hadn't felt the need to justify my actions to her. That I hadn't cared what she thought of me. Her regret is a symbol of my own weakness, a reminder that I let this thing between us progress a lot farther than it ever should have. I should have stayed far away, starting that second I spotted her standing at the bar.

But she's here right now. Inches from me. She's right. Willpower is nothing I'm known for. And she's the most devastating distraction I've ever encountered.

My right hand moves from the counter to her thigh, sliding up until I hit the hem of her dress. "Are you wet, Sophia?"

She doesn't answer, setting her chin stubbornly.

I slide my hand so I can rub my thumb against the inside of her thigh. Her dress is way too short, one of her imagine-what's-underneath outfits. My fingers are only a few inches from her pussy.

"You don't want to lie, in case I check. But if you tell the truth…that doesn't sound like being *over me*, does it?"

"Did you change your mind?" she snaps.

"No," I admit.

I'm just losing my mind. I can't think straight around her.

"Then, get away from me." When I don't move, she shoves my chest. "I mean it, Will."

Reluctantly, I step back, adding a couple of feet between us. "I didn't mean—"

"I don't want to play games."

She throws my own words right back at me, paired with a defiant jut of her chin.

Sophia might accept casual sex if that's what I offered, but that's not what she really wants.

I was partially right about her. She's not the poised golden girl or the polished princess some people see. But she does want pieces of the fairy tale, especially the prince.

And I'm a lot of things, but I'm no prince.

So, I just nod, not revealing the conflict churning inside of me.

Reminding myself of the sordid headlines with my name in them. Sophia deserves better than *casual*. Better than me. When she's happy with a responsible guy, she'll be glad this ended before it could really begin.

Sophia grabs her wineglass and then walks away. I exhale, rubbing the back of my neck a few times.

The last thing I feel like is sitting through a whole dinner with her family and the guy she might hook up with tonight. But I can't think of a good excuse to leave. And I'm trying to make a good impression on Adler Beck, not offend him by taking off early.

"Well, that was interesting."

I startle, glancing toward the second doorway. Saylor is standing there, studying me with a tilted head.

"Not interesting enough for me to mention it to my husband, if that's what you're worried about. But since you remind me a lot of myself, I will say this: Be careful. Becks are easy to fall for."

She turns and leaves before I can say anything in response, which is good.

I have no clue what I would've said.

CHAPTER TWENTY-ONE

SOPHIA

Dinner is awkward. Involving Noah in this evening was a terrible idea for reasons I hadn't even considered when I impulsively decided to invite him. He's hardly spoken a word since we arrived, even when my mom has tried to engage him in conversation. He's trying to act cool about being around my family, I think, and he seems to have taken it to the extreme of a near-catatonic state.

Despite his silence, I'm uncomfortably aware of Noah sitting beside me. Just like I'm painfully conscious of Will's presence on the opposite side of the table. Having a date here doesn't make me feel any better about seeing him. It makes me feel worse.

Will standing in the living room of Adler and Saylor's penthouse was a shock. For many reasons, not the least of which was that I'd decided I'd never see him again. Not up close anyway. I still have one more football game to photograph before Alex takes it back over.

No one gave me any heads-up that Will would be here. Adler's had teammates over before. But those are usually larger group gatherings, and those are guys he's played with for years, like Otto.

I'm guessing Saylor was the motivating factor. She sacrificed living near her friends and family after she and Adler got engaged. Moved halfway across the world for him and embraced a foreign country. She's carved out her own community here, but I'm sure she must miss home. Will's another person who understands what that culture shock must be like.

They've been chatting animatedly like old friends all night. Not surprising. Not only are they both Americans who adore soccer, but they also have similar outgoing personalities. They seem to know lots of the same people as well, swapping stories and making each other laugh while I down most of a bottle of wine.

I'm seated directly across the table from Will, stuck in the uncomfortable situation of not looking at him while not making it obvious that I'm avoiding looking at him. No one here knows that we've met before tonight, and I'd absolutely like to keep it that way. It's surprisingly hard, treating Will like a stranger. My attention is automatically drawn in that direction. Twice, I have to forcibly shut my mouth instead of responding to something he says.

I help myself to another serving of roasted veggies, then offer the plate to Noah. He shakes his head, so I set the dish back on the table.

"Are you okay?" I mutter under my breath.

I might be regretting bringing him, but at least I was right about him drawing attention off of me. No one has asked me anything all meal. Will hasn't spared one glance at me since we sat down, acting like our conversation in the kitchen never happened.

"Oh, yeah, I'm great," Noah replies. He leans back, to the point of almost toppling himself, then rights the chair with a red face.

I nod and then look back at my plate so he doesn't catch my eye roll.

We're eating dessert when the conversation turns, unfortunately, toward me. Well, half me.

"How did you two meet?" Adler asks, gesturing between me and Noah with his fork.

I'm surprised he's asking. He rarely makes much of an effort to get to know the guys I bring around. One guy I dated shortly before starting university, Karl, was particularly unpopular among my family. Adler jokes it's because he knows I'll kick them to the curb soon enough, but I think he's aware why Noah has stayed silent most of the night. Setting aside the fame and football, Adler inherited our dad's intimidating face. Most guys can't actually keep their cool around him; they just pretend to.

Some guys can though. Will's expression is carefully impassive, his head tilted to the side as he waits for the response, like everyone else.

Noah replies before I can, fumbling nervously, "We-we ran into each other, uh, getting drinks one night. Then, um, went to a friendly match together before Sophia got too busy with–with school."

That answer earns a variety of reactions around the table. Saylor's eyebrows rise when she realizes Noah's the same guy I told her about a few weeks ago. Adler and my parents look surprised, probably that I went to a Kluvberg scrimmage and didn't tell any of them. But Will's reaction is the one I home in on. His expression is stony as he looks down at his plate. But I catch the pulse of a muscle in his jaw before he reaches for his water glass and takes a sip. I take that to mean he's put together that Noah's the guy I was avoiding the day we met.

It shouldn't matter. I shouldn't care. He rejected me, told me we would never work.

"It was fun," I say.

Noah beams, the most animated he's looked all night. Adler shakes his head a little, but says nothing.

"So, Will."

I glance at my dad, startled, as soon as he speaks. He usually stays mostly silent during these dinners, chiming in on the conversation sometimes but rarely instigating it.

Will glances at me before looking at my dad. "Yes, sir?"

My dad's chest puffs up in response to Will's respectful tone even though he'd never admit he cared about it. "Interesting start to the season."

"*Terrible* start to the season."

Adler's mouth presses into a thin line, but he doesn't dispute Will's words. So far, this season has gone about the same as the last couple. Adler would never admit it, but I think football has become secondary to him. He still loves it, but he doesn't have the same intensity toward playing he used to. It's not everything to him, the way it was. The way it still is to Will.

"Leon is an old friend," my dad says.

Everyone who's anyone in the European soccer world is an old friend of my dad's, including Kluvberg's current coach. They played together at one point, I believe.

He's trying to intimidate Will, which I find interesting. Usually, his name is enough to make eyes go wide. Adler is a current attraction. My dad is seen as a living legend, no longer subject to the highs or lows of winning and losing. His legacy is frozen in time, infallible and impressive. Whenever people meet him, they're awed.

Will appears unbothered. He leans back in his chair, but keeps his balance. "Let me guess. You were one of the ten."

My father laughs. *Laughs.* "I was," he tells Will.

I have no idea what that means. I glance at my brother, but he looks equally confused.

"I might be changing my mind."

Will's expression is wry. "What did it? How well I've been practicing sitting on the bench?"

My dad still appears amused as he nods. "Leon rewards effort. He doesn't waste time or money. Or talent."

"Thank you, sir."

"Hans, please."

Adler looks stunned. I'm just as taken aback.

I've never seen my dad act so friendly. Him meeting Will was not an encounter that ever occurred to me. But had I given it any thought, I would have assumed they wouldn't get along. Will is loud and brash and opinionated, essentially the polar opposite of what I associated with my staid, serious father.

Will nods, taking it in stride. He has no idea this isn't how my dad normally acts. "Thank you, Hans."

I expect that to be the end of the bizarre conversation.

But my dad shifts in his chair, his attention still on Will. Studying him with visible interest. "I heard you scored thirty-three goals last season."

The corner of Will's mouth curls up as my dad keeps the surprises coming. I vaguely recall Saylor talking about Will's stats at our last family dinner. I didn't realize my dad was paying attention, much less that he'd memorized the exact number.

"I sure did, si—Hans."

"My final season with Kluvberg, I scored thirty-five. Club record."

Will's smirk grows into a full-blown smile. "I can't believe you retired after that. They would have had to carry me off the field a few years later, chasing thirty-six."

"My ACL was shot. Shredded it, taking all those shots."

"Let's not talk about injuries in a room of pro footballers, please," Saylor says. "Come on, Hans."

My dad smiles. "Just letting Will know what the record is. It's the only one of mine Adler hasn't broken. Did your folks play, Will?"

Without me consciously deciding it should, my mouth opens. "I think I hear Gigi," I blurt out.

Saylor sighs. "Crap. She must want her night bottle."

"We should get going, Hans," my mom says. She's been hiding yawns behind her hand for the past hour.

Around the table, everyone is suddenly standing and moving. Noah excuses himself to use the bathroom. Saylor goes to check on Gigi. Adler and my parents head into the kitchen, carrying some of the dishes.

Will and I are the only two people who stay seated at the table. I can feel his eyes on me, but I avoid his gaze. Interrupting was a reflex. I didn't want Will to have to talk about his family if he didn't want to, knowing it's a sensitive subject. But I didn't need to say something. I probably shouldn't have said something even though I'm relieved it essentially ended this uncomfortable evening. My first instinct was to...protect him, I guess, and I really wish I didn't know that.

I search my brain for something casual and blasé to say as we sit in silence, coming up entirely blank. So I just run my finger up and down the thin stem of my wineglass, pretending like I'm alone. There's nothing left to say and too much I want to. Keeping my lips pressed together seems like the smartest move.

Then, commotion surrounds us again, as my parents and Adler reenter the dining room. Saylor appears a minute later with a smiling Gigi on her hip. I guess she did wake up. The room fills with chatter, erasing the emptiness between us.

He wasn't supposed to fit here, I think petulantly.

He said we wouldn't work.

I stand slowly as the conversation transitions to goodbyes, not wanting to draw attention to my bad mood. Not wanting to answer questions about why I'm in a bad mood.

"Looking forward to seeing you play tomorrow," my mom is saying to Will.

My parents attend most of Adler's matches, but Will still has barely played since the start of the season.

"Thank you," he replies. "Hopefully, it'll be for more than a few minutes."

My mom smiles. "I remember the days of having to prove myself to a new club. Don't get discouraged."

Will nods. "I'm hoping Sophia will have some more goals to photograph."

I startle as soon as he says my name, taken aback by the casual way he mentions me. The nonchalant way he brings up photography when Saylor is normally the only one in my family who raises the topic.

I catch the split-second it takes my mom—and my dad—to realize what Will is referring to. They, like most people who attend football games, are focused on what takes place on the field. My small role is already diminished, and I've done everything I can to stamp it down further.

"She's a good sport, for helping out at the games," my dad says.

He smiles at me, meaning it as a compliment. My family has heard years of complaints from me about football. Of excuses to miss matches and sighs during conversations about the sport. They know photographing the games is a chore to me, not a task I took on voluntarily. But I'm *helping out*, in his mind. It's not a job, or a career. Not important. Not as important as the players on the field, at least.

"Your daughter is a very talented photographer." Everyone's attention, including mine, focuses on Will, but his is on my dad. "Have you seen the shots the team has been posting lately? All taken by her."

How does he know *that?*

One of the team photographers was sick last match, so they outsourced some of the photos they usually share on social media. A few of mine were chosen. But that's nothing I told him.

Worse than what Will is saying is the edge to his tone. The thinly veiled annoyance that sounds like he's offended on my behalf. I told him too much. He has insight into my perspective and my feelings that I haven't shared with anyone else here, not even Saylor.

"I've seen some of them," my mom says, saving my dad.

His silence tells me the answer to Will's question is no.

"But I didn't realize they had been taken by Sophia." She looks at me. "That's wonderful, honey."

"It's not a big deal," I tell her. "Just part of my internship."

My instinct is to downplay. Because I'm not confident in my abilities and because I know photography is not an interest anyone else in my family shares. But I'm realizing that has lasting repercussions. That I can't have it both ways. If I want them to care, I have to be brave enough to tell my parents that matters to me, rather than waiting for them to come around on their own.

Gigi starts crying—for real—and that pushes my parents out the door.

Will says goodbye to Saylor and Adler, then turns to me and holds out a hand. "Nice to meet you, Sophia."

There are layers to the five words, ones I don't have time to unwrap before he stops speaking.

I hold his gaze, my heart thundering in my chest. "You too. I love meeting fans of photography."

He smirks a little, still holding my hand. We stare at each other, same as we did when he first arrived.

I can't relax. The rasp of his skin against mine, the rush of having his whole attention—they're a shock to my system.

I don't think there's anything left to say between us. Or I *didn't* think there was. It feels like there might be now, the air thickening around us the same way it did every time we were alone in his apartment.

"Good night," is what he says before dropping my hand, but it sounds a little like, "Goodbye."

Tomorrow is my last match. After that, assuming another dinner doesn't get sprung on me—I'll be asking for the entire guest list in the future—Will and I won't see each other ever again.

Will heads for the door while I remain in the entryway, waiting for Noah.

I watch him leave and decide...

Will Aster is dangerous.

And it's not his cocky smirk or the tattoos that tell me I'm in trouble.

It's how I'm suddenly sure he's not only the guy you can't easily forget.

I'm certain he's the guy you never get over.

CHAPTER TWENTY-TWO

SOPHIA

I sit back on my heels, squinting at the screen as I flip through a few of the photos from the first half of the game. The second half is about to start, so my finger moves quickly as I assess the photos in a few seconds. I managed to get an excellent picture of Otto catching a shot. And a few of Adler that I should send to my family.

But my favorite is the one of Leon Wagner, the blur of several seated players behind him as he paces along the sideline.

I'm getting better at this, I think. More confident in my instincts and less concerned I'll do something wrong. It's easier to seek out certain moments and predict where the best opportunities will arise.

"That one is excellent," Alex says, glancing over my shoulder at the laptop screen.

He's continued coming to every home match with me, both as a thoughtful gesture and because Alex is the sort of pure fan who would hate to miss a game. I can't imagine a more perfect job for him than this, and I'm not surprised his injuries never kept him from coming, even if they did make it difficult for him to photograph.

"Thanks," I reply, continuing to study it.

The few times I've met Leon Wagner, he's been brisk and focused. Unsurprising for a German football coach. He's led Kluvberg's team for over a decade, an impressive tenure by any measure, and his animated expression says he loves his job just as much as Alex does. You can see the emotion—the love—in the photograph.

It might even be EPA-worthy. Might be. It's an option at least.

"Are you *sure* you don't want to stay on?" Alex jokes, still looking at the photo too.

At least, I think he's joking. Alex is supposed to get his wrist brace off tomorrow. I'll be reassigned elsewhere starting next week.

"I'm looking forward to trying something different," I say.

Which is true.

I should be relieved photographing games has come to an end. And I am. There are many other ways I'd prefer to spend my Saturday than at Sieg Stadium.

But...there are a few parts of this I'll miss. And not just the glimpses of Will.

I was annoyed when I first got this assignment, that football had managed to infiltrate my interest the same way it seemed to overtake everything else. But ever since Will mentioned my photos to my parents last night, I realized that was a pessimistic way of looking at it. That photographing football is a way for me to appreciate the sport on my own terms, in my own way. An overlap with the interests of the rest of my family.

Noise from the crowd alerts me to the fact that players are returning to the field. I close my laptop and stash it safely away before fiddling with the settings on my camera. Debate about switching to a wide-angle lens and decide to keep the 400mm on. Focusing on why I'm here is better than scanning the sideline, looking for Will. At least this is the last time I'll have to resist that temptation.

Ten minutes into the second half, Will gets subbed in. A little earlier than normal, which is bad news for me and good news for Will.

Wagner rewards effort, according to my father. And as I watch Will perform, it's hard to think anyone else on the pitch is working as hard as him.

He dominates the field. Sprints and kicks like losing is for other players. There's not the slightest bit of hesitation as he charges up the field. Then runs back down.

It's an endless back-and-forth as both teams fight for possession.

Müller, a forward, passes to Will just outside the penalty arc. I bite the inside of my cheek hard enough to taste blood, only remembering to press the shutter button when I hear the rapid clicks around me capturing the play.

I'm not religious. My family spent Sundays at football fields until I was old enough to do my own thing with friends or boys. But I pray, just like some of the fans in the stands probably are. Just this once, I pray a game will go a certain way even though there will always be another one.

Will shoots...and scores.

I hope the big camera blocks the wide smile on my face. Most of the other photographers here are locals as well. There's no question who most of us are rooting for. But we're not the club photographers. They're on the opposite side of the field, wearing Kluvberg's colors and logo. They're the ones who photograph the players arriving and take the locker room photos. Whose allegiance is clear. We're supposed to be less obviously biased. Or at least not draw attention if we are.

It starts to rain about ten minutes after Will's goal.

Twenty minutes remain in the match. Around me, other photographers pull out rain covers to protect expensive equipment.

Reluctantly, I do the same. It's harder to photograph with it on, and the equipment is built to be durable and withstand some elements. But it's better to be safe than sorry. I'm using my own equipment, not the paper's, and if something stops working, then I'll run into issues in my classes and with snapping last-minute options for the EPAs.

And this is my last chance to take photos of Will. I don't want my camera to stop working now either.

Since I'll be the one who goes through the card first, I don't bother to intersperse the snaps I take of him with other players.

I take hundreds of shots of him standing during pauses in play. Running. Waving his arms. In his element in every way.

One glance at him, and it's obvious how much he loves being on the field. Just like Wagner's feelings were on display.

I still don't *like* watching football. But I do love watching Will play.

I'll probably never admit that to him. I acknowledge it to myself, though.

One of the FC Bayern Söhn players gains possession of the ball and then sprints this way. He passes to another green jersey, who takes a shot that's deflected by a fullback—Braun, I think. And then the black-and-white ball is flying this way, closer and closer.

That's my only thought.

It's coming closer and closer.

I hardly have time to lower my camera before pain radiates the side of my skull. It *hurts*, and it's amplified by the shock.

No part of me expected to show up at the field today and get hit in the head by a football. I'm stunned—both physically and mentally—Alex's words from my first game replaying in my head like a taunt.

"Never turn your back to the pitch. I've seen pros get taken out by wayward kicks."

I didn't turn my back. I was looking at the field, and I was still too slow to react. Embarrassing *and* unfortunate.

I hear Alex's voice again now, nearby, high and worried. "Sophia! Sophia!"

All I can manage is a groan in response, lifting a hand to gingerly touch my head.

The pain is already dulling to a throb, but my brain is still struggling to catch up with what just happened. My camera is clutched to my side, one arm curled around it protectively.

There's commotion and activity around me, reminding me this is taking place in a stadium packed with thousands. Unfamiliar voices are talking, low and concerned. My parents are here, someplace, possibly seeing this spectacle.

And then there's another voice, one my body instantly reacts to despite my stunned state. A pissed-off one with an American accent, roughly demanding, "Let me the fuck through."

I force myself to sit up as soon as I hear Will, working to hide the wince as my head throbs from the movement. "I'm fine."

"Don't move," Alex tells me. He's crouched down next to me. "You might have a concussion. The team doctor is coming over."

"Okay," I say, deciding not making a scene is my best bet of getting through this quickly.

Hopefully, play will resume soon, and everyone's attention will shift off of me. I'm pretty sure I'm fine. My head hurts, but I can think clearly. My butt's getting wet from sitting on the damp grass, and the fact that I'm able to focus on that tells me that I'm probably okay.

Then, there's someone on my other side, and it's not the team doctor.

Will's expression is harsh, his dark eyebrows knit tightly together over his green eyes. They match the grass stain on his shorts. And they dart around, scanning my face urgently. "Are you okay?" he asks.

I nod quickly and immediately regret the movement. But I hide the grimace because he already looks worried enough. I'm not even sure how he got over here. There's a low barricade that surrounds the field, which we all stand behind.

"I'm fine. I just...wasn't expecting it. Got the wind knocked out of me."

A Bayern Söhn player approaches the small huddle around me, calling out, "*Ich fühl mich furchtbar. Es tut mir so Leid.*"

He's the guy who took the shot, I'm assuming.

I reply, accepting his apology, and manage a smile too, because he looks so dismayed. It wasn't his fault. Or Braun's, who's also standing nearby, wearing a concerned expression. Just an unfortunate angle.

Will doesn't move from my side, even after the other players walk away. And, God, does it burn at my insides the same way seeing him interact with my family last night did.

Because he had picked football. He told me nothing could ever happen between us because of football. But he's *here*, in the middle of a football game. I didn't get hit in the middle of an empty parking lot. There are other people all around, plenty of them helping me. But he's still here instead of taking a water break or talking to a trainer, like the rest of the players are probably doing during the delay of the game.

I can't handle him looking at me like this. Like he *cares*.

He ran over here.

He cares—at least a little.

And I wish he didn't. It would make this all a lot easier if he didn't.

"Go back to the game, Will," I tell him.

Alex clears his throat and then looks away, something in my tone saying this is a private moment.

"Sophia..."

"I'm fine. There's no reason for you to be over here. *Go back to the game*, Will." I don't leave any room for argument in my voice.

His jaw works as he stares at me for what feels like forever. Then he finally nods and stands, backing away. I close my eyes. Exhale.

The team doctor arrives a few seconds later, taking Will's empty spot and crouching down beside me. There are whistles on the field, but I can't see what's happening. A bunch of the other photographers have formed a loose standing circle around me. Blocking me from the view of the spectators and limiting my sight of the field. Protecting me.

I answer all the doctor's questions, and he determines me fit to stand up at least. I follow him off the field, Alex right behind me, carrying my camera.

Fighting an urge to look back at the field each step I take.

CHAPTER TWENTY-THREE

WILL

The mood in the locker room is euphoric. We beat Bayern Söhn three to one. And one of those goals was mine, which means *I* should be euphoric.

One more mark for me instead of against me. Another goal to add to what's been a disappointing tally this season.

Instead of thrilled, I'm anxious. I'm replaying the horrific second I realized the ball was headed straight for Sophia. The terrifying moment I realized it was going to *hit* Sophia. I don't know if the thud of contact was as loud in reality as it was when it echoed in my head, and it doesn't really matter. The sound will haunt me either way.

I'm tugging a clean T-shirt over my head when I hear, "Stay the hell away from her, Aster."

I exhale before turning to face Beck, having a good idea what this is about.

Guys have always groaned about how girls they know act differently around me. About the hair tosses and the fluttering eyelashes and the coy smiles.

This isn't the first time a guy—or teammate—has said that sentence to me because of jealousy or protectiveness.

But it *is* the first time I haven't replied, *Tell* her *that.*

Because as conceited as it sounds, that's always been the case. Their sisters or girlfriends or cousins or friends chased me, and I guess that partially applies to Sophia.

The difference is, I would care if she avoided me. I care that she's *been* avoiding me, which has never been the case before. And I would rather Beck punch me than tell Sophia I said she should leave me alone.

My shoulders square. "I don't know what you're talking about."

Beck's blond eyebrows knit together as he assesses me. Testing my sincerity, maybe. "No one else ran over there."

"Assholes," I toss back, lumping him in with the group.

Where was his protectiveness when Sophia was lying on the ground? Yeah, there were plenty of other people around, helping her. Wasn't good enough for me. It shouldn't have been good enough for her brother.

He studies me, a flash of surprise working its way across his face. I'm not sure when he'll stop underestimating me, but I hope it'll be sometime soon. The rest of this club reveres him. He's losing more of my respect each second this conversation goes on.

I should have anticipated me running over to Sophia earlier would attract attention. Just like I probably paid her too much attention at dinner last night. But neither is a crime, and I'm sick of always being judged first.

"I mean it, Aster," he tells me. "Stay away."

Even before this conversation took place, I could have easily guessed Beck would take offense to any guy when his little sister is involved.

A part of me admires it. I'd go to war for Tripp. And I want Sophia to have family members who look out for her. But I haven't fucking done anything—this time. I'm not the villain.

"Is Sophia okay?" I ask.

She said she was. She walked off the field fine. But Sophia is also the sort of stubborn that would do those things even if she was seriously injured.

Beck's blue eyes narrow, like he has some idea of why I care so much.

I understand why he's warning me away. Respect it even. If I had a sister, I wouldn't want her anywhere near a guy like me. All of my mistakes and my antics are part of the public record. They're splashed across magazines and newspapers, published online and discussed on social media. There's no disputing my reputation, and most of me agrees with Beck that it should stay far away from Sophia.

I still need to know she's all right.

"She's fine. She's also a kid. I mean it. Stay away, Aster, unless you want to be on a plane back to the States."

My jaw tightens to the point it might pop. I know what he's doing. He might as well be holding up a photo of Sophia and writing *off-limits* on it with a Sharpie. A younger version of me might have seen it as a challenge. Might have gone after her just to prove I could.

"I already said I would stay away from your *adult* sister, who I *talked* to during a dinner that *you* had invited me to. We're done here, *Captain*."

Beck stares at me for a minute longer, visibly annoyed by my mocking use of his title.

It's a reminder, more than anything. His appointed role on the team gives him the right to critique my decisions on the field. Not off of it. At least not out loud in the locker room for all the guys to hear. He's crossing a line, and he knows it.

"She's fine," he finally says. "Team doctor cleared her. I'm going over to her place to check on her."

Guess he's still miffed about my *assholes* comment, if he's bothering to tell me that.

"Good," I say.

Beck still looks irritated when he walks away. There's an excellent chance I might have just destroyed any goodwill he had toward me. Any chance of Beck going to bat for me about starting. Any cohesion on the pitch about fitting in better with the team. Right now, I don't care.

It seems like my sprinting across the field to check on Sophia is something he should be *thanking* me for.

I didn't do it for him, though. I saw her get hit, and I ran without thinking about it or deciding to. It was a reflex, the same way I always react on the field.

I don't regret it either. I wouldn't have been able to play the rest of the game, wondering how badly she was injured.

Otto approaches his locker next to mine a few minutes later. He claps my shoulder as I sit down on the bench and unlace my cleats.

"Good goal today, Aster."

I nod. "Thanks."

Maybe it'll be enough for the guys to stop looking at me as some marriage-destroying wild card. To finally thaw some of the frostiness from guys other than Otto, Fritz, and Olivier. Beck talks to me too, I guess, but I'm usually wishing he wasn't.

"Don't follow it up with any wrong plays," Otto cautions.

I glance over at him.

There's a knowing glint in Otto's eyes that makes me think he saw Beck over here and knows what we were discussing. That he had seen me run over to the sidelines earlier. And...he had been there at the club Fritz took me to. Had seen me approach Sophia.

And he definitely knows about the mess that landed me here. Everyone does, even if they don't explicitly mention it to me.

I'm pretty sure he's not talking about soccer at all.

I've always had the right moves on the field.

Off it is where I make the wrong plays.

All I do is nod at Otto again before turning back to gather up the rest of my stuff.

CHAPTER TWENTY-FOUR

SOPHIA

"Yes!" Mia cheers as I down another shot. I've lost count of which number it is, a sign I should stop.

But I'm celebrating. Today was the first Saturday in a while when I didn't have to hear a single word about football. I don't even know if the team won or lost today.

And I'm...happy about that. I think.

"Girl, what has gotten into you tonight?" Clara asks, giggling as I raise my empty glass in a silent cheers motion.

I've been going out to clubs since before I was legally allowed to.

For years, it's been part of my identity, how I spend my weekends. I'm not the athletic Beck. I'm the fun Beck. It was a constant as I was flipping through options of what else I wanted to be known for. Overcompensating maybe for my inability to maintain interest in one guy or one hobby.

I shrug, wiping my mouth with the back of one hand and possibly smudging my lipstick. "Just in a good mood."

I'm in a terrible mood. My classes have felt particularly

boring ever since I started my internship, theory and assessing others' techniques less interesting than taking photos myself. I still haven't decided which photo to submit to the EPAs, the pressure to pick one mounting more every single day. I've been avoiding texts from Noah, who messaged me multiple times this week. And I haven't been able to forget Will *hasn't* reached out to me once.

He raced to my side when I got hit and hasn't spoken to me since. I assured him I was fine, and I'm not his responsibility. My parents drove me home from the game after I was cleared by a team doctor, both exhibiting more concern than I'm used to seeing from either of them. I've sat beside them when Adler got tackled on the field, neither of them so much as flinching. But they both acted like a football to the head could have been fatal. Then Adler showed up at my apartment after the game with some of my favorite ice cream, which was sweet.

But Will hasn't even texted. Maybe I was too harsh when he came over. I was in shock and embarrassed and trying to avoid drawing more attention than I already had. Trying to pretend like he hadn't come over because then I wouldn't have to deal with how it made me feel.

He still could have messaged me. And that he hasn't makes me think he's moved on, the same way I told him I had. I showed up to dinner at Adler and Saylor's with another guy. I hadn't known Will was going to be there, but I didn't tell him that. And even not knowing, I still shouldn't have done it. Noah was happy just to be in the same room as my dad and brother, so I don't feel that guilty about bringing him. But it was an awkward conversation on the drive home, reverting to my *I'm super busy* excuse. One that didn't dissuade him, based on the messages I've been getting.

The two guys who approached our table earlier come back over with a fresh round of drinks. I reach for one, even knowing that I shouldn't. I'm getting too old for these kinds of wild nights, closer than ever to being an actual adult. Even though I can't decide which photo to submit to the EPAs. Even though I'm still flitting from guy to guy, unable to make interest last. I don't even remember the names of the men who came over shortly after we arrived.

"Hey, Sophia."

I look over my shoulder, Marie's features taking a few seconds to register. Yeah, I should definitely stop drinking.

"Marie!" I stand, giving her a big hug before introducing her around the group.

She's met a couple of them before, on past nights out. I've barely seen Marie the past few weeks, my Kluvberg assignment meaning I've hardly been in the office or used my assigned cubicle as of late. So, I texted her, letting her know where we were going this evening in case she was free.

Right after I finish introducing Marie around, Emilia lets out a loud, dramatic gasp before announcing, "Kluvberg players are here."

My grip tightens on my glass, but I refuse to glance over and engage. Tonight, I just want to be a girl in a bar. Not a famous footballer's sister or daughter. Just Sophia

I focus on the guy seated across from me, who rolls his eyes. When he realizes I noticed, he winks this way. I take another sip from my glass, reassessing him with fresh interest. He was probably just annoyed Emilia hadn't greeted him and his friend with the same level of excitement because he looks like the sporty type who might play football, but he seems to have more personality than most guys I meet. He smiles when I maintain eye contact. Hopefully, not looking over will prevent any Kluvberg players from coming over here like they did last time I was out with friends and ran into guys on the team.

"Who's *that*?" Emilia asks, her tone a mixture of shock and admiration.

I take another sip, still refusing to look over.

Marie is the one who replies, "That's Will Aster."

I choke a little, the sip I just swallowed solidifying into a lump of ice in my stomach. It didn't even occur to me *Will* would be one of the Kluvberg players here.

"*That's* Will Aster?" Mia asks. "The American with the sex scandal?"

Clara giggles. "But did you read the article? The woman did not stop talking about how good he was in bed."

I know exactly what article she's talking about. I tortured myself by reading all the coverage of Will's past that I'd been avoiding this week. In some attempt to move on, I guess. To understand his perspective, or maybe just to convince myself he's a lost cause who deserved to face consequences.

Coming here was supposed to be an escape from thinking about it all, and instead, it's the opposite.

I lose the fight against temptation, scanning the club until I locate Will. He's with a large group of other players, two of them grinning at him as they walk toward a corner booth in the VIP section. As expected, they're receiving a lot of attention. But none of the guys pause, all united as they head for the same spot. Until Will stops, looking over at a woman who has her hands cupped around her mouth to call out to him. I can't hear from here, but I can guess what she's saying. Will appears amused and unfazed, in his element here as much as he is on the field.

Quickly, I look away, right as the music changes. I feel warm and annoyed, buzzed on bitterness and vodka.

I can't escape him, it feels like. He's in my head. In my city. Maybe in my heart, which is beating twice as fast as it should be since he showed up.

"I love this song!" I shout, forcibly shoving any inhibitions away with any thoughts of Will. I'm here to have fun.

Everyone in the immediate vicinity looks over as I stand and climb onto the low, round table our booth is curved around, using it as a personal stage to shimmy on. This is attention I don't mind.

"Sophia!" Andrea screeches, reaching for her drink before I knock it to the floor.

The rest of the group does the same, clearing the smooth surface for me, their expressions delighted surprise.

Marie appears the most taken aback. When she and I have gone out together, the evening has been sipping on a drink and heading home early. But this behavior is more of what I'm known for. I don't hate the spotlight. I just resent when it's beaming because of football. Acting like this has always been the most reliable way to ensure that people aren't associating me with anything else. And right now, I'm also trying to forget.

I don't look away from the group gathered around me at how anyone else might be reacting. If they're even looking over here.

Ida climbs up on the table with me as the pop ballad continues to blare. Someone wolf-whistles nearby.

And me?

I continue to dance, focusing on nothing except the pulse of the music and the buzz beneath my skin.

CHAPTER TWENTY-FIVE

WILL

"**W**ill!"
"That's Will Aster!"
"*Hallo*, Will!"

It's safe to say I'm recognizable in Kluvberg now.

Olivier grins beside me as we walk through the crowd toward the VIP section, passing by lots of faces turned this way. Many of whom are pointing and shouting. Not at the group I'm with. At *me*.

A woman calls something out that has Otto snort-laughing before shoving a fist in his mouth.

I've really gotta learn German, I guess.

A waitress leads us over to a corner booth, immediately returning with an assortment of drinks. There's a smaller bar tucked back here, just for the VIP section.

This place was Fritz's suggestion, just like this outing. I played well today—*really* well. Wagner is still stubbornly not letting me start, wasting a sub to put me in for a part of the game. Today, I made that decision look foolish. I scored a hat trick—three goals—in the forty minutes I was on the field.

Finally, it feels like I'm showing off what I can do. This part feels good too—the celebrating with my teammates afterward.

The club is packed, just like the last place Fritz took me. Lots of women, many of whom haven't stopped looking over here since we arrived.

My eyes skim the crowd restlessly; I don't realize what I'm looking for until I find it. Not considering she might be here until I see her.

She's dancing on a table.

I'm positive it's Sophia, even though I can't see her face and don't recognize anyone she's with. A whole bunch of girls and two guys who are both laser-focused on her dress's short hem. The length designed to make guys imagine what's underneath, according to her.

I don't need to *imagine* it. I've seen it.

But I'm positive fantasies are exactly what's going through those guys' heads. Not just theirs. Lots of attention is aimed Sophia's way, that entire side of the club.

She's magnetic. Captivating. Blonde hair flying around as she spins in a circle, laughing and smiling at what the girl dancing with her is saying. Her heels make her long legs look endless.

She seems oblivious to the fact that the team is here. Part of the team, at least. There's only ten of us, some of the guys opting to head home or who had other plans to celebrate this afternoon's win. Including Beck, who left with his family. Saylor was waiting outside the locker room and congratulated me on my goals, saying we should get together again soon. I want to. I like Saylor. But it feels weird, knowing she'll tell Sophia. I'm trying to extract myself from her life, and she's making it damn difficult.

I'm not the only player who's noticed Sophia. Otto is looking that way, exchanging words with Olivier that have the Frenchman shaking his head. She wasn't on a table the last time I saw her out in this setting, but neither of the guys looks surprised by what's happening now.

What the hell is she doing?

Last weekend, she got nailed in the head by a soccer ball. She shouldn't be drinking, let alone dancing on a table.

Despite Beck's assurances she was fine, she wasn't at the match earlier. I've been debating texting her ever since it ended several hours ago, worried something was wrong or Beck was mistaken. But he seemed unbothered at the game earlier, which I took as a good sign. And I couldn't think of a single way to ask him about Sophia that wouldn't arouse suspicion. Wouldn't arouse *more* suspicion, that is. His warning after last week's game is still fresh in my mind.

The entire club—including its captain—is thrilled with me at the moment. And that's all I should be focused on, the wide smiles around me as the guys joke and drink. It feels like I'm a part of this team. Only time will tell if that's a permanent transition or if it's tied to how well I perform on the pitch.

It feels like a hollow victory, though. Because the blonde shimmying on a table to Shakira wasn't there to witness it.

I've never had anyone show up to see me play. *Me* play, not the soccer star. And I know Sophia was only there because of her internship. But I let myself pretend there were other reasons. She's been at every home game I've played here—until today.

And no matter how many times I tell myself I don't care, I can't make myself believe the lie. I *do* care.

The song's lyrics are fitting. Except I'm the one going mad.

She dances up there for another two songs while I try to focus on talking to my teammates. But as soon as she climbs down and then heads for the back hallway, I'm up and on my feet, glad I snagged the seat at the end of the booth.

I have no clear plan. I just follow her, passing two women talking in the hallway as blonde hair swishes ahead. She heads into one of the restrooms. I lengthen my strides, placing a palm on the door right as she goes to close it.

Sophia doesn't look surprised to see me when I step in and close the door, which I find interesting. I wonder when she realized I was here.

She crosses her arms, hitting me with a harsh series of German.

I have no clue what she just said, which she knows. So, I nod, offering a tentative, "*Ja,*" in response. I'm not here to argue with her, so agreement seems like the best avenue.

Sophia rolls her eyes. "This is the ladies' room."

"Where were you today?" I demand.

Twin lines form between her eyebrows. "What are you talking about?"

"At the game earlier. Where were you?"

The confusion clears from Sophia's expression. "Last week was my final game. I was just helping out the reporter who normally covers Kluvberg. He had gotten in an accident that made it harder for him to handle things. But he's fine now, so I switched back to photographing for different departments."

"Oh." I wasn't expecting the explanation to be so...simple.

Now that she's reminding me, I vaguely remember Sophia mentioning her assignment to Kluvberg was a temporary one. At the time, I didn't realize it would become the only time I got to be near her. I thought we'd continue to be friends who ate pizza together and talked.

"How did the match go?" she asks.

I'm not surprised she doesn't know. Today must have been a relief for her, a chance to finally escape football again.

"We won."

"That's great. How did the match go...for you?"

I hate that there's a difference in her head. That she's asking about my individual performance, knowing that's a separate metric of success for me. And I love it too. Especially knowing she has little investment in the sport. That she's only asking because she knows it matters to me.

"Three goals."

"That's amazing, Will. Congrats."

"Thanks." We stare at each other for a few seconds, me battling the urge to look down the entire time. The fucking dress she's wearing. "Nice dancing."

Her shoulders tense. "Just having some fun."

"You should be careful. Your head—"

Sophia laughs, but it's not a pretty sound. It's ugly and bitter, lacking any real amusement. "Oh, *now* you're worried about my head."

"What do you mean, *now*? I've *been* worried ever since it happened. If you forgot I came right over to check on you, then you're definitely not fine."

"I *am* fine. No need for you to be concerned."

If only it was that simple to turn feelings off. I have them for her, and I can't figure out how to get rid of them.

"Sophia..."

"What?" she asks. Her annoyance is faltering. I catch the

nervous fiddle of her fingers before she lifts a hand to tuck some strands of hair behind one ear.

I missed this. Even more than I realized, now that I'm experiencing it again. Talking to her. Looking at her. Simply being near her is a relief, healing an injury I didn't realize the extent of.

I step closer, drawn into her orbit. She smells like alcohol and a variety of perfumes. But beneath it all...Sophia.

"I'm sorry...sorry about what happened in Beck's kitchen." I'm sorry about a lot more than that, but this is the easiest apology. "I shouldn't have—I shouldn't have said anything."

She snorts. "You're sorry. Great. Okay then. Can you go now?"

I take another step closer. Sophia backs against the counter surrounding the sink, her stare defiant and her chin lifted as she holds my gaze. In her heels, she comes up to my shoulder.

"I'm trying—it's not—I just..." *Fuck.* I don't know what I'm doing. What I'm saying. All I know is I want to be here—with her—more than I want to be anywhere else.

She tilts her head to the side, her blue eyes searing into me like cyan fire. "Is this what it was like? With her?"

My breath stalls in my chest, lungs squeezing tight. There's only one *her* Sophia could be referring to. I never told her the pictures with Cassandra were of us leaving a restroom. Either she looked up the photos or someone told her. I never wanted her to know details. Never wanted that night to affect my relationship with her even more than it already had. I'm fighting this because I'm wrong for her. And I'm fighting this because it could be very bad for me. The only similarity between Sophia and Cassandra is that they're both connected to men with power over my career. I didn't choose to get involved with

Cassandra, knowing that. I didn't want her the way I'm desperate for Sophia.

"It was *nothing* like this," I tell her. "I didn't even know her real name."

"But you had sex with her. And you won't have sex with me."

I exhale. Those plain terms don't tell the whole story.

"She meant nothing to me. You...you mean something to me."

She scoffs. "That doesn't make any sense. I mean something to you, so you won't sleep with me?"

I exhale roughly, dragging a hand through my hair. "It's complicated. You deserve better than—"

"Shut up." She pokes my chest—hard. "I have an overbearing dad and an overprotective brother. I do *not* need another guy telling me what I deserve. That's my decision. You don't get to make that choice for me."

"You're right," I tell her.

My prison sentence has been lifted, essentially. I talked to an ecstatic Shawn earlier. Me playing well means Kluvberg has no incentive to cut ties with me. I earned some slack. I could get wasted tonight. Take home a random woman. How I've celebrated victories for years.

All I can focus on is Sophia.

I have no desire to talk to another woman, much less touch her. And celebrating with guys who have mostly ignored me before tonight doesn't sound that great either.

"Great. I have more tables to dance on." Sophia reaches down. There's barely enough room between our bodies for her to bend over. I don't realize what she's doing until I glance down and see the lacy fabric balled in her fist. She steps forward, shoves her underwear into my back pocket, then smirks. "A gift for all your goals."

She pats my chest, then slides to the left. I move with her. "Don't you fucking dare."

No *fucking* way is she going back out there to dance on tables, wearing nothing under her dress.

She's tipsy, pink cheeks and messy hair. She's also temptation and trouble and torment. I just got a taste of what playing well on FC Kluvberg is like. The roar of a seventy-thousand strong crowd cheering me on. The rare grin from Wagner, slapping my back as I stepped off the field. Teammates excited to party with me tonight, rather than acting like my presence in the locker room was an inconvenience.

None of that compares to standing in a restroom with her.

Sophia smirks. "What are you going to do about it? You just agreed I should make my own decisions—"

I slam our bodies together, our mouths colliding just as resoundingly.

Sophia kisses me back, her moan vibrating against my lips and encouraging the reckless energy shredding my self-control.

I shove a thigh between her legs, groaning when she rubs against me. Growling when I remember her panties are in my pocket and she's bare beneath this dress. My hands move to the short hem, playing with the edge of the fabric.

Her breathing is heavy now, her hips rocking against my thigh. Her hair is loose, falling in golden waves over her shoulders. My dick is throbbing against the zipper of my jeans, pounding to the point of pain. My balls are drawn up tight, eager to fill her.

It's been two weeks since we fooled around on my couch. Two months since I had sex.

There's no way I'm fucking her for the first time—for her first time—in a bar restroom.

But I can still make her come. Remind her how good it is between us, how electric and consuming.

I hoist her up onto the edge of the counter, admiring the sight of her swollen lips and hooded eyes as she stares at me. Her beauty, paired with evidence of how I affected her, makes me feel a little feral. My fingers trail up and down her arm, and she shivers, the texture of raised flesh obvious under the bathroom's bright lights.

She arches her back, thrusting her tits forward. I tug the thin strap of her dress off her shoulder slowly, groaning when it slips low enough for me to realize she's not wearing a bra either. I suck in a harsh breath before leaning down and biting the point of her nipple gently. She cries out, shifting so her body is even more exposed. Bent back like an offering.

"What do you want, Sophia?" I ask, exploring more of her skin with my teeth and tongue. I couldn't give a shit if I leave marks. There's this burning need to claim her, to know that this insanity I'm experiencing isn't one-sided.

Her breathing is heavy as she slips her fingers into my hair, raking her nails across my scalp. "I want you."

Not my fingers or my tongue or my cock. *Me.* This isn't casual sex to her, chasing physical pleasure, and that should scare me. It shouldn't make me want to fuck her even more.

I swear when my hand reaches the top of her thigh. She spreads her thighs, allowing me a glimpse of the shiny pink flesh. She's fucking soaked. I work one finger into her tight heat, then add a second. Her lids flutter, half covering her eyes as she moans with pleasure. It's an incredible high, watching her flushed, wet pussy stretch around my fingers. Slick and tight. I lean in and kiss her, simply because I want to, the swipe of her tongue against mine turning my blood into lava.

Someone knocks on the door, and I realize I've quickly lost track of how long we've been in here. Somewhere between seconds and hours. I kneel down, moving my hands to her hips so I can pull her center right against my mouth. She cries out—loudly—as soon as she feels my tongue trace her slit.

No one knocks again.

I want to savor this—her—but I'm no longer assuming this will be the only time I touch her like this. I'm focused on her pleasure, on making certain Sophia enjoys this. She's as bold as she was dancing on the table, rocking her hips against my face as I fuck her with my tongue. Her hand returns to my hair, tugging on the strands as she lifts her cunt closer to my mouth.

She comes quickly, slumping back against the mirror while her pussy is still pulsing. I straighten and kiss her—hard—letting her taste herself on my lips. Then pull her underwear out of my pocket and slip them back up into place.

Her blue eyes drill into me as I dress her, assessing and still aroused. I'm so hard that I can hardly think straight. I need to get the hell out of here.

"Keep those on, Sophia. I don't share."

Then, I turn and leave the restroom.

CHAPTER TWENTY-SIX

SOPHIA

There's a knock on my door as I'm pouring hot water into a mug for some tea. I peek through the peephole and exhale, trying to release some of the excitement that's appeared.

Will glances me over as soon as I open the door, his gaze as intense as I've ever seen it. Memories of last night trickle in, barely dulled by the hangover I woke up with. After he left me in the restroom, I spent the rest of the evening drunk on him, more than any other substance.

"Hey."

"Hey." He's wearing jeans and a white T-shirt, his dark hair still damp. He must have come straight from working out at the practice facility.

He looks very American, and I'm definitely fantasizing about pledging my allegiance. He still hasn't let me touch him. I was too dazed last night to even offer before he left the restroom.

Will's expression is unreadable as he shoulders his way into my apartment without waiting for an invitation.

I slam the door shut behind him. "Sure, come right on in."

I don't hate that he didn't wait for permission, though. I like his decisiveness. And it's not like I've never entered his place uninvited.

He glances around the kitchen and living room, then the open door leading into my bedroom. He's never seen the inside of my place before. Just walked me home once.

"What's wrong with your cabinet?"

"What?"

"Your cabinet." He walks over to the sink, focused on the cabinet door that's never fully closed.

"Oh. I don't know. It's been like that since I moved in."

"Do you have a screwdriver?"

"Uh...I don't think so," I say.

Will nods, opening one of the drawers and rummaging through it until he comes up with a small knife I've used with cheeses. He does something with it inside the cabinet, and then a minute later the door is shutting securely for the first time. "Hinge just needed to be tightened," he tells me, setting the knife on the counter.

"Oh. Okay. Thanks."

One corner of his mouth curves up. He's not paying attention to my apartment any longer, that green stare totally focused on me.

"How was your day?"

"Uh, okay. I did laundry."

I'm nervous, and it's a foreign, flustering feeling. I held my own last night—for a while there anyway, until his tongue got involved—but today feels different. Afternoon sunlight streams in through my apartment's windows, casting a golden glow over Will's expression. He's studying me the way I look at photographs, deliberation and admiration and a little disbelief.

Will nods, barely a bob of his head, then asks, "Do you like Indian food?"

"Indian food?" Not at all what I was expecting him to say. I know what I'm hoping him showing up here means, but I'm not sure if I'm right. Maybe he's just here to apologize again.

"Yep. Fritz recommended this place in Prinzregentenplatz."

His pronunciation is improving. Barely, but it's not any worse.

"Okay..."

He's looking for restaurant recommendations? Maybe I've been demoted back to tour guide.

Will exhales. Shakes his head once. "Remember when I told you I'd never given a woman my number before?"

"Yeah."

"Well, I've never done this part before either." He smiles. "I'm trying to ask you out to dinner, Sophia. On a date."

I stare at him, stunned. The excitement in my chest expands, registering the meaning before my brain can. "You're asking me out on a date?"

"Yes."

"Why?"

His grin grows, finding my reaction entertaining. "Because I want to."

"What about—"

"It doesn't matter."

My exhale is exasperated. Football—his career—doesn't matter? "Will—"

"I mean it. It doesn't matter. You matter, Sophia." Softly, he repeats, "You matter. You matter to me. And I'm so sorry if I ever made you feel like you didn't. I was trying to avoid old mistakes, and I ended up making new ones. But if you're willing to give me a second chance, I'd like to take you out to dinner tonight."

"You were right. If Adler finds out, he...won't be happy. I don't want you to—"

"He doesn't own the team. He might act like he does, but he doesn't. I don't think he can get me fired for dating you, and if he tries, then I'll fight it."

"You fought it in Seattle," I remind him. "And you still got released."

Will nods. "I know. But I fought it too late, and for all the wrong reasons. All I cared about was protecting my career. This is different. I'd fight for you too, not just soccer."

"But what if—"

He lifts his hand, brushing his thumb across my lower lip and effectively shutting me up. "You told me to let you make your own decisions, Sophia. Let me do the same."

"You're the one who demanded I keep my underwear on. That's you allowing me to make my own decisions?"

He gifts me with one of his full, unreserved smiles, his thumb continuing its torture along my lower lip. I'm fighting the urge to tremble. "Requesting you not flash your pussy at a club full of horny guys seemed like a reasonable request."

I glance at his crotch. "Does dinner mean you're finally going to let me touch you?"

"Are you saying yes to dinner?"

I don't have to think about it. "Yes."

"Yeah?" His smile is tentative. Hopeful.

I nod. "I like Indian food. And I like you, so...why not?"

His grin grows, looking more like the confident one I'm used to seeing. "I'll pick you up at seven, okay?"

"Why don't I pick you up? Seeing as I'm the one who has a car."

"I bought a car," he tells me.

"What? You did? When?"

"This week. It seemed like...time."

I smile, reading the subtext. Realizing Will has settled here a little more. Realizing he *chose* to settle here a little more. "Okay. I'll see you at seven."

He steps forward and kisses me. Softly, not like the possessive brand of last night. "I'll see you at seven."

———

"You should have worn flats," Will comments, as my hold on his arm tightens to a death grip for the hundredth time tonight.

I went all out for our date tonight. Styled my hair, full face of makeup, my skimpiest lingerie. Plus a short, strapless dress and shoes with a tall, thin heel that have threatened to snap off all night.

"You said you liked my outfit." Not only did he say that, he's barely looked away from me since picking me up a few hours ago.

"I love your outfit. I also love being able to feel my arm. You're cutting off circulation."

"Not my fault you had to park all the way down the street and there are cobblestones."

He sighs as I stumble yet again. "It would be faster to carry you."

"I'm fine with that," I reply.

One of my favorite things about Will is that he never backtracks. No matter the situation, he follows through. And right now is no exception. He pauses, and in a split-second, I'm literally swept off my feet. He continues walking like carrying me is completely normal, ignoring the startled looks from a few passersby. His hand brushes my ass before settling on my thigh. I know what he's doing even before he says, "You'd better be wearing underwear."

"You'd better check when we get to my apartment."

His hold on me tightens, and I smile.

Dinner was perfect. The food was delicious, and the company was even better. I had this part of the evening in the back of my mind all night, though. We both got mango lassis at dinner, neither of us having a drop of alcohol.

I could use some now to combat the nerves swirling in my stomach. I'm relieved Will already knows this will be a new experience for me. At least I haven't had to anticipate having that conversation all night.

He doesn't set me down until we're directly outside my apartment door. He's not even breathing heavily from the exertion, appearing totally nonchalant as I look through my bag for my keys. But then I catch a twitch in his jaw out of the corner of my eye as I disengage my lock, the tiny motion setting off a series of reactions in my body. My heart races and my fingers fumble as we step inside my apartment.

I flick on the light, he shuts the door, and then we collide.

Any worries about him not wanting this as much as me vanish as Will kisses me. His hands roam and his tongue explores, the press of his lips against mine so controlling and commanding. He's *consuming* me, it feels like. Ravaging my mouth.

He pulls away first, leaving me breathless and stunned. Panting and bereft, my pussy throbbing and clenching around nothing. In just a few seconds, I fell in love with what his mouth against mine felt like all over again. This feels like the first time I'm getting to touch him because it's the first time I haven't been worried he was about to stop.

We're dating. Sort of. Maybe. We just went on *a* date; the best one I've ever been on. And he told me he doesn't share, which felt like a claim.

His tongue licks a hot stripe down the side of my neck, making my knees tremble. It feels like I'm melting. Malleable. Overheated with arousal and overwhelmed with trust. I've never been able to fully let go with a guy before, always had reservations lingering in the back of my mind. But with Will, it's so easy to let go. I feel *safe* with him, cherished and protected. There have been other guys I was insanely attracted to. But I never felt this burning need to touch them.

I'm *dying* to touch Will. My palms dragging down the center of his chest feels like a form of relief. A *finally*. Even through the shirt he's wearing, I can feel the ridges and bumps of his abdomen, reminding me how ridiculously in shape he is. I reach the waistband of his jeans, fumbling with the button and zipper. My excitement rising when the denim parts. When he doesn't tell me, *You don't need to,* or another fucking, *It's fine.*

He has that defined V that points right to his cock, which I've never found that attractive before. It seemed like showing off, like a guy was vain and self-absorbed or more likely to spend time at the gym than thinking about you. But Will is this in shape because it's his job. On him, a professional football player, the distinctive ridges are insanely sexy. And I'm glad he has no idea what I'm thinking, because I'm sure he'd tease me about how much I "hate" the sport again.

My fingers brush through the dusting of hair below his belly button, following the line lower and lower. His entire body is a work of art, like one of the sculptures at the museum we visited together.

I sink to my knees right next to the rack that stores part of my sizable shoe collection, too eager to get all the way to my bedroom. Emboldened by the heated look that flashes across Will's face as he registers the movement and realizes my exact intentions. Hoping that means he's done holding back.

He fists his cock, running the flared head across my parted lips. My entire body feels like it's vibrating, so overstimulated that I can't focus on any one sensation.

The vein that runs the length of his shaft is raised and pulsing. His abs are clenched tight. My tongue darts out to lap at the bead of moisture on the thick head. Then I pull back a couple of inches, blowing on the damp tip. I've seen his cock before, but never this close. There's no way I'll be able to fit that many inches in my mouth. And I'm a little worried about my vagina, how he's possibly going to fit inside of me when we have sex.

"I've thought about doing this to you a lot," I confess.

Then lean forward, humming when I feel his thick length invade my mouth for the first time. The weight of his erection settles on my tongue, and I fight the urge to cough or gasp. I'm so *full*, the head hitting the back of my throat and cutting off my air. Will groans when I swallow, my throat tightening around the tip. I pull in a deep breath through my nose, my eyes prickling with unshed tears.

"*Sophia.*" My name comes out rough and ragged, tensed, like he's holding back.

I don't want him to hold back. I want to make him lose his mind.

I can feel him reacting to the suction as I hollow my cheeks, his dick hardening and swelling even more. He tastes salty and sinful, leaking down my throat. A persistent pulse pounds between my legs in response, hot and heavy. My hold on his thighs tightens, my nails pressing into his skin hard enough to leave marks, as I move my mouth along his cock.

"Fuck. You look—*fuck*." Will finally touches me, brushing the hair that's fallen forward back and away from my face. He wraps the long strands around his fist, his hips starting to rock in a steady rhythm. "You look so good with your lips around my cock. Is this what you've been wanting, baby? Why you were pouting last night? You wanted me to fuck this perfect mouth? You wanted to be on your knees for me like a dirty girl?"

I moan in response, feeling my throat open, feeling him slide farther into my mouth. Emboldened, I grab the base of his dick, gripping the firm flesh before slipping south to play with his balls.

His hips jerk, followed by a husky growl. And another, "*Fuck*," which seems to be one of Will's favorite words.

He's definitely not holding back now. A few tears fall. My jaw aches. And I'm so wet I can feel it between my clenched thighs, fighting the urge to reach down and touch myself so I can relieve the ache.

I'm doing this. I'm the reason Will Aster sounds like he's experiencing the most pleasurable sort of pain.

I pull back until I'm only sucking the bulbous tip. Flick my tongue through the slit at the end. He tugs at my hair harder, pulling me back.

"Wha—"

Before I can get the word out, he's repositioned us. I'm pressed against the wall next to the doorway that leads into my bedroom, my back to him. It takes Will about three seconds to lift my dress and lower my underwear. And then he's touching me *there*, not with his tongue or his fingers, but with his cock. He doesn't push inside of me, even once my hips start to move, seeking out a natural rhythm. His dick glides against my pussy easily, dampened by my saliva and all the arousal that's pooled there. Tormenting me, the rush of arousal like nothing I've ever experienced before. I lose all sense of reality, my world narrowing to nothing except him.

"Will…" I moan his name, clutching the flat wall and finding nothing to hold on to. Rocking back against him, seeking more, more, *more*.

"You're drenched. So wet, just from sucking me." He sounds happy about it. Proud. "You close?"

"*So* close," I breathe. I can feel it building inside of me, the heat and the pressure and the pleasure.

"Good. Use me. Make yourself come on me."

I slip my hand down my stomach, fingering my swollen clit while my hips continue rocking against his erection. Pinned between his muscular body and the solid wall. I've never been this turned on in my life. Nothing has ever felt so good, the rub of his hot skin raw against mine sinful and erotic and primal. All I can focus on or think about or feel.

I masturbate against his cock, my body moving faster and faster as biological urges take over.

Will's breathing turns quick and choppy, but he doesn't reach down to touch himself. He lets me use his body like a personal pleasure device, until I come with a loud cry in a dizzying explosion of release.

White-hot heat radiates through me, spreading through my whole body and leaving me limp. I slump against the wall, letting it hold up my weight. Barely cognizant of Will pulling my dress even higher. He marks my back this time instead of my stomach, and I love every filthy second of it.

CHAPTER TWENTY-SEVEN

WILL

S ophia sits up as I approach the bed. "What's wrong?"
"Nothing, baby."

I've called women baby before—when I forgot their name. Never as any sort of endearment, the way I've started saying it to Sophia.

She rolls into me as soon as I'm back under the covers. "Couldn't sleep?"

"No. I just had to take a piss." I did poke around her apartment a little. Looking at the framed photos, mostly. I haven't seen any of her work aside from the pictures the team posted from her internship. "You went to Africa?"

"Yeah. It was through the university. There was a program in Kenya." She pauses. "I'm dying to go back and take some more. I feel like I've learned so much since. And maybe then I could finally get a decent photo for the EPAs another year."

"The what?"

"It's a photography competition. *The* photography competition. It's like winning a gold medal or a World Cup for photographers. The photo has to be taken the year you submit it, and I can't—I can't come up with anything that seems good enough to send in."

"You will."

"Well, the deadline is coming up soon, so I'm running out of time."

"Well, you'll have more time now that you're not taking photos of footballers, right?"

"I guess." She sounds uncertain. "Does it bother you?"

"Does what bother me?"

"That I don't like football. Does it bother you?"

"No. Why would it bother me?"

"I don't know. I just thought it might."

I glance over, trying to get a better read on her. Moonlight is spilling in through the window, casting her room in a white glow.

Sophia looks ethereal and angelic, her blonde hair spread across the pillow like a halo. She looks over, catching me staring.

"I like you just the way you are, Sophia. Don't change. For me, for anyone."

She half smiles, but it slips away quickly. Her fingers brush my arm, using the limited light to trace patterns on my skin. "What's your favorite tattoo?" she asks.

"I don't have a favorite."

"Then why'd you get them?"

"I thought they looked cool."

"They do." Her fingers keep stroking, and I'm having a hard time keeping my body from reacting. "I don't have any."

"I know." I've touched, tasted, or explored every inch of her. There's not a freckle or a scar I don't know about.

"Right. Yeah." She giggles, and it's fucking adorable.

Her fingers still, and I close my eyes, trying to fall back asleep.

"Why won't you have sex with me?"

I tense as soon as Sophia asks the question, and I'm sure she can feel it.

I made her come twice more before going to bed, but we didn't have sex. She didn't push it at the time, too blissed out, but I knew the question was coming.

"I don't want you to rush into it, and I don't want you to think I'm only here for one thing. Your first time...I don't want you to regret it." *Regret me*, I add silently.

"Do you regret yours?" she asks.

I can see her face well enough to catch how she raises one eyebrow.

No, is the honest answer. Which I'm sure she knows.

"That was different."

"Because you're a guy?"

"No. Because I was a stupid, horny kid who couldn't play soccer twenty-four/seven and hated being at home. And because my decisions have rarely been good ones."

She shifts again, so she's staring at the ceiling. Her fingers graze her forehead, rubbing back and forth absently.

I clear my throat. "Sophia, I—"

"It's fine, Will. I'm just...deciding."

"Deciding what?"

"Whether I should tell you the truth."

"The truth about what?"

She's not a virgin, is my first thought. But why would she lie about that?

"I wasn't waiting for it to be special or to make sure I didn't regret it. I had a...bad experience."

Fury ripples through my body, locking my muscles into place. "What kind of bad experience?"

My tone is calm, but I'm not. *I'll kill him.*

"I should have known better. He was jealous of Adler. I should have known what it was really about."

"What happened?" By some miracle, my voice comes out a hell of a lot calmer than I am. I want her to confide in me, and freaking out and demanding an address for this asshole won't reassure her I'm worth confiding in.

"It was years ago, back when I was still in secondary school. He was older, at the academy."

The academy. Meaning he played football. Meaning he was good.

"We talked—flirted—for weeks. I snuck into his room the night we were going to...I was early, so I snooped around. Found the camera he'd set up and figured he'd planned to...well, you get the idea."

Yeah. I do.

"Tell me Beck beat his ass."

"Adler doesn't know. I never told him, never told anyone. I was...embarrassed, I guess. I knew Ansel had a reputation with girls. Knew he was jealous of my family. And the worst part was...none of it was about me. It wasn't a bet with his friends to prove he could get me in bed. It was about Adler. About football. That's why he wanted to sleep with me. To win."

Ansel. I memorize his name.

He's not on Kluvberg.

Does he play for another team? I want to ask, but I'm not sure I should. This is about her, not him.

"You have no reason to be embarrassed, Sophia. He should be."

"I should have known better."

"You were set up."

"So were you."

I still, surprised she's bringing Cassandra up. "That was different. I put myself in a bad situation. I was out partying. And I thought of myself as invincible. I was so arrogant; it never occurred to me there would be consequences, even after I found out who she was."

"She chose not to tell you who she was. She chose to lie about what happened."

Since the scandal that sent me here happened, I've been privy to lots of reactions. Social media's commentary was mostly disgusted and judgmental. My former teammates shunned me. Shawn was furious; Tripp was worried. My mom and I never discussed it, just like we avoid talking about most things.

Not one person *defended* me, like Sophia did just now.

I roll so I'm hovering above her, then kiss her.

She reacts instantly, winding her arms around my neck and pushing her fingers into my hair.

I slide a hand down her side and between her legs, finding her cunt by feel. I push one finger into her tight heat, feeling her breathing stutter against my chest as she reacts to my touch. Her legs spread, allowing me better access. I've never had this with anyone before. Talking and touching in the middle of the night, while the rest of the world is asleep.

I love seeing her like this, lying in bed beneath me, so responsive. Trust shines bright in her blue eyes as a pink flush steals across her face. Her lips part as her pussy pulses around my moving fingers.

She's perfect, and I'm terrified I'll ruin her. I've never had anyone rely on me before. My longest, most serious relationship has always been with soccer, and it's one-sided. The game can't love you back, and I've never needed it to.

"More," Sophia begs, arching into my touch.

I struggle to fit a second finger, and, fuck, is it a snug fit. She's still swollen from earlier.

She moans as my fingers find that secret spot, her grip tightening in my hair as she writhes beneath me.

I lean down and capture one nipple in my mouth, letting my teeth graze the sensitive bud. Sophia gasps, her fingers fighting to hold me in place. I chuckle, knowing she'll be able to feel the vibration against her skin. I keep fucking her leisurely with my fingers, feeling her walls flutter as she gets closer to coming.

I know her body so well by now. It's so easy to tease her right to the edge of release. To hold her there until the anticipation reaches a breaking point.

And it's so hard, after she comes, to not give her exactly what she's asked for. We're both naked, and I know she's willing.

I'm selfish. I always have been—unapologetically so. Most people are looking out for themselves—they're just less honest about it. But with Sophia, it feels like a chance I can't take.

I'd rather she hate me than regret me.

So, I kiss her and then roll away.

CHAPTER TWENTY-EIGHT

WILL

Fritz walks into the locker room right as I'm zipping up my soccer bag, ready to head out. Sensation is slowly returning to my body after the ice bath I ended practice with, the sore ache of my muscles satisfying. Proof I worked hard. I had a good talk with Wagner after practice, my teammates passed to me every chance they had, and I'm headed straight to Sophia's for dinner.

Life is good. I'm content, maybe even happy, and it makes me nervous something is bound to go wrong soon.

"You leaving?" Fritz asks.

I nod, slinging my bag over one shoulder. "Yeah. Have a good night."

"You're not coming to the club?" Fritz, and some of the other guys, made their evening plans common knowledge earlier.

Me, a year ago, me, a month ago, would have jumped on that. I've barely explored any of Kluvberg's nightlife, and the city known for being a party destination in Europe. Since moving here, I've gone out twice. But no part of me is tempted to change my evening plans. "Not tonight," I tell him.

Fritz smirks at me. "Too tired?"

For fuck's sake. I'm not *that* much older than him. "Too busy," I reply. "I've got other plans."

His eyes light up with interest, and I swallow a groan. I don't need Fritz—or any other guy on the team—poking around my personal life.

"Have fun. I'll come next time, okay?"

Olivier and a couple other guys return from their training sessions, distracting Fritz and allowing me to leave without any other delays. I head to the parking lot, tossing my bag in the back of the sedan and then starting on the route that's become very familiar. Heading to Sophia's after practice has become my new routine.

When I walk into her apartment, I find Sophia standing at the stove, which is a surprise. Normally, her kitchen seems to get just about as much use as mine. As in not much. I might have some furniture now, but the cabinets in the kitchen are basically empty. Sophia has pots and pans and dishes, but I've become accustomed to only using them to eat the takeout that one of us picks up. She turned down my offer to grab something for us on my way here, but I assumed that meant she was picking food up.

"You're cooking?" I ask.

I always thought I'd hate domesticity. In my mind, *settling down* was seeing my mom stare at the door, waiting for my dad to come home when he rarely did. It's much easier to just not open yourself up to that potential disappointment.

But it wasn't a conscious choice, opening myself up to it with Sophia. It just happened. Became harder to stay closed off than to let her in.

She shrugs casually, like it's no big deal. But her cheeks are red, and I don't think it's because of the steam rising from the boiling water on the stove. "Pasta is one of the only things I know how to make."

"Smells good," I say, walking over to her. I lean down to kiss the top of her head, smiling when I hear her breath hitch, and then walk over to the sink to wash my hands.

"How was practice?" she asks.

"We don't have to talk about football."

"I know. I asked."

"It was okay," I tell her. Then add, "I might be starting next game."

"Really?"

"Uh-huh."

Wagner was his typical stoic self, but I'm pretty sure I saw a twinkle in his eye when he stopped me after practice and told me to make sure I was well-rested before our next match. That, paired with excitement about seeing Sophia, is the main reason I didn't stay late, like I often do.

"Will, that's amazing." The excitement and enthusiasm in her voice tug at something right in the center of my chest. I'm as unaccustomed to having someone cheer me on as I was to sleeping in bed with a woman.

We take seats at the counter once the food is ready. Unlike me, she has stools. Whenever we eat at my place, it's on the couch or the bed. Both places where food often gets forgotten. We've been dating, I guess, for a couple of weeks. Unless I'm playing or training, I'm with her.

Sophia looks over expectantly as I take the first bite.

"It's good," I tell her.

It's bad. So, *so* bad.

The noodles are so undercooked that they're still crunchy. The sauce tastes like a super-salty tomato. The meatballs are bland and burned. Without a doubt, it's the worst thing I've ever tasted.

But Sophia made it. Made it for *me*. So, I take another bite, followed by a large gulp of water.

Sophia takes a bite. Makes a face. Looks at me. "Will, it tastes *terrible*."

"It's not that bad." I shovel more spaghetti into my mouth, fully committing to the act.

She watches me with obvious amusement. "You're a better liar than I thought."

"The point of being a good liar is, no one knows you're lying."

She points her fork at me. "So, you admit you're lying."

"Would people pay to eat this at a restaurant? Probably not." *Absolutely not.* I glance around her apartment. "We're not at a restaurant."

Sophia rolls her eyes. But there's something soft on her face as she watches me shove another bite into my mouth.

After we finish dinner, I stand up to do the dishes. Sophia hip-checks me out of the way playfully to load the dishwasher the way she wants it. I clean the pasta pot, dry it, then lean past her to set it back on the stove. She's standing directly in front of me, so I can't resist leaning down to press a kiss to the top of her spine.

I've been thinking about touching her all day. Touching her is *all* I think about, unless I'm actively playing soccer.

Sophia shivers, sinking back against me.

My hand skates down her side to the hem of the shorts she's wearing, easily sneaking beneath the stretchy fabric. Sophia moans, and I groan when I reach the wet spot in her underwear.

"Is this all for me?" I tease.

It makes me feel a hundred feet tall, how her body reacts to me. How she never guards herself or hesitates. I would understand her caution, after what she told me happened with Ansel, the dick I'd love to run into in a dark alley. But Sophia's never shy or reserved when I touch her like this. She never hides her reactions.

Her breathing is getting faster. More moisture is soaking the already drenched fabric. I pull my hand free from her shorts and yank them down, taking her soaked thong with them. Spin her around and back her up until her bare ass is pressed against the kitchen drawers.

She looks up at me, her expression so full of lust and trust that something clenches in my chest. Rather than analyze what that might be, I grab the backs of her thighs and lift her onto the edge of the countertop. Not super sanitary, but we're done eating. She is, at least. Her needy gasp is loud and surprised, inflating my cock, which has been half-hard since I got here.

"Who are you this wet for, Sophia?"

She leans back and opens her knees, letting me admire the wetness covering her cunt. "You," she gasps, her hands scrambling for purchase on the smooth counter.

"Right answer." I slip a finger inside of her wet heat, licking a line up the inside of her thigh.

She calls out, lifting her hips to give me better access as I spread her wide.

"I love how loud you are," I tell her, admiring the view of her pussy stretching when I add a second finger. "Hearing what you sound like when you're desperate to come? My favorite fucking sound. Being inside this tight pussy? My favorite place in the whole world."

The sounds spilling out of her mouth are a nonsensical mix of my name, "More," and, "Please."

I work my fingers faster, watching her writhe on the countertop. The couch would have been more comfortable, but she's at the perfect height here. And Sophia's too far gone in the haze of pleasure to care where she's lying. It would be so easy to tug my shorts down and slip the erection straining against the mesh fabric deep inside of her. She's given me the green light so many times. But I'm still unsure about taking that final step. I know it'll mean something to her, and I know it'll mean something to me. I'm terrified I'll somehow fuck it up.

So, I lean down and suck on her clit, knowing that'll push her over the edge. Her pussy clamps around my fingers, to the point that it's painful as she comes.

As soon as her cunt stops fluttering, she's sliding off the counter and pulling on the waistband of my shorts. Then, it's my turn to clutch the counter as she sinks to her knees and sucks my cock into her mouth.

Eagerly, like she's desperate for a taste.

I hit the back of her throat, and she hums approvingly, the vibration as incredible as the clench when she swallows. My knees almost buckle when she pulls back and circles the flared tip with her tongue, then traces the slit at the end. Her mouth moves down to my balls next, pulling the right testicle into her mouth and then moving to the left one.

We've both gotten good at discovering what each other likes, something I've never experienced with a partner before. I've never been with the same woman enough times to get to know those things. For her to get to know those things about me. Nothing about it is boring, the way I assumed it would be.

I let go of the countertop and push my fingers into her hair, paying no mind to the elastic as it pulls from her hair and falls to the floor. I just enjoy the feel of the silky blonde strands running through my fingers as I thrust into her mouth.

"Just like that," I tell her.

Sophia's hands run up the back of my thighs until she reaches my ass cheeks. Her nails dig into my skin as she physically pulls me deeper into her mouth. That's what pushes me over the edge, her acting like she can't get enough of my cock. Her taking me as deep as she physically can.

My groan is a low rumble as heat licks its way down my spine. My balls draw up tight. And then I'm coming, the muscles in my groin tensing and contracting as my dick jerks, filling Sophia's mouth with spurts of cum. Delicious throbs thrum through my body as she swallows everything I give her.

I slide out of her mouth, sated but not satisfied. One look at her—swollen lips and tousled hair—has raw need remaining, like a spark that's been blown at but not extinguished.

I can't get enough. With her, I always want more.

I reach down for my shorts, but Sophia snags my arm before I can pick them up.

I glance at her, surprised. This isn't part of our routine. We usually eat, fool around, hang out, fool around again, and then go to bed. Rinse and repeat.

"I need more," she tells me.

She's always insatiable and eager, often initiating intimacy between us first. But I know she's not asking for my mouth again. She wants *more*, that final step we haven't taken.

And I'm dying to fuck her, obviously. This is the longest I've gone without sex since I was a teenager. I'm insanely attracted to her, and stopping myself from pushing inside her is a form of torture every single time we get naked together.

But I also want more than sex from Sophia. I have feelings for her, and I'm nervous to mix that with what has always been forgettable and meaningless in the past. I don't know how to explain that to Sophia. I can hardly make logical sense of it myself. And I know she's reading it more as a rejection each time I hesitate.

Like I'm hesitating now.

I think of her angry words in the club restroom. How she can make her own choices, how this is her decision. Part of me is still trying to make that decision for her, each time we get close to this point. She's trusting me, and being worthy of that means facing my own fears.

I've experienced the physical act of sex before. But the emotional aspect is new to me, same as her. I don't know how to *make love* to a woman, as corny and cliché as that sounds.

"Okay." A simple, inconsequential word, for what feels like a monumental moment. But I'm bad about expressing myself with syllables; I always have been. It's probably why I always gravitated toward sports, where actions speak much louder. You rarely have to justify or explain. You just do.

I tug her up and into me, holding eye contact the entire time.

"Okay?" The question is whispered, like this moment is a bubble that might pop.

"I've been dying to fuck you since I saw you pouting in the stands, so it shouldn't be a hardship on my part."

Sophia rolls her eyes in response, but it lacks the normal nonchalance when I say something that amuses or annoys her.

She's nervous. I catch the twitch in her cheek as she chews the inside. Her fingers trail down to my wrist, and then her hand is on my slick, half-hard cock. My dick reacts, swelling, rapidly getting hard again.

She smiles smugly at the sight, as proud of my reaction as I'm enamored by hers.

Her hand drops, finding the hem of her shirt instead and pulling it over her head. She lets me look at her naked body for a few seconds, then heads for her bedroom.

I take a deep breath, then follow.

CHAPTER TWENTY-NINE

SOPHIA

A ir leaves my lungs in a surprised gust as Will lifts me and tosses me onto the mattress like I weigh nothing. I wiggle on the soft fabric of my comforter, trying to get comfortable and also find a position that seems alluring. Nerves are pinballing inside of me. I want this. I've *wanted* this. But I wasn't sure when he'd finally say yes. Will is treating this like a big step, which is making me even more aware that this is my first time.

Which is not a bad thing, I don't think, but it's definitely a noticeable one that's not helping with my mounting anxiety.

"You little liar," Will says.

I glance over.

He's staring at the table next to my bed. "You kept it."

It's not a question, so I don't answer.

He picks up the slip of paper and waves it toward me. "You said you lost this."

I smirk. "Well, then I found it again."

I'm lying, and I'm sure he knows that. But I'm vulnerable enough right now, my bare body entirely on display to him as I lie here waiting for him to join me in bed. About to have sex for the first time. Maybe I'll eventually tell him I've memorized every crease, letter, and number on that ticket. That I've kept careful track of it ever since he handed it to me. But I'm not admitting any of that right now. Or sharing that I've hidden the ticket in the pages of a book every other time he's come over to avoid this exact conversation.

"*Section 336. Row E. Seat 4,*" he reads.

"Lots of better seats available..."

His laugh is low and throaty before he sets the ticket down, then climbs onto the bed. "No, there weren't. You weren't in any of them."

"That would be sweeter if I hadn't actually been sitting in your seat," I say, rolling into him.

Our legs tangle together naturally. This isn't the first time we've lain together like this. But my heart is beating rapidly, giving away the fact that this isn't going to be like those other times.

Will's fingers weave into my hair, tugging at the strands gently as he sifts through them. "I'm glad you texted me."

"Me too." I drag my hand down his chest until I reach bare skin, skimming my fingers along one of his hip bones before finding and fisting the heavy weight of his cock.

Will sucks in a sharp breath, his fingers no longer moving. "Since I got here, I've been trying to be smarter, be better, to do the right thing. Not just for me—for *you*. When you said it was your decision...it is. I've resented the hell out of anyone who tried to tell me what to do my whole life. And I never want you to feel that way. That I don't trust you or don't believe in you. I don't trust *me*. Don't believe in *me*. I want you, Sophia. I want you so fucking bad."

I shift so I'm fully on top of him, keeping my hold on his erection and guiding it between my legs. "You have me."

I've never felt this way around anyone before, like he controls my heartbeat. There's a permanent section of my brain that's stuck on thinking about him, regardless of whether we're together or apart. A giddy rush whenever he looks at me that shares the same weightless sensation with falling.

Will studies me, and I stare back.

It's, without a doubt, the most intense moment we've ever shared.

His Adam's apple bobs as he swallows. And I'm blushing. I can feel my cheeks radiating heat in response to his close inspection of my face.

"I'm not going to ask if you're sure. But if anything changes, if it hurts or something just...doesn't feel right, promise you'll tell me."

All of a sudden, I'm certain. The nerves fade, torched into nothingness by burning need.

I'm so, *so* certain. I can remember the cocky arrogance Will was cloaked with during our first meeting perfectly. That indifferent player, slouched and scowling, is not the guy you look at and think, *Perfect candidate to take my virginity.* Maybe when it comes to experience, but not tenderness. He's the guy who leaves as soon as he comes, who acts like your hymen is an inconvenience. That's the kind of guy Will seems like he is. But he's not. He's so much more.

He's all I want and everything I need.

"I promise."

Will nods, then repositions us so that I'm the one on my back beneath him. He strips off his shirt before crawling over me. Slowly, putting on a show of rippling muscles that I don't even think is deliberate. I slide my hands down the front of his chest, over his shoulders, and down his bunched biceps, feeling his muscles tense as he reacts to my touch.

"I'm already worried about how long I'll last, baby," he tells me. "You touching me is not fucking helping."

I like him calling me baby. Like it way too much.

"Sorry." I smirk, unabashed, my hands continuing to roam across his hot, firm skin.

I shiver with excitement when he cups my breasts. Squirm when his head bows and he sucks my left nipple into his mouth until it's a sharp, aching point, then moves to my right.

I lift my knees as high as they'll go, wrapping my legs around his waist in an effort to speed up the process of getting him inside of me. Impatient to finally experience what it'll be like. As amazing as his tongue on my breasts feels, it's not the first time.

His laugh is throaty as his lips move along my neck. "You *just* came."

"So did you, and you're hard."

"You're naked. Of course I'm hard."

My nails dig into his back. "*Please.*" I don't care about being coy or aloof, not with him. I want him to know how badly I want this to happen.

"God, you're so fucking gorgeous." His calloused fingers run down my ribs, leaving a trail of goose bumps in their wake.

"Will," I whimper.

All I can focus on is the throbbing between my thighs. He's touching me everywhere, except where I *need* him to. It feels like every other time we've hooked up has been foreplay, building up to this moment.

"Please," I beg again.

His hand moves between us. I feel him *there*, the thick head of his erection pressing directly against the entrance of my pussy. All I focus on is that one point of contact, concentrating so hard the slightest shift seems like an explosion.

Will suddenly freezes, dropping his head into the crease of his elbow next to my shoulder. "Fuck. *Fuck.*"

It's not his *that feels so good* fuck. He sounds frustrated and disappointed.

"What? What's wrong?"

"I don't have a condom with me." He lifts his head, his features twisted into a grimace as he glares at the bed beneath my head. "I haven't been—I wasn't thinking... I'm assuming you don't have one?"

I shake my head. Then bite my bottom lip, deliberating my response. "Do you...need one?"

His attention sharpens, gaze snapping from the comforter back to me. "What do you mean?"

"I've been on birth control for a few years to help regulate my periods. So, if you want..."

I trust him. Which I think he already knows, but I'm telling to him. Practically shouting it.

Will's expression is tormented amusement. "You're asking if I want to fuck you for the first time bare and then watch my cum drip out of you?"

My entire body reacts, basically vibrating with arousal. I love his dirty mouth and his brash words. Love hearing his unfiltered thoughts. Love that he's treating me like a seductive woman, not an inexperienced girl.

"If you don't want to..."

His chuckle is dark. Dangerous. I know exactly what's about to happen before it actually takes place. And I'm ready for it to. Will might think he's a wrong choice; I'm certain he's right.

Finally, there's a stretch.

The first inch is uncomfortable. The second one stings. The third one burns. But there are no alarm bells blaring in my head in response to the flaring pain. Logically, I know what's happening, why my body is protesting.

I'm being conquered, but I'm not sure it really counts since I'm willingly handing myself over. And beneath the building discomfort is the biological urge to be filled like this. A need that's always been there and never been satiated. An itch that's been rubbed before but never been scratched.

The burn between my legs sharpens to a pinch, the burst of pain sudden. It's too much, space being filled I'm not sure exists. My insides feel like they're being spread so much that internal stuff must be getting rearranged. I press my lips together, forcing my breaths to stay even as he pushes deeper and deeper.

It seems like I can feel every centimeter as it slips inside. Each vein pulsing in his cock. My instinct is to rebel against the intrusion. Shy away from the pain. Will hisses when I tense, my inner muscles clenching to fight the urge to move away. His fingers dig into my hips, his face as concerned as it was when I got hit by the football. The way he's invading my body feels violent, but the expression on his face is achingly tender.

"Okay?"

I manage a nod. His hips have paused, but the discomfort hasn't disappeared. I don't look down to see how far in he is, because I'm not sure I want to know the answer.

Will's thumb rubs a soothing circle above my hipbone before his hand moves to the spot right above where he's entering me, massaging there gently. A spark of pleasure breaks through the agony.

"You're so fucking tight," he tells me. He sounds happy about it.

Me, not so much. I'm glad it feels good for him, but I'd be on board with being a little loose if it meant feeling the way I usually do when he touches me. I just have to trust this is the worst part. I should have asked for some advice from my friends, maybe, rather than acting like I knew what they were talking about.

"I'm a virgin," I remind him.

Will smirks. "Not for much longer."

It's exactly what I need from him—confidence and reassurance. *He's* exactly what I need. I can't imagine doing this with anyone else.

"Keep going."

Another inch.

"Do I want to know how much is left?"

"Probably not." His fingers rub against my sensitive clit again, which helps. "You can take it, baby. You're doing so well."

"You're so *big*," I moan. I'm not sure I'll be able to walk tomorrow.

Right now, it feels like I'll never forget what having him inside of me feels like. I've seen his dick. Touched it. Sucked it. I knew the size when I begged for this. But it seems physically impossible that more can fit inside of me.

There's worry on Will's face again. I'm not a masochist, so I'm positive I don't look like I'm enjoying myself. "We can stop."

"Fuck no." Not only do I hate backing down from a challenge, I don't want to endure getting to this point again. "Fuck *me*. For real. Don't hold back."

Decisiveness flashes across his face. And then, with one quick thrust, he bottoms out. My legs are spread wide enough that I can feel his groin brushing my clit. It *hurts*, the pain of being split apart a sudden stab that steals my breath. But it also feels good, the primal part of me that's been craving this, savoring how it feels to be filled. A missing piece, snapping into place. I'm complete without Will, but he makes me feel whole.

His expression is strained, the tendons of his neck drawn tight. But his eyes are soft as he tucks some of my hair behind one ear, then slides his hand down the length of my body until he reaches my knee, hooking it over his hip. Something shifts inside, the burn of being stretched transitioning to sparks of pleasure. The pain starts to fade as my body adjusts to the new sensation.

I moan. "Do that again."

He moves inside of me again, the slow drag of his cock a thousand times more arousing than anything I've ever experienced. Basic instinct overtaking reason, a much deeper urge than chasing pleasure or escaping pain.

Will starts to actually fuck me, sweat building between our bodies as they move together. *Good* turns into pure pleasure, pain fading to a distant memory. My nails dig into his shoulders and my legs wrap around his waist, trying to get as close to him as is physically possible.

The smell of sex fills the air, salty and musky and arousing. I feel the pressure in my pelvis expanding, tendrils of heat spreading through me as my muscles tighten and then start to shake. All I can focus on is the hardness inside of me, the stretch less foreign with each thrust.

He senses the shift in my reactions, angling his hips and finding a spot that immediately makes my body detonate in an exquisite burst of sensation. It feels like I'm floating—thoughtless and weightless—nothing registering except a deluge of pleasure so intense it's numbing. My pussy is pulsing around *something*, instead of nothing, and the difference is astounding. So consuming that I barely register another foreign feeling—the throb of his dick deep inside of me, followed by a seep of warmth. I come again, or I'm still coming, everything about this moment hazy and dreamlike. His strokes slow, then stop.

The mixture of our releases is already leaking out of me. I reach down to touch the sticky mess, my fingers smearing through the wetness as I brush against the spot where he's still inside if me. I can feel how stretched I am around him, how wide he's holding me open. The coarse rasp of his pubic hair and the smooth skin of his balls.

Neither of us say anything. This is a moment that doesn't need it, shimmering and intangible. Meant to be savored silently, because it won't last forever.

He kisses me, soft and sweet, still inside of me.

And I know Will Aster just wrecked me for anyone else.

CHAPTER THIRTY

WILL

I'm lacing up my left cleat when my phone buzzes with an incoming call. I glance at the screen out of habit, already deciding not to answer it since we're about to head out to the pitch for warm-up. Freeze, when I register the name on the screen.

Mom.

She never calls me. I try to do some quick math in my head and figure out what time it is there. I can't think fast enough to come up with an estimate even.

Heart racing, I answer. "Hello?"

"Will."

From that one word, the worried way she says my name, I know something is wrong. I knew it before I answered, based simply on the fact that she called at all.

"What's wrong?" I ask.

Olivier walks past, his expression creasing with concern as he glances over at me.

"Tripp was in an accident. The police just called...I'm on the way to the hospital..." Her voice drifts in and out, either because of poor reception or the deafening rush of blood in my ears.

"I'm on my way." The words come out automatically, without me deciding to say them, a sigh of relief on the other end of the line echoing loud and clear across the Atlantic.

"He's at Mass General," my mom tells me.

"Okay. I'll be there as soon as I can."

I hang up the phone. Kick off the cleats I just put on and step into my sneakers instead.

"You okay?" Fritz asks from his spot two lockers down.

My, "No," is abrupt.

I'm in shock, I know. I should have asked my mom more questions about what exactly happened. How seriously Tripp is injured. But it was bad enough for her to call me, which tells me all I need to know. Which means time listening to details would have been time wasted. "I've gotta go."

"Go?" Fritz looks confused. "Go *where*?"

I don't answer. Don't have time to explain.

I grab my keys and my wallet, make sure I'm still holding my phone. Leave the locker room, ignoring all the questions called out behind me. Fritz isn't the only one who's noticed my strange behavior. We usually leave the locker room as a team, not alone.

Wagner is standing out in the hallway, talking with one of the equipment managers.

I walk right up to him. "I can't play today."

His bushy brows lift, the only shift in his stern expression. "You're starting, Aster. You asked me for this. Haven't shut up about it since you arrived."

The disappointment is crushing. I had a feeling—a hope—that this was coming. But I didn't know for sure until now.

I just shake my head. "I have to go." Keep walking.

There's a short list of things I prioritize above soccer, but there are *some* things. My baby brother is one of them.

"Aster!"

I turn back. Every second seems precious right now, but Wagner deserves some explanation. "My brother was in an accident. He's in the hospital."

Wagner's face softens a fraction. "I'm sorry to hear that."

I nod, then turn to go. He didn't give me permission to leave, but I'm not waiting for it.

"Aster."

I glance back again, since he sounds sympathetic. Not that he's about to ban me from leaving this building.

"You need something, you call. Okay?"

"Okay," I reply.

The drive to the airport is a blur. So is the conversation at the desk with an airline worker who manages to get me on a flight to Amsterdam that's leaving in twenty minutes with a connection to Boston.

Getting through security is a breeze with no luggage. I stopped at my apartment to grab my passport, but didn't bother to grab anything else.

My flight is already boarding by the time I make it to the gate. The two-hour layover in Amsterdam is the worst part of waiting. I debate on calling my mom. She hasn't reached out to me again, and I'm not sure if that's a good or a bad thing. Maybe she overreacted, then showed up at the hospital to find out Tripp just had a broken arm or something. My phone dies during my deliberations, which makes the choice for me. Rather than buy a charger at one of the stores, I doze in an uncomfortable chair until it's time to board my second flight.

It's dark out when I land in Boston. I grab the first taxi I see and direct the driver to head to Mass General, ignoring the sympathetic look that destination receives. I don't think many people rush to the hospital for any joyous reason. I never have. And I'm sure my grim expression conveys I'm not rushing to see a baby's birth, which is the only happy occasion I can think of.

According to the clock on the dash, it's almost midnight. It feels like it's been several days since I left Germany.

My knee bounces for the entire half-hour drive, a mixture of relief and dread swirling inside of me when I spot the line of ambulances parked outside the huge building. I hand the driver my credit card, then head for the main entrance as soon as the payment is processed.

Inside is chaos. An announcement blares out of the loud-speaker. A baby is screaming. A man is shouting. I have to wait for a woman accompanying a little girl cradling her left wrist to discuss paperwork with the man behind the desk before I can ask about my brother. He tells me to take the elevator at the end of the hall to the third floor before answering one of the three ringing phones on the desk.

The layout on the third floor is almost identical to the one downstairs. A large reception desk in the front of a waiting area. I start toward the desk.

"Will."

I turn, looking at my mom for the first time in months. I came to Boston for Christmas last winter, mostly to see Tripp. But she was there too, hovering in the background. Smiling when she saw us joking around together.

"Hi, Mom."

"You really came." She sounds surprised as she stands from the chair she was sitting in, and it pisses me off. I've always shown up when it really mattered. She can't say the same.

"Yeah. How is he?"

"Out of surgery. In recovery now. He hasn't woken up yet."

"Should he have?"

She shrugs, a small, helpless motion that annoys me even more. I don't deal well with uncertainty. If it's bad, I want to know it's bad. If it's okay, I don't want to be worried it's bad.

I look around the mostly empty waiting room. There's a middle-aged man in a chair by the tall windows, but no one else in sight. "Where's his doctor?"

"They said they'd give me an update when they know more, Will. Don't make a scene."

My molars grind at the subtle chastisement, but I take a seat without saying anything. After a pause, my mom sinks back down beside me.

"How...how have you been?"

"Fine." My response is short as I stare out the window at the bright lights of Boston. Of home, technically. But it's never felt like it. Nowhere has.

"Your new team is...going well?"

"Yes." I rub a thumb along the textured plastic handle, wishing she would stop talking.

"Germany. That's exciting. Europe is supposed to be beautiful."

My mom seems incapable of staying silent. She's nervous. We haven't spoken in months, and I know she's worried about Tripp.

"What exactly happened?" If we're going to talk, I'd rather it be about my brother than me.

"A driver didn't see him when he was changing lanes."

I swallow, hating the mental image that comes to mind. Crunching metal. Screeching tires. Broken bones.

Tripp got a bike because I did.

It should be me, lying in a hospital bed. I've done so much reckless shit in my life. But somehow, I've never even broken a bone.

"Is the driver here too?"

"He was. He...didn't make it."

"He's dead?" I ask, like that could possibly mean something else. Suddenly, I'm certain my mom wasn't exaggerating or over-reacting.

"Mrs. Aster?"

My mom immediately stands to face the approaching woman. She's wearing scrubs and a white coat. And an exhausted expression.

"How is he?" There's a note of panic in my mom's voice that's new from when she was just speaking to me. She's scared, more scared than she was showing me.

Again, I think, *It should be me.* Tripp would be much better at this role. He'd know what to say, how to comfort her.

"No change," the doctor says. Her voice is low and melodic. Soothing. So, it takes a moment for it to sink in that she's delivering bad news. "But your son is stable. His body just went through an incredibly traumatic ordeal. Both the accident and major surgery. His body is in shock. He'll be monitored closely throughout the night. I'd suggest you go home, get some sleep, and come back in the morning. If anything changes, we'll call you immediately. I promise."

My mom nods. "Thank you, Dr. Johnson."

Dr. Johnson gives my mom's shoulder a reassuring squeeze, smiles at me, and then heads back toward the double doors.

Impulsively, I follow her, ignoring my mom's exhausted, "Will."

"What are the odds?" I ask her. "The odds that my brother wakes up?"

Dr. Johnson pauses. Turns around. She's a little younger than my mom, probably in her early forties. "I'm a surgeon, sir. Not a gambler. Tripp is young and otherwise healthy. We're doing everything for him that we can. Medicine is science, but it's not an exact one."

"But...you must have some sense. An idea, at least, of what his chances are."

"I can tell you that most people with your brother's injuries wouldn't have made it this far. The fact that he survived surgery and is stable now is a major win. Let's focus on that for now."

She offers me another smile; one my facial muscles can't seem to react to.

I let Dr. Johnson walk away this time, her sobering words leaving me in a state of shock. I spent the whole trip here worried. That fear has only gained roots and spread since I arrived at the hospital. Paired with the growing panic that I could have come all this way for a *funeral*, not an emergency. My father chose to leave. I've never lost someone who wanted to stay, and it's a far more devastating notion.

"Come on."

Numbly, I follow my mom into the elevator and through the lobby.

"Did you bring any luggage?" she asks as we exit the hospital and walk into the sticky evening air. Boston's humidity feels like it's at about one hundred percent.

"No."

She nods like that's the answer she was expecting. "I still have some of your old clothes in a box somewhere."

"You didn't get rid of them when you turned my room into

your drawing space?" My mom's expression is startled, so I explain, "Tripp mentioned it."

She still looks surprised. I guess the possibility that my conversations with my brother involved her isn't one that occurred to her.

"I'll drive," I say when we reach her old green sedan.

Getting into a car is the last thing I feel like doing right now. But I'm guessing my mom wants to drive even less. Sure enough, she hands the keys right over, smiling gratefully before she rounds the bumper to climb into the passenger side. I open the driver's door, sliding the seat back as far as it'll go before getting in as well. Turn on the car, grateful when the air-conditioning begins blasting right away.

"I, uh..."

I glance over at my mom, who's twisting her fingers together anxiously.

"It's nice to see you, Will," she tells me.

I swallow the lump that rises in my throat. Clear it.

The last time my mom and I were at a hospital before tonight was because of that day we don't discuss. The day I found her on her bed with an empty bottle of pills on the carpeted floor. The day our relationship morphed into...this.

I don't think I'm the only one who realizes that.

"It's good to see you too, Mom," I say, then pull out of the parking lot.

CHAPTER THIRTY-ONE

SOPHIA

FC KLUVBERG STATEMENT FROM HEAD COACH LEON WAGNER

Will Aster has requested and been granted an indefinite leave of absence for personal reasons. The club has no further comment at this time.

I reread the press release for the fifth time, almost colliding with another student as I exit the building and pass the fountain. I mutter an apology, my eyes immediately returning to the phone screen.

Will hasn't replied to a single one of my messages. He never came over last night, like he was supposed to. This morning, I found out he hadn't played yesterday. And now, Kluvberg has released a statement that tells me absolutely nothing, except that something is wrong.

There's no one I can ask for more details—at least not

without arousing suspicion about why I care. Based on Wagner's statement, I'm not even clear if he knows what's going on.

I take a seat on one of the stone benches surrounding the fountain and then tap his name, twirling some of my hair around one finger anxiously as I listen to it ring.

And ring.

And ring.

I've decided he's not going to answer when I hear a click, then a croaked, "Hey."

"Will?"

There's a muffled thud on his end, followed by a low, "Fuck." He clears his throat. "Did you mean to call someone else?"

"Why haven't you answered any of my texts?" I demand. There's an edge of hysteria to my voice, twisting it into a sound that's almost unrecognizable. My feelings seem just as alien.

I know I like Will. I care about him. I'm sleeping with him. But this...this frantic panic feels like something more than lust or familiarity.

A rustle in the background this time.

"I haven't seen them. My phone died on the way here."

Way where?

"Oh. Are you...okay?"

Will exhales, and I know from the sound that the answer is no. Knew it from the second I heard he hadn't stepped on the pitch, actually. He was so excited about starting. No way he would have missed that for any trivial reason.

"My mom called right before the game yesterday. My brother was in an accident. I flew to Boston as quickly as I could."

"Is your brother all right? Will he be all right? How bad was the accident?" The questions fly out rapid-fire, all the worry that's had no outlet tumbling out in a rush.

"He hasn't woken up yet, as far as I know. I didn't get to see him before the doctor told us to go home and sleep."

Go home and sleep…

"*Fuck.* I woke you up."

I should have realized as soon as I heard his groggy tone. The rustling was sheets. It's ten here, which means it's the middle of the night where he is.

"Not even sure I'd fallen asleep yet."

Will is lying. I'm certain. He flew all night to see his brother and was fast asleep. He's not sure if Tripp will be okay, and he's trying to make *me* feel better.

"I'm *so* sorry. I just…you didn't come over last night or play in the game, and you weren't answering my texts. I got worried. Sorry, again. I'll let you get back to sleep. Let me know how Tripp is doing. You know, when you have the chance. I'm sure there's a lot going on…"

He clears his throat again, and I think he's going to ask about the game yesterday. Whether Kluvberg won without him.

Instead, he tells me, "I'm sorry, Sophia. I should have texted you before heading to bed. I didn't think…I didn't mean to worry you. Everything happened so fast, and then it was the middle of the night for me, and I didn't think through that it wasn't still the middle of the night for you."

"It's fine," I say quickly. As long as *he's* fine.

"If you didn't show up when we had plans and weren't replying to my messages, I would have called 110."

The smile appears automatically. I don't realize I'm smiling until my cheeks stretch. "You sound like a local."

"Yeah, well, I had a good tour guide."

There's a beat of silence. But it's not awkward. It's more like we're both weighing what else to say.

Will speaks first. "I'm not used to having someone to text."

My heart clenches painfully. There's a fluttering feeling in my chest too.

I've learned more than where Will is during this conversation. I've discovered the size of my feelings for him, and it's not tiny.

"I'm not used to...texting," I tell him.

The sentence is clunky. It doesn't make perfect sense, and maybe I can blame it on English technically being my second language. But I know exactly what I'm trying to say. I just don't know how to say it or whether this is the right time to.

These feelings are far more foreign than any language. I'm not used to caring, is what I mean. I've always flipped through guys easily with no lingering attachment.

And it's as terrifying as physically falling, realizing just how far I've traveled from indifferent.

I'm more scared to tell Will I'm in love with him than I was about having sex for the first time. That was only new to me. From what Will is saying, I think this is new to him too.

Will doesn't laugh or tease. Without seeing his face, I know that means he understood what I was really saying. That there haven't been other guys I was worried about and reached out to. That there are big feelings.

"Thanks for calling," he says softly. "I'll, uh, when I know more, I'll let you know, okay?"

He sounds as uncertain as I feel, which is both comforting and concerning.

"Okay."

"Bye, Sophia."

"Bye, Will."

I hang up, then stare into space for a while until I have to get up and head to the *Neues Kluvberg* offices.

CHAPTER THIRTY-TWO

WILL

My fingers tap anxiously against the plastic arm of the chair as I study the painting on the wall. It's a meaningless mess of shapes, no matter how long I stare at it. Or at least, I think it is. Maybe Sophia would see something different if she were here.

But this isn't an art museum. It's a hospital. Someone, somewhere, probably slapped a bunch of paint on a canvas, and then it was mass-produced for people to stare at while they waited to hear if their loved ones were still living.

My mom returns from her trip to the coffee maker, a steaming cup in one hand. I've already downed two myself despite the fact that it tasted like motor oil.

"Any news?" she asks.

I shake my head. I would have gotten up and found her, if there had been. Which she probably knows. But it's something to do—asking—and we've had nothing to do since we arrived two hours ago. There's been no sign of Dr. Johnson, and the nurse at the front desk says someone will update us "soon" each time I ask.

The only upside I can think of is that it means there are no updates. That Tripp is still alive, asleep in one of the rooms lining the long hallway past the front desk.

A half hour later, a young woman in scrubs approaches. "Are you here for Tripp Aster?" she asks.

My mom leaps up faster than I can. "How is he?"

The woman's smile is kind. "I'll take that as a yes. He's awake. I'll take you to see him. Dr. Johnson got pulled into an emergency surgery, but she's set some time aside later this morning to talk you through some of the rehabilitation..."

After *awake*, I barely hear a word that's being said.

He's awake. *Alive.* The relief spreading through me is staggering. I've never felt so grateful. So humbled.

People say it all the time—that life is short. I've said it to justify some of my selfish decisions. But *saying* something and *realizing* something are two different things. My brother could have died yesterday, in a split second. Life can change—*end*—in a split second. It's as sobering as any thought I've ever had, as uncomfortable as sitting in the hard chair, waiting for news, has been.

"I'd recommend going in one at a time," the woman tells us as we walk down the hallway. "He's on several different medications, and he will likely be disoriented."

I nod, stopping when she does. "You go, Mom."

She surprises me by shaking her head. "He'll want to see you."

It doesn't sound like the *you never come home* dig I could take it as. My mom and I have gotten along remarkably well since I arrived. Part of it is that we've had a mutual focus—worrying about Tripp. But it's also more time than we've spent together—just the two of us—in a long, long time. All it took was a horrific accident.

Horrific doesn't seem like a horrible enough adjective when I step into Tripp's hospital room. He's lying on the narrow, slightly elevated bed, the side railings and blue bedding blocking most of his body. What I can see is bruised or scraped or both.

His head turns slowly toward the sound of the door closing behind me. I fight to hide the shock that wants to appear in response to his appearance, sure it's the last thing he needs to see.

"Hey, little brother," I say, walking deeper into the small room.

He has a window at least, and there's a chair beside the bed that I head toward.

"Will." My name is a rusty rasp, like he hasn't spoken in a long time. "You came."

There's surprise in his voice, and it hits me differently than my mom's did. Instead of anger, I feel shame.

We're close. But we don't talk every day. Or every week, even. Especially since I've been in Germany, our conversations have been sporadic.

"Of course I did." I keep my tone light as I lean over and kiss the top of his head before sinking down into the chair. It's the same fucking kind as what's out in the waiting room, unfortunately. "I'd been wanting a vacation, anyway."

Tripp rolls his eyes. Even that looks like it might be painful. The surrounding skin of one is swollen and puffy, and the other will turn into a nasty shiner.

"You must be missing stuff," he tells me. "Practice or even a game—"

I shake my head. "I'm missing nothing. This is where I want to be."

Tripp exhales. "How's Mom?"

"Worried. We both have been. She's right outside. The nurse thought both of us might be overwhelming."

"Was the nurse blonde?"

"Uh, maybe?" I can't come up with any recollection of what she looks like.

"She didn't ask you for an autograph?"

I scoff at his teasing, pretending not to notice how he winces after smiling. "She'd better just be focused on helping you heal. You scared the shit out of me, Tripp."

He nods, his expression somber. "Wasn't how I wanted you to come home."

Home. There's that damn word again. It was strange, sleeping in my childhood bed last night. It's even tinier than I remember. Even when I was sprawled out at an angle, my feet were hanging off the side of the mattress.

"How's Germany?"

"About the same as when we last talked. I'm playing pretty well."

"That's awesome, man. Who are you playing next?"

I appreciate the way he's feigning interest. Tripp has never shared my love of soccer. He's asking because he knows I care about it, not because he does. Just like Sophia.

So, instead of answering, I tell him, "I met someone."

"What? Really? Where?"

If we weren't having this conversation in a depressing hospital room, I'd laugh at his excited expression. The way he's perked up like a little kid getting candy. Tripp came out in college and has gone through a steady line of serious boyfriends ever since. His relationships have always lasted several months at least. Until Sophia, mine never lasted past a night. Me mentioning a woman to him is the equivalent of Tripp telling me he joined a futsal league.

"I met her at the team's stadium, technically. She's, uh...I don't know quite how to describe it. She's just different."

That's the only way I know how to explain the warmth in my chest when she called earlier. When I realized how worried she was. How much she cared.

"Are you actually dating her, or is it just sex?" Tripp asks.

"It's not just sex."

"Wow. I'm happy for you."

"Thanks, Tripp." I stand. Kiss the top of his head again. "Let me go grab Mom. Give her a chance to see you. We can talk more later."

Tripp nods.

I smile, squeeze his shoulder, then head for the door.

"Will."

I stop and glance back. "Yeah?"

"I can't feel my legs."

I'm frozen, experiencing the same thing. My entire body is numb. "You mean..."

"They're running tests. But, yeah, probably. They think sensation would have come back by now. You know...if it was going to."

"*Fuck*. Tripp..." I grip the back of the chair, needing something to stabilize me.

"I won't need a swivel chair when I'm treating patients, at least. Good thing I'm not studying to be a surgeon, or they'd have to put the operating table on the floor."

I swallow, still struggling to comprehend. Trying to fight

through the shock and the sadness so I can make jokes about this the way Tripp is. Not being able to walk...to *run*...I can't fucking imagine it.

"And you know I hate going to the gym, so I have a good excuse now," Tripp continues. "But if I can never get hard again and have to pee into a plastic bag for the rest of my life...that'll really suck. That's most of what the tests are for."

Jesus Christ. I didn't even consider any of that. My frozen brain hadn't gotten that far.

"I'm so sorr—"

"Don't apologize like it's your fault instead of shitty fucking luck. And don't tell Mom yet. I want to know exactly what the prognosis is first."

"Okay. I'll call Shawn, find out what my options are for getting out of my contract with Kluvberg."

"What? What the fuck are you talking about?"

"You just told me you're *paralyzed*, Tripp. You seriously think I'm going to write a *Get Well Soon* card and head back home like nothing's changed?"

"That's exactly what you're going to do. Except you can skip the card because all you ever do is scribble *Love, Will* inside."

I snort even though he's not wrong. I've never been better at written words than spoken ones.

"You're not a doctor or a physical therapist, Will. What the fuck are you going to do? Mom will already be around, hovering. I don't need you doing it too. What I need is to watch my big brother doing what he loves. What I need is for you to show that bastard in Seattle what a mistake he made. What I need is for you to go *home* and tell that girl you're in love with her because I'm positive you haven't done that yet."

I exhale. "Tripp..."

"I mean it, Will. I need to act like this is no big deal to get through this. I need *you* to act like this is no big deal to help me get through this. Mom and I were planning a surprise trip to come see you play in the spring. Except I'm maxed out on surprises now, so I guess it won't be one. But I still want to visit. I'm still going to visit, and I can't do that if you're not there."

It feels so wrong, agreeing to change nothing about my life when my brother's has just been totally upended. But I nod because I don't know what else to do. Then head out into the hallway, trying to hide the sorrow from my expression when I spot my mom. She heads inside the room, and I remain in the hallway, staring at another one of those senseless, stupid paintings on the wall.

———

"I thought I'd find you in here."

I grunt, taking a swig of the whiskey I found hidden in the bottom of one of the toolboxes I pulled out, next to a wad of cash. Nothing's changed in the garage. My mom hasn't cleared this place out in the eighteen years since my dad left us—first forced, then voluntarily.

We spent all day at the hospital with Tripp, not leaving until he was pumped so full of painkillers that he couldn't keep his eyes open. My mom made meatloaf for dinner—one of my childhood favorites—and then I came out here.

Retreated to the garage, just like my dad used to. I've been sitting on the hood of the old, dead Pontiac that's parked in here ever since. Shocked it's still here. I've stayed with Tripp the past few times I came to visit, avoiding this place for a long list of reasons. When Tripp mentioned our mom was cleaning out the house, I assumed this had been hauled away a long time ago.

"Why haven't you gotten rid of this?" I ask, nodding toward the useless muscle car. "It might be worth something. At the very least, you could get someone to haul it away for free."

"I want to keep it."

"Why? Isn't it just a reminder of—" *Dad* is right at the tip of my tongue. But I can't quite make myself say it. Not in this garage, where his memory is strongest. Where he spent the most time. Pretty sure he loved this car a hell of a lot more than he ever loved us.

"It's a reminder things can take a while to fix. But that you shouldn't stop trying."

I don't think we're talking about cars anymore.

I don't meet her gaze, focused on the chipped paint I'm sitting on instead. This is too much right now. Talking to Sophia last night and realizing how serious this thing between us has become. Relief that Tripp is alive and heartbreak about how his life has been forever altered. I can't deal with my mom and our messed-up relationship right now.

She doesn't leave, like I'm expecting. She shuts the door that connects to the rest of the house and walks closer, hauling herself up onto the hood beside me. Takes the glass bottle I'm holding, surveying the label.

"Would have been a week's worth of groceries."

"Dad was never great at sharing."

My mom makes a sound of amusement. "No, he was not."

Then, to my surprise, she tilts the bottle back and takes a sip. I've never seen her have more than the occasional glass of wine. My father didn't leave a lot of space for other people's indulgences. He was the irresponsible parent, so my mom had to shoulder all the responsibility of raising us.

"I'm going to stay for a few more days, as long as that's okay."

As far as I know, none of the tests of Tripp's motor function have come back yet. Until they do, I can't picture leaving. Hell, even once they do, I'm not sure how I'm supposed to fly back to my life. He's right that there's little I'd be able to do. But it's a level of selfishness I'm not sure I'd be able to stomach, not changing my life at all when his has been totally toppled.

"Of course that's okay, Will. This is your home."

"I hate this house," I tell her candidly.

My mom sighs. "I hate it too."

"Is it like the car? You're holding on to it out of some twisted affection?"

She sips more whiskey, then hands the bottle back to me. "Moving's a hassle."

I snort.

"And it feels important to wake up every morning and look at the place where I thought I was going to die. To wake up and be grateful that I didn't."

I still, the bottle halfway to my lips. Shock spreads slowly. We've gone eighteen years without mentioning that day. Part of me assumed that meant we would *never* discuss it.

My mom exhales. "I'm sorry, Will. I know it'll never be enough, but I am. I was in a dark place before your father left, and I went to an even darker place after he did. I made a mistake —a big, selfish one. You boys were so young, and I was so scared, and I...I've never forgotten the look on your face in the hospital. Never forgiven myself for how I pulled you into that dark place too. I thought staying, living, would show you that I knew what a mistake I'd made. That it would fade over time. Shrink in size. But it's always stayed between us, and I'm sorry about that too. I should have been braver. Should have at least *asked* if you wanted to talk about it instead of pretending it never happened."

My whole life, I've considered myself more similar to my dad. Our self-destructive personalities, our selfishness. But for the first time, I consider I might be more like my mom. Because I've made mistakes. Big ones. And I've regretted them. I've tried to make up for them.

My dad never did that. He was so self-centered he probably thought going to prison was some personal vendetta against him, and he did the opposite of asking for forgiveness after getting released.

"I don't know what to say," I admit.

This has been a mindfuck of a day, to put it mildly. It feels like I've been spun around in a circle and the whiskey isn't helping.

"You don't have to say anything, honey. I just needed you to hear it."

I nod a couple of times. Blow out a long breath. Then, I reach out and grab my mom's hand, squeezing it three times. It was our secret language when I was little, when my dad was yelling or raging. A quick, *I love you*, or, *It'll be okay*, or, *Do not worry*. It's why I tap my thigh three times before every shot.

It calms me, cuts through the noise, no matter what else is going on.

She squeezes my hand three times back.

"I'm glad—" I clear my throat. "I'm really glad you woke up, Mom."

There's a quiet sniffle, and I know she's crying. I keep my

eyes forward, at the closed door of the garage, giving her a little privacy. Letting her have a moment. Hating the sight of this garage a little less.

Because it feels like I just got some small piece of my child-hood—of my mom—back.

CHAPTER THIRTY-THREE

SOPHIA

There's a knock as I'm pouring coffee into a travel cup.

"Coming!" I call out, capping the cup, licking some creamer off my thumb, and then heading for the door.

Will is standing in the hallway, an exhausted expression on his face and a duffel bag slung over one shoulder.

I still the second I see him, the fact that he's actually here taking a moment to sink in.

"Hey." My voice comes out funny, so I quickly clear my throat.

"You got bangs."

"Yeah." I finger the shorter strands covering my forehead. "Wanted to try something different. What—what do you think?"

"You always look gorgeous, Sophia."

My heart does a strange pitter-patter when I register the sincerity in his voice. He sounds *so* tired, but sincere.

"Can I come in?"

"You don't usually ask for permission." I step aside so he can, shutting the door behind him.

Will half-smiles in response, but it collapses quickly.

We've texted back and forth in the week he's been gone, but he never mentioned a return date or told me when he was flying back here.

Will drops his bag on the floor, runs a hand through his hair, and then turns to face me. Apprehension rushes through me in response to his serious expression, joining the warmth that accompanies the realization that he came straight here from the airport.

"You packed light." I nod toward the bag, which is sagging flat now that it's off his shoulder.

"I didn't pack at all. Brought this back from my mom's. Some old stuff I forgot I had."

"How's Tripp?"

Last Will told me, his brother was awake, but the doctors were still running lots of tests to determine the full extent of his injuries.

"He's...he's alive, which is the most important thing. But, uh, he'll never walk again." He looks away, out the window. Toward Boston maybe. "So, uh, I don't even know if I've processed that yet. The whole time I was there, I was trying to pretend things were okay. It's hitting me more now that I don't have to worry what he's seeing on my face. He'll have to relearn how to live his whole life."

I suck in a deep breath. I figured it was bad. If Tripp's injuries had been minor, Will would have come back sooner. But I had no idea it was that serious. That permanent.

"Do you want a hug?" I ask. It's the only thing I can think to offer him.

Will looks at me, one corner of his mouth curving up a tiny bit. "Yeah. A hug sounds great."

I step into him, wrapping my arms tightly around his waist.

He smells like fast food and exhaust fumes. But beneath it... Will. Grass and laundry detergent.

His grip on me is just as tight as mine is on him. Tighter maybe, fusing our bodies so closely together that you couldn't slip a piece of paper between us.

"I'm so sorry about your brother," I whisper.

"Thanks."

"Is there...is there anything I can do?"

"You're doing it," he tells me.

I relax into him even more.

I'm glad he went home. Glad he saw his mom and was there for his brother. But I'm so, so happy he's back. I didn't realize how many cracks in my life he'd filled, until they all reappeared in his absence.

"I missed you," I whisper.

I feel his chest heave with an exhale before he pulls back just enough to look at me.

"I've been fighting this—us—because I'm concerned about the future. My future in soccer—I mean, football."

I can't even muster a proud smile when he self-corrects. I'm too caught up in what he's saying, where this could possibly be going.

"Your future with another guy, someone who would be a hell of a lot better for you than I am. And I realized..." He swallows. "I realized, when I was sitting in a hospital in Boston, that worrying about the future assumes there will *be* a future. I've done a lot of things I regret, Sophia. But I know—I *know*—that fighting this will be my biggest one. So...I want you to know that I'm in. I'm all in with this thing between us."

There are questions I could ask him in response. If he's still planning to return to the States after this season ends if an

American team wants to sign him. If he's okay with telling my brother about us, knowing it could affect his relationship with his teammates. If his brother's injury means he wants to leave here even more.

But those are all external forces, some of which neither of us has any control over.

What I have complete control over is my feelings for him. Telling him what those feelings are.

"I'm pretty sure I'm in love with you."

He tilts his head, his expression a mixture of surprise and amusement. "Pretty sure?"

"Yeah. Pretty sure. I've never been in love with anyone before, so I'm not totally sure what it feels like. But this..." My voice lowers, turning into a whisper. I've been vulnerable in front of Will many times. Sharing this with him is stripping myself bare.

He's held the power to hurt me for a long time. But admitting it to him is almost unbearably intimate.

"I think this is it. When you're not here, I think about you. When I'm not talking to you, I wish I were talking to you. When I'm not touching you, I wish I were touching you. So...I'm in love with you. I love you, Will."

His expression softens, the worried lines in his forehead completely easing. My body relaxes in response.

"I'm not great with words or talking about how I'm feeling. I thought part of it was how I grew up, never having a great example of what a healthy relationship was supposed to look like. But Tripp has never had that issue, so maybe it was just an excuse." His fingers find my chin, and he tilts my head back slightly, rubbing his thumb back and forth just below my lower lip. "I was *pretty sure* I was falling in love with you when you got hit by that football. But I was completely certain when my mom called me about Tripp. There are two times I've left a game when I should've been on the field. Once for my little brother and once for you. If you needed me, there's not a fucking thing that could keep me from getting to you, including a football game."

My eyes feel hot and prickly, moisture gathering in the corners. I'm not normally a crier. But Will telling me he loves me? That makes me want to sob from happiness.

I sniffle. "I needed you that day. I was just mad that you ran over. That you were acting like you cared after telling me you didn't want me."

"Wanting you has never been the problem, baby. I promise." Gently, his thumb moves higher, catching one of the tears that escaped my eye. His tender expression turns teasing. "Do you need me to show you how much I want you?"

"Aren't you tired?" I ask.

He must have flown overnight to be here this early.

Will chuckles, low and husky. His hands are already roaming, igniting nerve endings everywhere. "I'd have to be in a damn coma to be too tired to fuck you. Even then, I could probably still get hard."

I scoff, but it's quickly silenced by warm lips covering mine. Will lifts me up in his arms, walking us into my bedroom. I might be late for class, but this will absolutely be worth it.

He lays me down onto the mattress, and then his hot tongue is demanding entrance to my mouth again, skillfully finding mine. His hands slip under my shirt. Shivers skate across my skin as his palms brush over my stomach and up past my rib cage.

The bra I'm wearing is flimsy lace, decorative with little

function. It feels like there's no barrier between his hands and my boobs as he cups them, the heat of his skin searing into mine. The part of me that feels like it's been missing since he left snaps back into place, a warm, content glow burning bright in the center of my chest. His body covers mine completely, the firm planes pressed against me protectively.

His thumbs find my nipples, using the lace to rub them into hard points.

I moan into his mouth, surrendering completely. My body is melting into the mattress, turning into a pool of lust beneath him. I lift my hips, seeking the delicious friction of his cock.

"*Fuck*, I missed you." He kisses a line down the side of my neck, his hot tongue sucking the skin in a few spots.

I moan when he discovers a particularly sensitive spot. Or maybe he didn't find it. Maybe he knew it was already there. "Me, or my mouth and pussy?"

"All of you," he replies, tugging the front of my shirt down until the lace of my bra is visible. "I missed all of you. You make me forget about all the bad shit." He kisses the curve of my breast, then slides a hand down to the waistband of my shorts. "I wish you'd been there, in Boston." He tugs at the button of my shorts until the fabric gives way, allowing him access to my underwear. "I told Tripp about you."

"You did?"

Talking is becoming increasingly challenging. I don't know what to focus on—what he's saying or how incredible it feels to have him touching me again. I became addicted to this in an alarmingly short amount of time. I crave Will more than I thought was possible. Knowing he loves me heightens sensations that were already overwhelming.

"Mmhmm."

I gasp when his fingers stretch me, the feeling less foreign but still shocking. Will grunts, exploring how ready I am for him. I think of him every time I touch myself now, but it's never the same. He knows my body better than I do. Owns it in a way no one else ever will.

Electricity sparks across my senses. Pulsing and powerful, like a tangible presence between us.

Will sits up and pulls me into his lap.

Our faces are so close that I can't see all of his.

"I love you, Sophia," he tells me.

The warmth in my chest flares, burning brighter and hotter. Expanding until it feels like it's too large for my body to contain. Too much to bear in the best way.

My hips rock against his. I can feel him between my thighs, thick and hard. Thickening. Hardening. The throbbing between my legs is growing to an unbearable ache. My pussy is heavy and swollen, desperate to be filled.

"I love you," I say, pushing my fingers into his hair so it's off his forehead. Testing the words. Tasting them in this moment that they've never been a part of.

I've told my family I love them. Friends, usually while drunk, departing from bars. But never a guy. Never in the romantic sense.

"Tell me in German."

"*Ich liebe dich.*"

"*Ich liebe dich,*" Will repeats. Then again, his lips brushing my shoulder as he whispers the words against my skin like a secret meant only for me.

My hands dip beneath the hem of his cotton T-shirt, lifting the fabric and revealing the carved muscles beneath. I run my fingers over the stacks of muscle, memorizing each dip and groove all over again. An endless spread of warm golden skin, covering muscles so harshly defined that you could hurt yourself on them.

I lean back on my heels, looking at him. Mussed hair. Exposed abs. Big bulge. He's so *masculine*, an urge that's primal and feral tugging low in my stomach as I stare at him. "You're really hot."

Will laughs, a ragged rasp that settles in my stomach. That tells me how much I'm affecting him. "Is that what put *pretty sure* over the top?"

"I was sure. I just...I didn't know how you'd react."

His expression turns serious. "I haven't done this before."

He rubs his thumb across my lower lip, my awareness narrowing to that one spot where he's touching me. His other hand leaves its spot on my hip, drifting down to my knee and then back up again. Only this time, he doesn't go over the material of my shorts; he slips under it. My heartbeat races as he draws nearer to the apex of my thighs, setting each spot he touches ablaze. It feels like liquid heat is flowing through my veins, flushing my skin and burning away oxygen. My breathing turns choppy and is embarrassingly fast.

"I haven't either," I manage to say. Something he knows, yet feels important to say.

"I want all your firsts, Sophia. You're *mine*."

My moan is loud, the combination of his possessive words and his intimate touch a heady cocktail.

Will's eyes darken to a shade of green that's nearly black as he takes in my reactions. My hips are moving against his hand, but I need more than his fingers.

I lean forward and close the gap between our mouths again. When I bite down gently on his bottom lip, he groans, sliding his hand from my chin into my hair and angling my head. Will kisses the same way he does everything else—skilled and confident. Aggressive yet controlled. It shocks my system like a shot of adrenaline, except a thousand times more powerful. Everything builds between us—the urgency, the desire, the want.

The perfect sort of numbness spreads. I'm unaware of anything else. Drowning in desire and breathing in him.

And then he's pushing inside of me from a deeper, different angle. My gasp is startled, surprise quickly ebbing into pleasure. I'm so wet I can hear him working in and out of my body. Will's pace is steady, but not rushed. My body adjusts, meeting each thrust.

His lips move to my neck, caressing and nipping and sucking at the skin. I feel on display in the best way. Like I'm the main attraction and the only focus. I can feel the pressure tightening and strengthening. Building and forming. Simmering and spreading.

He's a high I never want to come down from.

But every fall has a landing.

CHAPTER THIRTY-FOUR

WILL

Wagner obviously made some sort of announcement to the entire team about my absence because I catch a lot of sympathetic looks during my first practice back. None of my teammates mention anything to me about it directly, just some version of how it's nice to see me or they're glad to have me back. I'm relieved by the slight detachment. I'm not close enough to any of them to talk about my family, and I don't want their respect because I left to see my injured brother. I want to earn it on the field.

Even Beck offers me a smile when he spots me instead of sticking with his typical stoicism, which makes me feel a little guilty about how I'm secretly sleeping with his sister. The *secret* part makes it seem like Sophia is something I'm ashamed of, that we're something to be ashamed of, and I hate that. Sophia is no longer a choice. She's woven so deeply into my life it's nearly impossible to remember what it looked like without her in it. She's worth any consequences Beck might throw at me. But I'm still apprehensive about what those might be. Sophia hasn't brought up me remeeting her family members, and I've been focused on getting resettled in Kluvberg and checking in with Tripp ever since I returned to Germany.

Tripp's out of the hospital now, at a rehab center that's supposed to be the best in Boston. He protested when I paid for it, until I told him it was either I pay or I move back to Boston. After that, he didn't raise any more complaints about me footing the bill.

Practice ends, and it's a relief. The summer heat has faded, but I'm still drenched with sweat. I didn't work out once while I was gone, and it's been a rough transition back to the exhausting regimen here. Plus, I have better places to be. I'm not headed home to an empty apartment.

Fritz asks me if I want to grab a beer once we're in the locker room. Since I begged off last time and have been gone for the past week, I agree, even though I'd really just like to head straight to Sophia's apartment like I was planning to. I text her, letting her know I'll be late, then head out with Fritz. Olivier and a couple of midfielders end up joining us. It's fun and relaxed, a dynamic similar to what it was like with my team-mates in Seattle. An easiness I wasn't sure I'd ever experience here. They rib me about ignoring the women approaching our table until they're occupied themselves.

I leave as early as I can without seeming rude. In Seattle, I never had anyone to go home to. Anyone I was missing.

Sophia's already in bed when I let myself into her place.

It's past eleven, but none of the other guys seemed likely to head out soon. It'll be interesting to see how they fare during practice tomorrow. I drink a glass of water and then head into her bedroom. Sophia's not asleep yet, clicking through photos on her laptop with an adorable furrow creasing her forehead.

"Hey."

"Hey." She glances up. "How were drinks with the guys?" She beams like a proud mom, asking me that.

I roll my eyes. "Fine."

I strip, then head into the bathroom to brush my teeth. When I return to the bedroom, she's closed her laptop.

"Really? It was fun?"

"Yeah." I climb into bed, tucking one arm behind my head.

Sophia leans over to kiss me, then wrinkles her nose. "You smell like perfume."

"Must be Fritz's."

She snorts. "He has expensive taste."

"He did pick the bar. Cost me twenty euro for the beer he recommended."

A scoff this time. But nothing else. No teasing mention of my salary.

I roll my head to the side, staring at her profile. "Yes, there were women there. Yes, they were wearing perfume. But I didn't touch a single one of them. Didn't even talk to them. That's nothing you ever have to worry about."

She's still staring at the ceiling, instead of me.

"What's wrong?" I ask.

"Nothing. I'm glad you're settling in with the team more."

"Sophia, just say what you're really thinking."

She exhales. "You're only signed for one season. You only want to stay for one season. And I just...selfishly, I'm hoping that'll change."

I knew this conversation was coming, and I've been dreading it.

"I don't have complete control over my contract," I tell her. "There's still a lot of the season left. Whether Kluvberg wants to keep me...whether another team wants to sign me...there's a little I have a say in and a lot that I don't."

"I know."

"When I told you returning to the US was my first choice—that was before us. This isn't temporary to me. But...it's a discussion we'll need to have, once I know what the options are. Until I retire, there will be unknowns about where I play."

"I know," she repeats.

She *knows*, but I'm not sure if she's okay with it. She told me she doesn't like change, that permanence is one of the things that drew her to photography.

"I wouldn't just pick up and leave." *Like I did to come here.* My contract was the one thing holding me to Seattle. I'm more tightly tied to Germany than I ever imagined being, all because of her. "*Sophia.*"

Finally, she looks at me. The uncertainty on her face stalls the breath in my chest. I never want her looking like that when she's focused on me. I want her to see me as solid and safe, not shaky.

"You, uh, you like it, right?" she asks. "The sex?"

I blink, stunned. I thought we were discussing my complicated soccer career. The change in topic throws me, the shift in subject to sex even more unexpected. "What?"

"I know you...come, but is there other stuff you're wanting to do? Like, I don't know...but if you did know, would you tell me? Stuff you used to do or like to do or...something?"

I blink again. Say, "What?" again.

She sighs. "Never mind."

I sit up. "What are you talking about?"

"I just...I know you're more experienced. I want to make sure you're still...enjoying it."

"You think I'm *not enjoying sex with you*?"

Where the hell is she getting this from? I come harder and faster with her than I ever have with anyone else, and I thought how often we have sex made it obvious how attracted I am to her.

"No. I don't know. It's different for guys, right? I just didn't know..." Her voice trails off, and I want to shake whatever she's trying to say out of her.

"I have *no idea* what you're talking about. What's different for me?"

Her cheeks pinken as she studies the ceiling. "I went out for drinks with some friends after you texted, saying you'd be later, and they were talking about different guys they'd been with and different stuff they'd done and..." She exhales. "You're the only guy I've been with, so I could be bad in bed and not know, and I know you have lots to compare this to, and I just...you're used to something else. I don't want you to be unsatisfied." The last sentence is quiet. Followed by a fresh flame of red in her cheeks. "Forget it. Turn off the light. Let's go to bed."

Yeah, right.

I roll over so I'm hovering above her. "It was before you, Sophia. All of it. I wasn't *satisfied*. I was bored. I didn't know this existed. Wasn't aware you were out there. I can't compare you to anyone else because it's never been like this for me before. I thought ending up here was a punishment—turns out it was the best thing that could've happened to me. I only have to think about you, and I'm hard, Sophia. These pouty lips ..." I trace her lower lip with my thumb. "These tits ..." I cup one. "This perfect pussy ..." I lower my hips, letting her feel my growing erection. "I've *never* wanted a woman the way I want you. I love you. This isn't just sex to me, but it's the best fucking sex I've ever had."

She searches my face, testing my sincerity.

"I won't lie to you," I tell her. "Never. If you want to know anything, just ask me. I'll be honest, always. I worked hard during practice earlier because I'm hoping Kluvberg will consider keeping me. Those women wearing perfume earlier? All I could think about was coming back here and getting in bed with you."

"You promise?"

"I promise."

I study the face that's become so familiar to me. The features I've memorized.

Sophia has two freckles below her left eye. A dimple on her right cheek. A thin, short scar in the center of her chin.

"If you need me to fuck you until you believe you're the best sex I've ever had, I'm fully prepared to do that."

She smiles, some of the tension finally relaxing. Her hand rises, tracing my jaw and then my lower lip. "I want to be with you, and I want to be enough for you."

I lean down and kiss her. "We'll figure the first one out, and you never have to worry about the second one."

Leaving Kluvberg at the end of this season is no longer the ideal outcome. Playing well this season is an incentive because it means they'd consider keeping me, not only so I look like a worthwhile risk to American teams.

A thought that's been in the back of my mind for weeks. Sophia's fears have pushed it front and center, reminding me my decisions don't only affect me any longer.

It feels like a monumental realization to have.

Most of my life, I've been selfish. I've never had anyone relying on me or expecting anything.

Everything is different now.

Because I can't imagine anything worse than letting Sophia down.

CHAPTER THIRTY-FIVE

SOPHIA

I click through the last ten shots, making sure at least a couple of them are good options. More like six of them.

I glance up at Otto, nod, and smile. "You're all set. Thanks."

It's not until Otto responds in German that I realize I spoke to him in English. It's become second nature from spending so much time around Will.

Plus, I'm distracted right now. I've kept track of every player who's been sent in here, and there's only one left.

Hopefully, Otto will discount any giddiness as nerves or excitement about today's assignment.

I'm sure Adler had some part in getting me this gig—taking portraits of this season's team. I'm sure someone on Kluvberg's immense staff was responsible for this task in the past and is probably resentful of my role now.

But if I'm stuck with the disadvantages of being a Beck, I've decided I might as well enjoy the perks as well. And these are the official photos. They'll be displayed around the stadium. On the team's website. On the Jumbotron during the games. Maybe they're not the thought-provoking, curated photographs I'd like to be known for, but they're shots that thousands of people will look at. And that's the primary objective of most artists—to be seen. To have people witness your work.

I still haven't gotten an official offer to join the *Neues Kluvberg* staff, and I figure any publicity this garners can't hurt.

Otto leaves with a final friendly smile. Aside from Will and Adler, he's the player I know best on the team. Practically a second brother.

I busy myself with adjusting the equipment unnecessarily until the door opens again.

I feel the shift in energy immediately. Know it's him without turning around. Before warm lips graze the back of my neck, taking advantage of the high ponytail my hair is pulled up in.

"This is highly unprofessional." There's no incrimination in my voice, though. Just breathiness.

"You're the one with the job that involves taking photos of half-naked men."

"Everyone..."

His lips travel to my collarbone, sucking gently on the juncture of my neck and shoulder. I struggle to recall what I was saying, complete thoughts slipping away like water through cupped hands.

"Everyone's kept their clothes on."

"So far." Will's hand lands on my thigh, heat burning through the silk dress I'm wearing.

It looked professional in the mirror this morning. He watched me put it on.

His palm creeps up my thigh. I inhale sharply, the slow simmer of arousal spreading across my skin. How he affects me this much—this easily—I'll never understand. Plenty of guys I photographed today were objectively attractive. But this electricity is unique to Will. An awareness that hasn't diminished with repeated exposure.

"We can't do this here."

We're in the team's locker room. There's a sign on the door, telling people not to come in and interrupt the photo sessions taking place, but that doesn't mean no one will.

"Do you want to?"

"Yes," I admit.

He promised he'd always be honest with me, and I'm just as transparent.

He laughs lightly, then steps away. The spot where he's supposed to stand in front of the screen has been marked by a black X taped to the floor. Will walks over to it and turns, waiting for me.

My motions are clumsy as I pick up the camera, remnants of arousal humming in my blood.

Will looks totally unaffected as he picks up the football on the floor and tucks in under his left arm, wearing his Kluvberg uniform and a devilish half smirk I already know means his photo will receive the most views of all that I've taken today. The shutter clicks over and over again as I try not to notice the intensity in his gaze. The way it burns through the barrier of the camera and seems to penetrate my soul.

I lower the camera, flipping through the photos with the same cursory look that I did with every other player. Most of the guys required adjustments, suggested changes in stance or expression. I'm not surprised Will nailed the first try.

"All set," I say.

"Great." Will pulls his shirt over his head, then tugs down his shorts.

"*Will*," I hiss, glancing at the closed door.

No one has come in during any of the other sessions. But still...we're in Kluvberg's *stadium*. Both here for jobs.

When I look back at him, he's sitting on the bench that lines the front of the old lockers. Totally naked, his impressive physique on display and his dick half hard. It twitches under my gaze.

"Come here, Sophia."

God, that voice. That husky, commanding tone that narrates my fantasies.

Will's infected my body to the point that I don't know how I'd ever separate him out, even if I wanted to. This shouldn't be happening here. And there's a tantalizing thrill to the forbidden, a temptation far more powerful than caution.

I toss a worried look at the door, then obey. He's stroking himself now, his huge hand moving up and down the engorged length of his cock. His thighs are spread as he lounges with all the casual confidence of a king on a throne, watching me approach.

"I locked the door," he tells me. "Don't worry."

I am worried, but not about me. No one knows about us.

Will's been focused on football and keeping in close touch with his brother as Tripp continues to recover from the accident. He also talks to his mom a couple of times a week, encouraging the improvements in their relationship that appeared during his visit to Boston. I've had a flurry of new assignments at the paper, and I still have to decide what photo to submit to the EPAs before the deadline next week.

Will chose me over football, regardless of the consequences. But that's much easier to do when there haven't been any. I want to tell my family about our relationship, but I have no idea how they'll react. I'm not confident my dad or Adler wouldn't leap to conclusions and decide Will was taking advantage of me and use their connections to affect his career.

It's easy to forget about all that as I walk over to Will.

But I still feel guilty, realizing he's risking everything and I'm risking nothing.

I know exactly how our relationship would be portrayed publicly. Will, the troublemaker and womanizer. Me, the naive victim.

But I've been that before. And it felt nothing like this. I know Will, and I know he would never take advantage of me in any way.

"Hey." His fingers are on my chin, tilting my face so I have no choice except to look at him. Not letting me hide. "What's wrong?"

"Nothing."

I glance at the door. My other sessions lasted about fifteen minutes, and I have no idea how much time has passed since he walked in.

Will's presence removes things like time and logic and reason. And he might have locked the door, but if anyone discovers that, it'll result in questions. Eyebrows I'd rather not get raised.

"Sophia." His tone is flinty now. Bossy in a different way than his commands earlier.

"You're risking more," I blurt. "You and me...when people find out...you're risking more."

I don't want to share any similarities with the woman who forced Will's move here. But I know there's a major one. That our association will cause more problems for him. And I hate that.

"My decision to make," Will tells me. "Remember?"

Before I can respond, he's pulling me down into his lap and yanking my underwear to the side, and there's the stimulating surge as he stretches me open.

Suddenly, there's only this. The slight burn as my body adjusts. The dark possessiveness as Will watches where our bodies are joined, seeing me take him. The promise of pleasure as he pushes deeper, hitting a specific spot that makes heat unfurl in my abdomen.

"The only thing I want you to worry about is staying silent," he says.

My fingernails dig into his shoulders as the pressure builds, his hands on my hips guiding my movements. No matter how many times we have sex, my body manages to forget how huge and deep he feels, filling me so there's no space for anything else. Everything about the way he's fucking me is skilled and confident. Forcing me to absorb the shock of each upward thrust, to drown in the consuming pleasure of it. No hesitation. No stutter like he's second-guessing.

Euphoria soars through my veins.

I had no idea sex—intimacy—would feel like this. I'm floating and falling. Aware of everything and feeling one thing. Breathing becomes hard. Everything starts to feel detached. All I can focus on is the sensation of him pounding me, the friction that's both natural and otherworldly.

We both come quickly. I press my mouth against his shoulder to muffle the sound of my moans. I'm still breathing heavily as I stand and adjust my outfit, my legs shaky. I'm so sensitive, each small motion a reminder of what just happened.

"Not a bad day at work, right?" Will teases as he pulls his shorts up.

He grabs the football before his shirt, bouncing it on one

knee. Kluvberg jerseys hang on the wall behind him, ready and waiting for tomorrow's match.

"Wait," I say as he leans down to grab his shirt. "One last photo."

Most guys would probably question it. Get self-conscious.

Will Aster is not most guys.

He remains in place as I grab my camera, holding the ball loosely against his side. The waistband of his shorts hangs low, showing off the impressive topography of his chest. He glances at me, and the shudder clicks in rapid succession. And I know, without looking at the result, that these will be some of my favorite photos I've ever taken.

Photography is all about emotion, and this picture is brimming with it. The focus on Will's expression, the harsh edges of his muscles, the coiled power of a predator about to strike—they're all captivating.

Not that I'm biased.

I smile. "Got it."

CHAPTER THIRTY-SIX

WILL

I'm in the middle of unpacking when my phone buzzes in my pocket. We're in London for a Champions League match, the first time I've ever been to England. The first time I've been anywhere in Europe, aside from Germany.

It's Sophia.

I glance at Fritz—I'm bunking with him on this trip, thanks to a last-minute mix-up about the number of rooms needed—who's sprawled out on his bed, busy scrolling on his phone. We just got back from dinner, which was a long meal. It's already almost midnight.

"Hey," I answer.

"Hey. You made it."

She knows I did. I texted her when we landed, and the fact that she's still calling makes me wish Fritz wasn't ten feet away and I could talk without thinking twice about what I'm saying. Makes me smile, knowing she called just to hear my voice before falling asleep.

"Yeah. It was a pretty easy trip." The first time I've traveled outside of Germany with the club, and it was on a private jet.

"I miss you." Her voice dips low, seductive and teasing.

Fuck. I recognize that tone, and hate hearing it when I'm this far away from her.

"Soph—Stop."

Fritz glances over, then away. Curious but not suspicious.

She giggles in my ear. "Don't you miss me too?"

I head into the bathroom, making sure the door is shut tight behind me. "You know I do. You also know I'm bunking with Fritz, because I mentioned it in my text."

Sophia hums. She's in bed. I can tell from the rustle of fabric in the background.

"Are you touching yourself?"

"Maybe."

"*Sophia.*"

"Why do you think I called you? I wanted to hear your voice as I..."

She lets out a breathy moan, and the loose fabric of my sweatpants isn't enough to contain my hardening dick. It strains against the soft material, leaving me with the options of either walking back into the room with a huge hard-on or taking care of this while I'm on the phone with Sophia.

I opt for option two.

"Don't you dare come," I tell her, opening the glass shower door and turning on the spray. For the sound and because I'm probably going to need to rinse off after this. "Not yet."

I switch my phone to my left hand and then tug the band of my sweatpants down with my right one.

"Are you jerking off right now?"

"Working on it." I fist my throbbing erection, the skin pulled tight and burning hot. "Tell me exactly what you're doing."

"I'm touching myself."

"Specifics, Sophia. Are your fingers in your pussy or rubbing your clit?"

"My clit. I'm pretending you're sucking it, but you keep pulling away because you don't want me to come until you're inside of me."

Jesus, fuck.

She's too good at this. *Way* too good at this. I can picture exactly what she's describing, teasing her until she's desperate for my dick.

"How would you want it? Hard and fast, or slow and sweet?"

"Hard and fast," she gasps. "Oh God, Will. I'm so close."

I can hear the slick sound of her fingers. Her rapid breaths. Imagine exactly how she looks, legs spread and pink pussy glistening.

I'm not there. But it's so easy to imagine I am. How she smells, how she tastes—it's all imprinted in my brain now. She moans again, and my dick swells even more, growing longer in my hand. Blood is rushing to my cock so fast that I feel dizzy, the haze of pleasure overtaking everything else.

My cock is fully erect, pre-cum beaded at the tip. My balls are drawn up high and tight, not even caring they're about to empty into a tissue instead of her tight cunt. My grip tightens, beating off so hard that she can probably hear me too.

"If I were there, I'd be inside of you. Watching you spread around me. You always take me so well, squeeze me so tight until I'm pumping you full of my cum—"

She's coming, her moans and pants and my name pushing me over the edge too. The pressure at the base of my spine explodes, heat zinging along every nerve ending as my cock swells and jerks, white ropes of cum coating my hand then dripping on the floor. I grab some tissues from the box by the toilet, using them to clean up the mess.

I'm still breathing heavily when I toss the tissues in the trash, gripping the cool marble edge of the counter surrounding the sink as my racing heartbeat starts to slow to a normal rhythm.

"Fuck. I need a shower."

"I'd lick you clean if I were there."

I groan as I kick off my sweatpants. "You're gonna get me hard again."

"Sorry."

She doesn't sound the least bit sorry. She sounds happy. Satisfied.

I grab the edge of the counter again, tightening my hold as I deliberate how—if—I should bring this up. I decided against it, until she called.

Sophia speaks before I can. "I submitted my photo to the EPAs."

"Yeah? Which one did you pick?"

She narrowed it down to three last night, two from the national park where we had gone hiking last weekend. I'd carried her camera equipment for most of the trip, and my shoulder is still sore.

"The one of the park, in the Nature category."

"That's awesome, Soph. Congrats."

"Thanks."

"We're playing Manchester tomorrow," I blurt with absolutely no preamble.

"I mean, I knew that since you're in London."

A pause, where neither of us say anything.

I clear my throat. "Is it the same guy?"

The star player on Manchester right now is a German—named Ansel Fischer.

Another pause. A long pause that tells me the answer before she speaks. "It doesn't matter."

My grip tightens on the marble even more. "The fuck it doesn't."

"It *doesn't*. It was a long time ago. I'm over it. Over him."

I exhale. "Okay."

"I mean it, Will. I don't want you to do anything. Let it go."

"It's a contact sport. Remember how getting hit with a soccer ball felt? I kick harder than anyone on Bayern Söhn, and sometimes, kicks can be unpredictable."

Her exhale almost sounds amused. "If you get a red card, no sex for a week."

"That's a punishment for you too, baby."

"Because I *mean it*. I want you to win. But he's not worth you getting injured or penalized."

"I said okay."

"Promise me, Will."

Dammit. She knows me too well. Knows I won't break a promise, not to her.

"I promise I won't do anything stupid."

"Okay." She sounds satisfied. "Good luck tomorrow."

"I love you."

I can hear the smile in her voice. "I love you too."

I hang up, then step into the shower.

———

"Where've you been?" Fritz asks when I walk into our shared hotel room the following morning.

I hold up the coffee I'm carrying. "Got a tattoo."

"You *what*? Where?"

I turn my wrist so he can see the numbers and letter there. The skin surrounding them is still pink. I'll have to cover it with a bandage before the match.

"*Three hundred thirty-six. E. Four*," Fritz reads. "What does that mean? Some sort of code?"

I ignore the question as I drain the rest of my cup and grab my soccer bag. "You ready to go?"

"Yeah. I was just waiting on you."

I nod, making sure I have everything before we leave the room and head for the elevators. Most of the team has already boarded the coach bus that's waiting. It's a short trip to Manchester United's stadium.

The sky is gray and gloomy as we disembark, almost ominous-looking. England's infamous rain appears imminent. The grim backdrop makes it easy to get lost in my own head until we're on the field, warming up, my entire body humming with the anticipation of an upcoming game. All soccer fields look the same, no matter where in the world they're located. A piece of home scattered across the entire globe.

I'm stretching my hamstrings when a guy with light-brown hair jogs by, calling out something in German I'm certain is an insult based on the bristling all around me. Otto shouts something back. I know I'll see *Fischer* on the back of his maroon jersey even before he turns.

I'd hate him no matter what. I hate him even more, catching the flash of a smug smirk.

"Watch out for Ansel," Beck advises beside me. "He's a bit of a dick."

"So I've heard," I mutter.

"What?"

"Some of the other guys were saying the same thing," I say.

Beck nods, believing me. I understand why Sophia never told her brother what happened, and I'd never betray her confidence by telling him myself. But I wish he knew, if only because I know there would be no *but* about it. That he'd be just as focused on decimating Manchester's star as is my motivation for this game.

I want to win, like always.

But I also want to embarrass them in their home stadium. For there to be no question at all who is the superior team.

From that one glimpse I caught of him and the one night Sophia told me about, I'm confident Ansel is the inferior man, not just the worse player. Planning to record a woman during sex without her knowledge isn't just abhorrent. It tells me that he never appreciated or adored Sophia the way she deserves. You couldn't do that to someone you like, much less love.

The captains meet for the coin toss. Manchester wins it, opting to take the kick-off. In a happy coincidence, Ansel gains possession of the ball quickly. I barrel toward him, immediately challenging him. I haven't forgotten my promise to Sophia. I'm not going to cross any lines. Give him the beating he deserves, the sort I learned how to deliver in Boston's back alleys. I'm positive Ansel Fischer is the same exact breed of rich and entitled asshole that used to tease Tripp until I taught them how to shut up.

I'm not going to take this as far as I could—as I want to. But I'm still going to make this the most difficult game Ansel has ever played in. Not only is he going to lose, but he's going to lose badly.

I steal the ball from him, jamming my elbow into his ribs and hearing his harsh exhale.

When I spin and get a glimpse of his expression, it's confused. He has no clue why I'm coming after him, and that pisses me off even more. He should have lots of regrets. But he's probably like my dad, disregarding them.

I sprint away, leaving Ansel behind and heading straight for the goal.

We beat Manchester, four goals to one.

CHAPTER THIRTY-SEVEN

SOPHIA

To: sbeck@universitätrhein.de
From: admin@europeanphotoawards.org
Subject: Category Reassignment

Dear Ms. Beck,

This email is to notify you that your submission to the Nature category for this year's awards was moved to the Sports category after review. No further action is required on your part.

Sincerely,
Adele Allard
Chairwoman of the European Photography Awards

My heart drops into my stomach as soon as I read the first line of the email. Frantically, I scroll through my sent messages until I reach the one confirming my EPA submission.

I didn't send the photo of the stone bridge I'd intended to submit.

Instead, I sent in the photo I took of Will after the official team portraits. Probably because it's one I stare at a lot. It came out even better than I had expected, overflowing with intensity, but it was not the photo that was supposed to be my submission. It's rough and raw, not the precise photo that was supposed to showcase all that I know about sunlight and angles. I took a hundred versions of the photo I planned to send in. One of Will.

I quickly look up the public number for the EPAs and dial it on my phone, praying under my breath as I listen to it ring. I can't be the first person who made this mistake, right? Or maybe I am. I waited until the last possible second, pressing Submit right before midnight, when I was tired and stressed.

"Hello?" a woman answers.

"Hello. I'm calling because I just received an email that my submission to the awards was moved to a different category. When I looked up what I'd submitted, I realized that it was not the photo I'd intended to send. I'd like to replace it with the correct submission?"

"What's your name, ma'am?"

"Sophia Beck."

An ominous pause.

"Miss Beck, I'm sorry, but all submissions are final."

Panic swamps me. "I understand that's your policy, but I need you to make an exception. The photo I submitted was not the one I'd meant to. It was a mistake."

"There was a very small window when that could have been rectified," the woman responds. "We receive thousands of submissions, and judging has already entered the third round. If we allowed photographers to swap out their submissions this late, we would have to redo hundreds of hours of review that has already taken place. Especially in this instance."

"What do you mean, especially in this instance?"

A sigh. "Changing your submission would affect the process, Ms. Beck."

A lightning bolt of excitement races through me when I register her meaning. If it would affect the process, that means my photo is still under consideration. *I made it to the third round.* There are five rounds before finalists are announced. Halfway is a lot further than I anticipated making it.

"Would you like me to remove your photograph from consideration?" the woman asks.

My excitement dims a little, remembering the reason I called in the first place.

"Uh, no. Thanks for your help."

"Have a good day."

The woman hangs up. I set my phone down slowly, staring at the photo on the screen, undecided about what to do next. Taking photos of football was one thing when it was an assignment for my internship. But the EPAs were supposed to be my shot at proving my worth as a serious photographer. About pursuing a career with no connection to sports. It's ironic—the story of my life, really—that I thwarted my own efforts.

And then there's the unfortunate fact that if I possibly manage to make it to the finals, that intimate photo of Will would be released with my name attached.

———

Will's in a great mood when he comes over. Kluvberg beat Manchester United, four to one. An impressive, dominant performance by any measure.

I meant what I told him—that Ansel means nothing to me. There's not even any resentment or anger there any longer. Just scorn for the person that he is. Or was. I hope he's changed, but I doubt it.

I'm happy Kluvberg won. Apprehensive about telling him I made a mistake with my EPA submission. Relieved he's home. All those emotions shift to secondary when Will sets the bag of takeout he brought over on the counter, and I catch the flash of black on the inside of his right wrist. All of his tattoos were contained to his left arm, until now.

I grab his forearm, twisting it so I can see it better. So I can tell if it says what I think it does.

It does.

He got the seat numbers on his ticket—the exact spot where we'd met—tattooed on his arm.

"Will..." That's all I can manage to say—his name.

One corner of his mouth turns up. "If you hate it, don't tell me. It's permanent."

"I don't hate it. I love it. I just...I can't believe you did it."

He shrugs, pulling boxes of takeout from the paper bag he brought over. "None of my tattoos meant anything. I wanted one that did."

I rise up on my tiptoes, pressing a kiss against his cheek. "I have to tell you something."

He glances over. "Okay ..."

"Remember the photo I told you I sent into the awards?"

Will nods. "Yeah. The one from the park."

"Yeah. Except I, uh...I found out this morning that's not the photo I'd submitted."

A line of confusion appears between his eyes. "What do you mean?"

"I submitted a photo of you, accidentally. The photo I had taken in the locker room, after your portraits."

"The one where I'm shirtless and holding a soccer ball?"

"*Football*, and yes." I bite my bottom lip. "I called earlier, as soon as I realized. They can't swap submissions at this point in the process. Either I withdraw or..."

"Or?"

"Or there's a chance I could win. Not a *big* chance because they receive thousands of submissions and a lot of those are from talented veterans who know exactly what they're doing instead of a university student who sent in a shirtless photo of her boyfriend by accident. But there's *a* chance, so I felt like I had to tell you. I'll withdraw it, if you want, and then there's no—"

"Don't withdraw."

"Are you sure?" I search his expression. "If I miraculously win, this contest is a big deal. In certain circles anyway. Our names will be linked in the press. Kluvberg will definitely hear about—"

"About how I'm your *boyfriend*?"

I feel the heat in my cheeks, radiating like twin suns. I was hoping he'd missed that slip of the tongue. "That's what most people will assume."

"I don't care about most people. I'm asking you."

"Yes."

He grins. "Good answer. Because I just told my brother I'm bringing my girlfriend to meet him next weekend."

CHAPTER THIRTY-EIGHT

WILL

I look away from the swings creaking in the wind and glance over at Sophia. "This is where I learned to play soccer."

We're at the park in my neighborhood where I spent most of my childhood. It looks better than it did when I was a kid, but not by much. They put in a new playground with fresh wood chips, added a few new picnic tables. They must have swapped out the old soccer goals at some point because I don't think that those would still be standing. But they're no longer new, worn and weathered from the elements.

This whole place—the entire neighborhood—has seen better days.

I'm not embarrassed about having Sophia see it. Aside from visiting Tripp, my main motivation for taking this trip was showing her my world the same way I've gotten to know hers. She knows more about my childhood than guys I went to college with. More than my brother knows, even.

But standing beside her in this spot, I'm definitely aware of our different backgrounds. She's used to much nicer places, and it's vulnerable to show her my rougher parts. She wouldn't be in the States, wouldn't be in a park with a soccer field, if not for me. I've always disregarded other people's opinions pretty easily. But hers is different. Hers matters to me.

Sophia says nothing as she stares at the field. Going to Seaport or Harvard Square would have been a lot more enjoyable for her.

"Let's head back to the house," I say. "We can—"

"Let's play some football."

I blink at her. "What?"

Honestly, that's the last thing I ever expected to hear her say.

"Let's play. There's a football right there by the swings."

"What are you—"

She's already walking away, toward the soccer ball she spotted.

I follow her, still in a state of shock. My mom isn't supposed to be home from work for another hour, and we both wanted some fresh air after being stuck on an airplane. This was the first place I thought to bring her to.

Sophia's pulling her hair up into a ponytail when I reach her.

"You really don't need to do this," I tell her.

"I know I don't. Just like you didn't need to spend hours walking through galleries with me. I *want* to."

"When was the last time you played football?"

She smirks. "I'm a Beck, baby. Soccer is in my blood."

I grin back. I know she's doing this for me, and it makes her bravado even hotter. "I didn't think Becks called it soccer."

"I'm adapting to the local culture." She dribbles a few yards away. I actually have no idea if Sophia has *ever* played soccer before, so I'm impressed by her ease. Maybe an aspect of it is intrinsic, just like she teased. "First to ten?"

"Sure." I'd agree to anything she suggests, whether soccer is involved or not.

It's a perfectly crisp New England fall day. Leaves litter the grass, crunching with each step, the sun's warmth the perfect complement to the slight bite to the air.

Sophia starts dribbling, her blonde hair streaming behind her like a flag.

I let her score first, and a quirk of her lips tells me she knows that. How well she plays doesn't matter to me. I would have no idea how to manage any of the settings on her fancy camera. It's enough—more than I ever expected—that she's on this field with me. That she's making this effort because she knows I love this game, even though it's always represented different things to her.

Soccer saved me. It suffocated her.

But I think that, maybe, she views it a little differently now. There's no sign of boredom or resignation on her face as we run up and down the grass chasing after a worn checkered ball.

Just like my view of the park we're in is shifting. Instead of desolation, I see resilience. I see how far I've come from the little kid who spent so much time here. I've played in the important stadiums I always dreamed of. But I also came back here. I didn't forget about this place.

And seeing how far you've come is much more astounding when you're standing in the spot where you started.

CHAPTER THIRTY-NINE

SOPHIA

W ill's mom is wonderful.

I wasn't sure what to expect, based on what little I knew about her. Since Will's trip here following Tripp's accident, they've kept in regular communication. Discussions about his brother's recovery have filled what used to be silence, but they don't just talk about Tripp. I've heard Will mention football to his mom. Places around Kluvberg. Me.

Delilah is warm and welcoming and curious, asking me endless questions about myself as we eat the meatloaf she made for dinner. It's Will's favorite, apparently, and I'll have to remember to ask her for the recipe because it's a hell of a lot better than the spaghetti I cooked for him. She's worked in the same job as a secretary at a dentist's office since before her sons were born, she tells me, but always had a passion for art.

As soon as she finds out I'm a photographer, that leads into a whole other discussion. I'm expecting Will to look bored, but there's a small smile on his face as he squirts ketchup on his dinner and listens to his mom and me talk.

Delilah invites me into her studio after we finish dinner,

which turns out to be her bedroom. Will opts to stay in the kitchen and clean up.

"I usually keep all this more organized in the spare bedroom," she tells me. "It's a little scattered right now."

"You didn't have to move all this," I say, feeling guilty for the effort she's going through to host us. Even though the room is small enough that it was probably necessary. We barely fit our suitcases in there as it is.

"Nonsense. I loved doing it. Love having Will here. And you, of course."

I smile in response. It's obvious to me how much his mother loves him, and I hope it's something Will is starting to see again as well.

Delilah shows me a few sketches that look like they're of the inside of this house. A chair. Vases filled with flowers. Bowls of fruit. A park—called Boston Common, she tells me. The last piece of paper she hands me is a drawing of her two kids.

I recognize a younger Will immediately with a smaller kid who must be Tripp beside him. I haven't met Will's brother yet. We're going to visit him at the rehabilitation center where he's recovering tomorrow. But I can easily see the similarities between the two of them—the dark hair and the cheeky smiles they share.

"This is incredible," I tell Delilah. "You're very talented."

"It's just a hobby," she replies, her cheeks turning pink.

Words I've said before.

"I mean it, Delilah. There must be some galleries in the city. You should bring a few of these by some of them. I'm sure they'd be interested."

"Maybe," she says in a way I think means she won't. And that's okay. Maybe a hobby is all she wants—needs—this to be.

Will isn't in the kitchen when we return. The dishes have all been washed and put away, suggesting we were looking at Delilah's drawings for longer than I realized.

"I've got to switch a load of laundry in the basement," Delilah tells me. "Will probably headed out to the garage. Straight down the hallway, on the left."

"Oh. Okay."

I follow her directions, opening a door and stepping from hardwood onto a concrete floor. Sure enough, Will is out here.

He glances back when I close the door behind me. "Hey."

"Hey." I walk over to him, stepping into his side when he lifts his arm.

Will kisses the top of my head. "You good?"

"Great. Your mom and I talked art."

He smiles, the soft, tender one that is my second favorite to the cheeky grin he never grew out of. "I could hear some of it down the hall."

"So...this is it?"

There's an old car taking up most of the garage, dwarfing the space so it's impossible to miss.

"This is it," he confirms.

"It's nice."

"It's useless. My mom should get rid of it."

I'm sure there's a reason she hasn't, just like I'm certain there's a reason Will came out here to stare at it. "You could fix it," I suggest.

"I don't know that much about cars."

"You could learn."

"Maybe," he says.

We stand in silence for a few minutes, Will playing absently with some strands of my hair as he studies his dad's old car.

"My friend Wyatt called, asking if I wanted to hang out tonight. I was finished in the kitchen, so I came out here to talk with him, and then... I kinda got stuck out here." He clears his throat. "You up for going out for a little bit?"

"Yeah, sure." My phone vibrates in my pocket, so I pull it out. Then almost drop it as the words on the screen register. "Oh my God."

"What? What's wrong?"

I blink rapidly. "They just announced the finalists for the EPAs. I'm one of them, in the Sports category."

"Sophia! That's amazing!" When I don't respond, Will's voice turns concerned. "Isn't that amazing?"

"No. I mean, yes. I just...they publish the finalists' photos ahead of the ceremony, Will. I just received the email, but once they officially announce...it will be news."

"So, that means..."

"That everyone will know that I submitted a shirtless photo of you? Yes."

CHAPTER FORTY

SOPHIA

I've never been this nervous, arriving at my parents' house. They're hosting this family dinner instead of Saylor and Adler. Will offered to come with me, but I have no idea how this evening is going to go. I'd rather he officially met my family as my boyfriend after I've had the chance to explain some things to them.

My dad is out front when I park, trimming some of the shrubs that line the path. I showed up extra early intentionally, hoping to talk to my parents alone before Adler got here with his opinions.

"Hello, Papa," I greet.

He pauses his clipping to kiss both of my cheeks. "How are you, Sophia?"

I exhale. "Okay."

"How was your trip?"

"Fine."

As far as my family knows, I spent this past weekend at Fashion Week with my friends.

"Is Mom around?"

"She's inside."

He walks up the gravel path with me.

"The yard looks nice."

Gardening is where my father funneled his attention after retiring and raising two kids. The land surrounding the house where I grew up used to sit mostly empty. Now there are patios and topiaries and gardens.

"Thank you."

My mom's in the kitchen, working on dinner. She abandons whatever is in the pot on the stove when I appear, coming over to hug and kiss me.

"How was Fashion Week?" she asks.

I take a deep breath. As good of an opening as any I considered on the drive here. "I didn't go. I lied."

"Oh?"

My mom glances at my dad, and they share a silent conversation. I've always been pretty honest with them because they allowed me the freedom to mostly do what I wanted to do anyway. There was no need to be duplicitous. And when I *did* lie, I didn't admit to doing so.

"I went to Boston with Will Aster." I pull my phone out of my pocket. "I'm dating him. And I submitted this photo of him to the European Photography Awards, and I was selected as a finalist. The ceremony is in a month, in London, and I'd really like it if you both came with me."

Total silence follows. My parents exchange another look, this one longer than the last. They don't look disappointed, at least. Just stunned.

The sound of the front door opening is what interrupts the quiet.

"We're here!" Saylor's cheerful voice calls out.

"I'll be right back," I say. "I need to talk to Adler for a minute."

Adler and Saylor are still in the entryway when I walk out of the kitchen. It's gotten cool enough out for coats, and Gigi is bundled up in a pink corduroy jacket. I kiss her cheek, then hug Saylor.

"I can't wait to hear all about Fashion Week," she tells me. "I'm so jealous."

I hide the grimace, force a smile, and then glance at Adler. "Can I talk to you outside for a minute?"

Saylor's eyebrows fly upward at the odd request, but she says nothing when Adler nods, just continues toward the kitchen with Gigi.

Adler follows me back out the door, into the front gardens my dad was just manicuring. This is harder to admit to him than it was to my parents. Not only is he more closely connected to Will, he's never shied away from sharing opinions about my life. When my parents have shaken their heads about me showing up in a short dress, he's suggested I put on pants. He's always done his best to look out for me the best way he knew how.

And he has no idea about me and Will, I'm certain. If he did, he would have mentioned it by now. I wasn't sure exactly when—or how widespread—the announcement about finalists would be, and it's been hovering over me like a ticking time bomb ever since Will and I returned from Boston.

"I'm dating Will Aster." I spit it straight out, same as I did with my parents.

Instantly, the confusion on Adler's face transforms into anger. "You're *what*?"

"It's been going on for a while now, and I didn't tell you

because I was worried this is exactly how you'd react." I wave toward his face.

Adler huffs. "Sophia, he's—"

"I know *exactly* who he is, Adler. He is a good person."

"He's also conceited and impulsive and—"

"This isn't a debate. I'm telling you as my brother, not the captain of FC Kluvberg. I expect you to be happy for me, for *us*, and if you're not, then you and I aren't going to have a whole lot to talk about anymore."

Adler looks shocked. "You can't seriously—"

"Remember how I reacted when you met Saylor? I was happy for you. I got to know her."

He rubs a hand across his mouth, like he's trying to keep choice words inside. "She's my wife, Sophia."

"You think I'd be telling you this if it wasn't serious between us? It's very serious. It's different with him than it's been with anyone else. He doesn't care about my last name. Or that—"

My brother exhales. "Sophia, that isn't—"

"Let me finish. That's not the only reason why I'm with him. But most guys *have* cared. They've wanted to meet you. Or they've been jealous of you and tried to use me to—"

Adler's gaze sharpens. "Use you to what?"

I say nothing. I didn't mean to mention Ansel. He wasn't supposed to be any part of this conversation. I decided I'd never tell Adler what happened a long time ago.

"Use you to what?" he pushes, sensing I'm holding something back.

"There was a guy who...he pursued me because he wanted to hurt you. It doesn't matter anymore. It was a long time ago."

"It was Ansel Fischer, wasn't it?"

I swallow. Nod. "Yes."

"And you told Will. That's why he went after him nonstop when we played Manchester."

"Yes," I admit.

A little of the anger dissipates from Adler's expression. He looks more contemplative than mad. Realizing I confided in Will about what happened with Ansel, that Will took it upon himself to dole out some revenge—that seems to have given Adler more pause than anything else I've said. Maybe it's a footballer thing, because I wouldn't have guessed that would matter.

"I love him," I say. "And I know you love me. So, I need you to let this be. Did I tell you that you were making a mistake when you chased after Saylor? Did I judge you when you were stumbling out of clubs with models? Trust that I know what I'm doing. And don't let this affect anything related to the team. My relationship with him has nothing to do with Will as a soccer player. It's his career. It's important to him. He loves it like you and Saylor do."

My brother studies me for long, long minutes. Finally, one eyebrow lifts. "You call it soccer now?"

I might be blushing a little. "I played," I tell Adler impulsively. "Will brought me to this park by his mom's House. It's where he learned to play. It was...fun."

The last time I played football was here, with my brother. There was a very narrow window before Adler started taking it too seriously, before he—and I—understood the expectations, where we would kick a ball around together.

"Okay."

I exhale, a rush of relief.

"I will do my best to...accept this. And to only threaten Aster a couple of times."

"No threats."

He shakes his head twice. "Never thought you'd date a footballer."

"Me neither." I bite my bottom lip. "Uh, one other thing."

He looks wary. "What?"

"Remember the photography awards I was talking about?"

Adler nods his head, even though I'm not sure he really does remember. Saylor is the one who's asked me about them the most.

"I'm a finalist in one of the categories."

The concern totally disappears from Adler's face. He beams. "That's incredible!"

"Yeah, it is." I smile, the praise feeling really nice. "And the, uh, photo I submitted is of Will."

I don't mention he's not wearing a shirt in the photograph. I feel like I've dumped enough on Adler already.

A little of the enthusiasm has dimmed from my brother's expression, but not all of it. He nods once. "Congrats, Sophia. Really."

"Thanks."

"That's everything, right?"

I laugh, relief making me giddy. The only person left to tell is Saylor, and I already know how she'll take the news. There's a reason I saved her for last.

"That's everything," I confirm.

He exhales. "Good."

We head back toward the house. Halfway there, his arm lands on my shoulders, squeezing me against his side. A way we haven't walked in a long time. "I looked up some of your photos. The ones you took of the games at the start of the season. They're amazing, Sophia."

I smile, warmth that has nothing to do with the weight of his arm spreading through me. "Thanks."

"I'm sorry I haven't asked about your photography more. Looked at your photos before."

"It's okay."

"No, it's not. I want to see more. Maybe after dinner?"

I have to clear my throat twice, to get rid of the lump that's appeared there. "Sure."

Right before we reach the door, Adler tells me, "You're too good for him. But I like him more than any other guy you've brought around."

I rest my head on his shoulder for a second. "Thank you."

He squeezes me again, and then we head inside together.

CHAPTER FORTY-ONE

WILL

Cameras flash as we walk toward the doors of the hotel. Kinda ironic since we're here for photography awards. I wonder if any of the people photographing us now submitted to the EPAs.

Sophia's grip on my hand tightens as we walk into the lobby of the London hotel where the awards are taking place. She's anxious, but I doubt anyone else here can tell. She's walking with all the regal confidence of a queen, her blonde hair pulled back in a deceptively simple knot that I know took twenty minutes. But I can spot the strain in her smile. The stiff line of her shoulders.

Her parents and Beck and Saylor are already inside. We just came from a mixer before the actual awards ceremony, where Sophia was a popular attraction. People paid more attention to me than I was expecting them to as well. I guess photographers don't normally show up with their subjects as their dates. There's been a lot of fascination with me and Sophia ever since her photo of me was released.

My face is partially cut off in it, but the Kluvberg jerseys in the background—not to mention Sophia's last name—were a big giveaway as to what club was associated with the photo. And it's not the first time I've been photographed with my shirt off. Both because of antics during games and from different ads I've done. Add in my recognizable tattoos, and it didn't take very long at all for people to figure out it was me.

I don't really care what anyone else thinks of our relationship, but it's nice that the response has been mostly positive. That no one has mentioned the name Cassandra Owens. There was some ribbing from the guys—someone papered the inside of my locker with printouts of the picture—but I think that's a good thing. A sign of acceptance, if not respect.

And Beck, who I was most worried about reacting poorly, has handled me dating his sister better than I expected. He's mostly treated me the same as before, which was a best-case scenario.

He's smiling now, same as Saylor and Sophia's parents, as we approach the table where they're all seated. More and more people continue to fill the big ballroom where the ceremony is set to take place, chatter emanating all around us. I had no idea what to expect from tonight, since it's my first photography awards event. The turnout is impressive, and the setting is sophisticated, which I know is adding to Sophia's nerves.

Sophia's cheeks are flushed as she leans forward to explain some of the categories to her parents, the silk dress she's wearing clinging to every curve and reflecting the candlelight. She's practically vibrating with nervous energy, so I reach under the table and rest my hand on her knee. She relaxes some, her hand finding mine under the table as she continues talking to her parents. I'm so glad they came, that they're showing up for Sophia this way after years of attending Kluvberg games.

She's nervous about tonight. Wanting to win. But I know part of her apprehension about these awards—the reason she took so long to decide what to submit in the first place—is that she thought she needed to prove something to her family. I hope them being here is all the assurance she needs that photography is the right path.

A few minutes later, the lights dim, one on the stage glowing brighter. A woman walks up to the lectern and gives a long speech that's honestly a little boring. Partly because I'm almost as anxious as Sophia. Anxious for Sophia. I want this win for her more badly than I've ever wanted to win a game myself. This moment when she has her entire family here, supporting her passion. Cheering her on at her version of a football match.

They run through the categories alphabetically, each winner getting announced and the recipient going up onstage to receive their award.

Finally, the Sports one is up. The same woman who's introduced each category speaks up, talking about all the amazing entries and how inspiring sports photography can be. All the finalists' photos get flashed up on the screen, Sophia's last. It remains on the screen, and that's how I know who the winner will be before it's actually announced.

The woman leans forward and declares the winner is Sophia Beck.

CHAPTER FORTY-TWO

SOPHIA

Metal rumbles as suitcases continue to appear on the conveyer belt running in an endless circle. I'm trying to keep an eye out for my luggage, but I'm also so exhausted that I can't even remember what color my suitcase is right now.

I hide a yawn behind one hand. "I'm *so* tired."

"You should have slept on the plane," Will tells me.

"I *tried* to sleep on the plane."

I wore an eye mask, I had a glass of wine, I put on noise-canceling headphones. Nothing worked.

He grins. "You're cute when you're grumpy."

"I'm not grumpy," I grumble.

Will hums what sounds suspiciously like a strong disagreement, but he's smart enough not to say anything else. He slept the entire flight and now appears relaxed and well rested.

I'm excited about this trip. So, so excited. I've wanted to come back to Africa ever since the program I participated in, and this time, I get to bring Will with me. But I forgot—purposefully—how much traveling for twelve hours straight sucks. I was up packing late last night, so I've averaged about five hours of sleep in the past forty-eight hours.

Will steps forward and pulls one of our bags off of the belt. We're traveling with three suitcases—two of which are mine. One is my photography equipment, painstakingly stored to make sure it made the journey safely. I hide another yawn as Will retrieves our two other bags.

"Need me to carry you too?" he teases as we head for the exit.

I roll my eyes, but I'm a little tempted to say yes.

The wheeled suitcases roll seamlessly over the wood flooring.

It's just past two a.m. local time, the sleepy passengers from our flight are the majority of the people inside the Kilimanjaro Airport.

As soon as we step outside, it's obvious how far we've traveled. Rather than the cold draft we left behind in Kluvberg, the air is warm and dry. At least twenty-five degrees Celsius. It's a welcome—and unfamiliar—experience for January. We traveled to Boston to spend the holidays with Delilah, Tripp, and Tripp's boyfriend, Jayden, and it was just as chilly in Massachusetts as it'd been back home.

A smiling man wearing a green linen shirt is waiting for us outside the airport, the logo of the company we booked the safari with emblazoned on the side of a beige van. He greets us warmly and then loads the luggage for us. Three other couples climb into the van as well, filling up the rows of bench seating.

I doze against Will's shoulder for the entire drive, the darkness making it hard to see much of anything past the sides of the road. I rouse when we reach the campground where we'll be staying. When I went to Kenya through the photography program, we stayed in a lodge, exploring a nearby park by Land Rover to spot impalas, rhinos, buffalo, lions, and more. We also were able to experience some local culture and attend a weekly festival of an indigenous tribe. I was part of a community within the program, and that was reflected in where we stayed.

So far, Tanzania appears to be more isolated. The shuttle stops in front of a small cluster of platform tents. We all climb out. I'm not the only one smothering yawns as another man and a woman appear, not looking nearly as exhausted, even though this is the middle of the night for them. They must get accustomed to welcoming visitors at all different times of the day.

We're assigned to tent five. My phone buzzes in my pocket. I pull it out to see a message from Saylor. It's three a.m. here now, so one a.m. in Germany. She's probably up with Gigi, who's still teething.

SAYLOR: You there?

SOPHIA: Yes! Sooo tired, but we made it.

She replies instantly.

SAYLOR: AND? Any ring yet?

I roll my eyes. She's been convinced Will is going to propose on this trip ever since I first told her about it. I'm certain she's wrong. Yes, we've been together for over a year. Yes, we live together. Yes, we love each other. But I don't know that any of those are reasons to get married.

Will is in his second season with Kluvberg. He made the decision to extend his contract sound like an easy one, although I wasn't entirely sure it was. Selfishly, it's the one I wanted him to make. I wanted to stay close to my family, and I was offered a staff position at *Neues Kluvberg*. From my perspective, it was perfect. From Will's, I'm not as certain.

> SAYLOR: Did you check his pockets? That's
> how I found mine.

I roll my eyes, then unzip my suitcase so I can put on pajamas.

Will heads into the bathroom, the shower turning on a few seconds later.

When I walk into the bathroom, he's lazily soaping his shoulder. I watch the white suds slip down his wet skin, avoiding his cocky smirk as he watches me check him out. I thought I was too tired to make it through a shower, but the sight of Will, naked, is rapidly waking me up.

I slip out of the nightie I just put on and step under the spray with him.

"Thought you were *so* tired," he tells me, smirking.

The tiles are cool against my bare feet, the spray of water warm, but not too hot. I step into him as water beats against my back, pressing my face to my favorite spot on the side of his neck.

"I love you."

His lips press against my wet hair. "I love you too, my little grump."

He fucks me lazily. Leisurely. Then shampoos my hair for me before we both grab towels. I brush my teeth, then climb into the comfy bed, expecting to fall asleep instantly. But there are too many unfamiliar sounds. I hear a loud thud in the distance and am instantly awake, recalling all the open land surrounding these tents.

"How close do you think we are to wild animals?"

"Close," Will mumbles.

"But, like, how close?" I press. The lodge where I stayed last time was very different than this. Practically a hotel with solid walls instead of canvas flaps.

Will groans, then climbs out of bed. He spins it so his side is closer to the entrance of our tent. "Happy? They'll eat me first."

"That was very sexy," I tell him, rolling half on top of him once he's settled back under the sheets.

His laugh is a low rumble against my cheek. "Good. Are you going to be able to fall asleep now?"

"Saylor thinks you're going to propose on this trip," I blurt. "Bet Beck you would."

Will's still and silent. "What'd your brother say?" he finally asks.

I can't get a clear read on his tone, and I can't see his face either. "He said you weren't going to."

"Interesting."

"Why is that interesting?"

"Because I asked for his blessing, after I got your dad's. Figured he was too competitive to keep that to himself if it meant losing to Saylor."

"*Oh.*"

I wasn't expecting Saylor to be *right*. She's never going to let me live this down.

"Was that a good *oh* or a bad *oh*?"

"A surprised one. I didn't, um...we haven't talked about it."

There's a pause. "Shawn thinks a US team is going to make me an offer next season."

"A US team made you an offer this season."

"I know," he says. "But the team that wants me now...

they're in Boston. I'm happy in Kluvberg. Your whole life is there. So, I decided I wasn't going to bring it up until...it didn't feel fair to ask you to marry me without discussing that first. And I won't know for a few more months if it's a real option or not."

I'm silent, processing.

"I shouldn't have said anything," Will says. "We can talk about it more when we get home. Let's just enjoy the trip, okay?"

I hesitate before saying, "Okay."

There's more I feel like I should tell him, but I haven't sorted through my thoughts yet. Will's already rolling over, and knowing him, he'll be asleep in minutes.

I lie awake, listening to the strange noises.

———

Breakfast is a blur. I'm tired, not having slept well last night.

Neither Will nor I bring up last night's conversation. But it's there, hovering between us as we talk about today's itinerary. As we climb into the Land Cruiser and head across the Serengeti.

It's an eventful morning. We pass herds of wildebeest and zebras, then pass several crocodiles sunbathing in the Grumeti River. After spotting a few gazelles, we head back toward the camp for lunch. The incessant bouncing over the rough terrain helps me keep my eyes open, at least.

I glance over at Will. He's backlit by the sun, the illumination making his profile glow. It's so similar to the first time I saw him, towering over me in the top section of the stadium's stands.

My eyes fall to his wrist, the tattoo there a permanent reminder of that fateful moment.

He looks over like he feels my eyes on him, his expression visibly softening when he catches me staring at him. "What?"

I shake my head, feeling almost shy. I feel like I've known Will forever. He knows me better than anyone else. But I still experience the giddiness and butterflies of a crush around him too.

He quirks a brow in another, silent question.

"You can ask," I tell him.

"What?"

"The question you were thinking about, before the Boston's team offer came up. You can ask because where you play won't change my answer."

"You'd move to Boston?"

I nod. "Photographers can work anywhere, remember?"

One corner of his mouth curves up as I quote the words he told me a long time ago back to him. "I remember."

I nod. "Okay then."

"Okay then," he repeats.

Will leans forward and kisses me. He always says he's bad with words, but I disagree. He tells me everything I need to know, everything I want to hear. But he also communicates a lot with his actions. I can feel the love and the relief in the press of his lips against mine, like the seal of a promise. A silent vow about the future—about *our* future.

He grins when our mouths separate, and I snuggle into his side, tucking my head under his chin and pressing my cheek against his chest. I can hear the steady thud of his heartbeat buried beneath layers of skin and muscle. Solid and warm and alive.

We ride like that the rest of the drive back to camp. And I've never felt more content.

EPILOGUE
WILL

S everal cameras flash as I adjust the microphone, tilting it down and toward me.

"Anticipation about tomorrow's final is at an all-time high right now, Will. How are you maintaining your focus, headed into such an important match?"

As soon as the first question gets called out, there are a few more flashes.

I run a hand through my damp hair before answering, "I've never had trouble maintaining focus during any game. Tomorrow won't be any different. If you take a look at our performance throughout the tournament, I think that gives a good idea of what to expect from me and the rest of the US team. Our one goal is to be the team raising that trophy."

"Even considering who your opponent will be?"

"Even then."

"You played for Leon Wagner for two seasons while you were under contract with FC Kluvberg. Do you feel like that gives you any advantage, going into the final?" another reporter calls out.

"I think that Germany will be a tough opponent, and we'll be prepared for a challenging match."

"Not only are you facing off against a former coach tomorrow, but you'll also be playing against your brother-in-law. How have you handled that dynamic?"

I exhale. I knew I'd get these questions once our opponent in the final was determined, but having to answer them is still irritating. "I'll be shooting to win, same as I would no matter whom I was playing against. Knowing Beck, I'm sure he's doing the same."

"Do you have any insights into the rumors that Adler Beck will be retiring soon and this will be his last international tournament?"

"No, I don't. I think that German football will suffer a huge loss whenever Adler Beck steps off the field for the final time and that whether he retires in a year or ten, his place in the history books was cemented a long time ago."

"You're married to Beck's younger sister, Sophia."

I wait, but there's no question that follows. "Yes, I'm aware of who my wife is."

Ripples of laughter work through the crowd of reporters.

"Will beating her brother and her home country land you in hot water with your wife?"

"All's fair in love and football," I respond, drawing more laughter from the crowd. "As captain, my role is to lead a very talented team of Americans toward what we all hope is a victory. If we are the ones lifting the trophy tomorrow, it will have been from a group effort."

I answer a few more questions, and then my time with the media is thankfully up. At least no one brought up Seattle or Cassandra Owens. If anyone had asked me years ago, I'd say that was a cloud I'd never shake. But all people want to ask me now is about my connection to Germany's famous family and about football, which is fine with me.

I'm done for the day, so I grab my stuff and head out into the lobby. Sophia is waiting, talking on the phone. She says something and then hangs up when she sees me approaching.

"Nice jersey," I tell her.

"Nothing else fits," Sophia hisses. "I mean, it fits, but it shows...stuff."

I smirk, briefly covering the small bump of her belly with my hands before I lean down to kiss her. She leans into my touch.

"We need to start telling people," she mumbles into my neck. "Saylor's getting suspicious. And the only thing worse than throwing up three times a day and not being able to drink spritzes is having to hide that you're vomiting and pouring drinks into plants."

"What about tonight?" I ask. "Your family is here. My mom is here. We can call Tripp to tell him."

"It's the final tomorrow."

"So?"

"So, you and Adler should be focused on football."

I snort. "I'm focused. So is he. But some things are more important."

"They are, huh?"

I kiss her again. "You know they are. Come on."

The hotel where we're staying is within walking distance of the stadium. We both shower and change, then head to the restaurant where we're meeting our families for dinner.

My mom flew from Boston to be here. Tripp and his boyfriend were supposed to come too, but his boyfriend's mother fell and broke a leg, so they ended up staying in Boston to care for her. Beck is obviously here, and so are Saylor, Hans, and Erika.

Everyone's in high spirits as we take a seat on the outdoor terrace that offers a stunning view of Rome.

We've barely sat down when Sophia clears her throat. "Before anyone asks if I want to have wine, I can't."

Saylor shrieks. "I knew it!"

My mom gasps.

Erika beams.

Adler and Hans look confused.

"I'm pregnant," Sophia confirms. She glances at me. "We're pregnant, I guess, but Will is having a way easier time of it."

"Amen to that," Saylor says. "Beck is trying to talk me into another one, but his only contribution was the fun part."

"Saylor," Beck groans.

The rest of dinner is filled with congratulations and predictions about the match tomorrow. We have the terrace to ourselves, so I wander over to the edge at one point to take in the full view of the city. My mom comes over to give me a tight hug, visibly emotional about Sophia's pregnancy.

Right after she heads back to the table, Beck sidles up to me. "If you think the fact that you knocked my little sister up means I'll take it easy on you tomorrow, think again."

I smirk at him. "Ah, come on. You've already won two Cups. You're going to deprive me of getting to brag to my son about winning one?"

"It's a boy?"

Shit. I glance over one shoulder, making sure Sophia is still farther down the terrace and out of earshot. "You did *not* hear that from me. Sophia wants to throw a big party and shoot off blue confetti."

"I can keep my mouth shut."

"I've yet to see any evidence of that."

Beck grins. "Seriously, congratulations, Dad."

Dad. No one's ever called me that before. I can't pin down a memory of saying that to my own father even though I must have.

"Did you feel ready for it?" I ask seriously.

"Fatherhood? Fuck no."

Somewhat reassuring. Saylor and Beck have kept their kid alive for five years.

"But Saylor was freaking out about it. We...Gigi wasn't planned. And I know neither of us would change anything. We figured it out. But I felt fucking guilty, knowing how much it would affect her career and that it wouldn't change mine the same way. Saylor's mom had left when she was young, so I knew she was worried she didn't have an example to follow. Basically, I faked it until we made it. You guys will be fine too."

"My dad left when I was ten," I state. "I don't have an example to follow either."

"You'll figure it out, just like she did."

I nod. Exhale.

"Will!"

Sophia is standing, and everyone is gathered by the door, ready to depart.

I hold a hand out to Beck. "I'd say good luck tomorrow, but..."

He grins. "Yeah. You too."

We shake, and then I head toward a waiting Sophia.

"Everything good?" she asks, glancing at her brother.

"Everything's great," I tell her.

We take a cab back to the hotel since Sophia insists on wearing heels and then complains about her feet. I've learned just to nod along in agreement when she says she should have known better.

She leans into me as soon as we're inside the elevator, and I'm certain it has nothing to do with her feet. She kisses the length of my jaw, one hand dropping to my crotch to rub my cock.

We don't even make it all the way to the bed in our hotel room.

Our sex life has always been extremely active, but it's ramped up to a new degree since Sophia's pregnancy. She's insatiable.

The bathroom is closer to the door, so I end up lifting her onto the counter. She's already a step ahead, her hands busy working the zipper of the slacks I wore to dinner. As soon as she gets my cock free, she's guiding the head to her entrance, working the tight clasp of her cunt over my erection. We're both breathing heavily, my balls already drawn up high and tight as she takes me.

I tug the straps of her dress down, the fabric slipping down to her waist. She arches her back, offering her breasts to my eager mouth.

Heat floods my groin, tendrils of fire racing up and down my spine. My thighs tense and tremble as she takes all of me, making breathy, needy sounds, like it's the best thing she's ever experienced.

Her nails dig into the back of my neck as her thighs spread even wider, taking me as deeply as she possibly can.

She's the sexiest thing I've ever seen. Mussed blonde hair, pouty lips, bouncing tits.

I barely hold on until she's coming too. She keeps kissing me, working down the line of buttons on my shirt until I'm shirtless and then tugging her dress over her head and flinging it away.

We end up in the shower this time, hot water pounding my back as I press her against the cool tiled wall. My cum is still dripping out of her from the last round. And she's so wet, soaked from the mixture of her release and mine. So responsive. So ready. For my cock, the only one she's ever taken.

Her legs are spread wide, her blonde hair plastered to her skin as she leans her cheek against the white tiles. I watch her expression change when she feels my erection growing again, the immediate flare of pleasure. She moans my name, and I'm done for. It doesn't matter that we just had sex. There's nothing I want more than to be back inside of her. The tip of my cock finds her entrance, and I thrust, the sensation of her spreading around me like nothing I've ever experienced.

I don't know how I lived without it. I don't ever want to live without her, and I wonder if that's how my mom felt. How she ended up in such a dark place. Maybe one day, I'll be brave enough to ask her. We're in a much better place than we used to be, but our relationship won't ever return to what it looked like before that day.

Sophia cries out, and it takes me a second to realize that she's already coming again. That all she needed was me inside her.

I fuck her through it, then pull out while she's still fluttering and spin her around before pushing back inside. I can hit deeper this way. Can watch each tiny shift in her expression. Can kiss her, which is what I do. She kisses me back eagerly, digging her fingers into my shoulders.

She's so wet, but she's so tight too, those two things working against each other.

I come so hard that the edges of my vision blur to black, her pussy contracting around me and milking my release. I come and come, so much that I can feel my cum leaking out of her.

She laughs. "I feel *so* good right now. I don't even think I can stand."

"You don't have to stand. I'll hold you."

"Will you shampoo my hair too?"

"Of course."

We finish cleaning up and climb into bed, neither of us bothering with clothes. I don't think I can physically go another round, but Sophia has woken me up in the middle of the night before, and I've risen to the occasion—literally—every time.

"Do you think you'll win tomorrow?" she asks me, then yawns.

"Yes," I answer immediately.

She giggles. "That's what I thought."

"Trying to decide who to bet on?"

"No. I want you to win. I always want you to win."

I kiss her forehead. "*Ich liebe dich.*"

She sighs, sleepy and content. "I love you too."

I think we'll win tomorrow. But even if we lose, I already have everything I want most in the world.

THE END

ABOUT THE AUTHOR

C.W. Farnsworth is the author of numerous adult and young adult romance novels featuring sports, strong female leads, and happy endings.

Charlotte lives in Rhode Island and when she isn't writing spends her free time reading, at the beach, or snuggling with her Australian Shepard.

Find her on Facebook (@cwfarnsworth), Twitter (@cw_farnsworth), Instagram (@authorcwfarnsworth) and check out her website www.authorcwfarnsworth.com for news about upcoming releases!

ALSO BY C.W. FARNSWORTH

Standalones

Four Months, Three Words

Come Break My Heart Again

Winning Mr. Wrong

Back Where We Began

Like I Never Said

Fly Bye

Serve

Heartbreak for Two

Pretty Ugly Promises

Six Summers to Fall

King of Country

Rival Love

Kiss Now, Lie Later

For Now, Not Forever

The Kensingtons

Fake Empire

Real Regrets

Truth and Lies

Friday Night Lies

Tuesday Night Truths

Kluvberg

First Flight, Final Fall

All The Wrong Plays

Holt Hockey

Famous Last Words

Against All Odds

From Now On

Printed in Great Britain
by Amazon